DICTIONARY OF MATH

DICTIONARY OF MATH

Shivanand Tiwari

ANANYA PRAKASHAN
Delhi

Publisher
Ananya Prakashan
E-17, Panchsheel Garden
Naveen Shahdara, Delhi-110032

ISBN : 978-93-89191-01-1

Price : 350.00
Edition : 2024

Printed at
Harsha Printers,Jagatpuri, Delhi

Contents

A

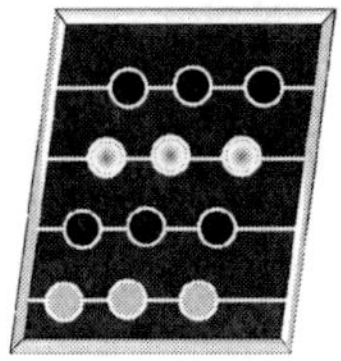

Abacus *(एबाकस)* A calculating frame with balls of different colours. गिनती सिखाने का यंत्र जिसमें तारों में रंग बिरंगे लट्टू लगे होते हैं।

Absolute Value *(परम मूल्य) निरपेक्ष मान* The positive value for a real number. वास्तविक संख्या का धनात्मक मूल्य। जैसे $-|3| = 3, |-6| = 6, |0| = 0$.

Abstract number *(अव्यावहारिक संख्या)* Any number which has no specific units. वे संख्यायें जिनके साथ इकाई संयुक्त नहीं होती है।

Acceleration *(त्वरण)* It is the rate of change of velocity with time. If the change in velocity of particle is, dv with change in time dt then, acceleration will be $a = \frac{dv}{dt}$. समय के साथ, वेग परिवर्तन की दर त्वरण कहलाती है। $a = \frac{v_2 - v_1}{\Delta t}$

Account *(गणना)* An account is a record of financial transactions. वित्त संबंधी हिसाब-किताब।

Accuracy *(यथार्थ)* Accuracy means exact, precise without error, usually referring to numerical computations. अंकगणित गणनाओं में इसका अर्थ विशुद्ध संख्या को प्रदर्शित करता है जिसमें गलती न हो।

Acre *(एकड़)* An acre is a unit of area used to measure land. एकड़ क्षेत्रफल मापने की इकाई है, जिसके द्वारा भूमि की माप की जाती है।

Acute angle *(न्यून कोण)* An acute angle is an angle that is smaller than 90°. वह कोण जो 90° से कम होता है।

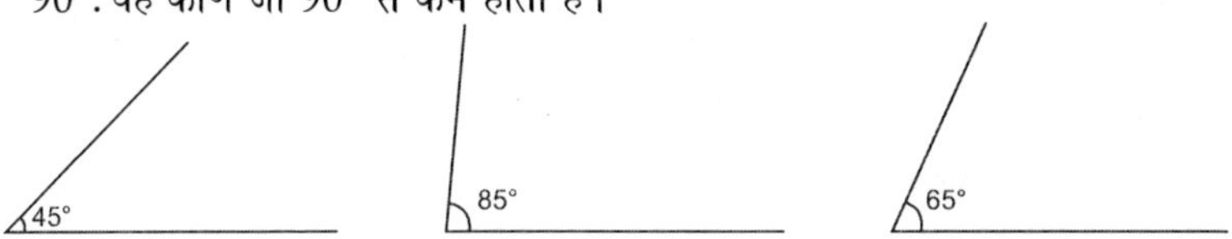

Fig. Acute angle

Addend *(योजक)* The number being added in addition question. संख्यायें जिन्हें जोड़ा जाता है।

5 + 8 = 13
Addendum sum

Addition ***(योग)*** Addition is a kind of arithmetic. It is used to find the total or sum, of two or more numbers put together. The sign for addition is '+' which is often referred to as 'plus'. अंकगणित की वह विद्या जिसके द्वारा दो या दो से अधिक संख्याओं को जोड़ा जाता है। जैसे $2 + 2 = 4$, $-6 + 4 = -2$.

Addition of formulae ***(सूत्रों का योग)*** The formulae that is related to trigonometric functions of sum of difference of angles with individual functions of these angles. त्रिकोणमिति से संबंधित सूत्रों के योग और अन्तर को प्रदर्शित किया जाता है।

If A and B are two angles, positive, zero or negative. यदि किसी त्रिभुज के A और B दो कोण है जो धनात्मक शून्य या ऋणात्मक है तब–

(*i*) $\cos(A - B) = \cos A \cos B + \sin A \sin B$

(*ii*) $\tan(A + B) = \dfrac{\tan A + \tan B}{1 - \tan A \tan B}$

(*iii*) $\cos(A + B) = \cos A \cos B - \sin A \sin B$

(*iv*) $\cot(A - B) = \dfrac{\cot A \,.\, \cot B + 1}{\cot B - \cot A}$

(*v*) $\sin(A - B) = \sin A \cos B - \cos A \sin B$

(*vi*) $\sin(A + B) = \sin A \cos B + \cos A \sin B$

(*vii*) $\tan(A - B) = \dfrac{\tan A - \tan B}{1 + \tan A \tan B}$

Addition of Vectors ***(सदिश राशियों का योग)*** It is different addition because in case of vectors we have magnitude as also the direction. यह एक भिन्न प्रकार का योग है क्योंकि इसमें दिशा और परिमाण दोनों का ध्यान रखा जाता है।

Adjacent angles ***(आसन्न कोण)*** Adjacent angles use two angles that direct at the same point or vertex and which have one side in common. ऐसे दो कोण जिनका एक ही शीर्ष बिन्दू होता है तथा एक उभयनिष्ठ भुजा होती है।

$\angle AOC + \angle COB = \angle AOB$

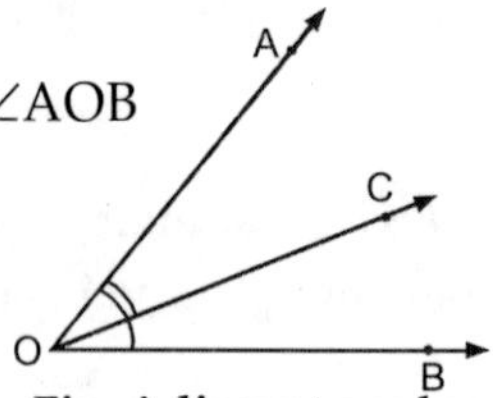

Fig. Adjacent angles

Algebra ***(बीजगणित)*** Algebra is a kind of arithmetic. It is a way of working out number problems using both letters and numbers. The letter can stand for any number. Algebra is used to work out an equation such as $y = 2x + 7$. गणित की वह शाखा जिसमें अज्ञात पद को ज्ञात करने के लिए अज्ञात पदों का समीकरण बनाते हैं। जैसे $y = 2x + 7$

Algebraic function ***(बीजीय फलन)***–An expression containing or using only algebraic symbols and operations such as $x^2 + 2x + 4$. जो फलत किसी चर की विभिन्न सांख्यिक घातों से प्राप्त पदों से बनता है उसे बीजीय फलन कहते हैं –

उदाहरणार्थ– $x^2 + 2x + 4$.

Alternate angles ***(एकान्तर कोण)*** Alternate angles are the angles made when two lines are crossed by another straight line. Alternate angles are always in pairs. यदि दो समान्तर रेखाओं को एक तिर्यक रेखा प्रतिच्छेदित करती है तो एकान्तर कोण बनता है। ये हमेशा युग्म में होते है।

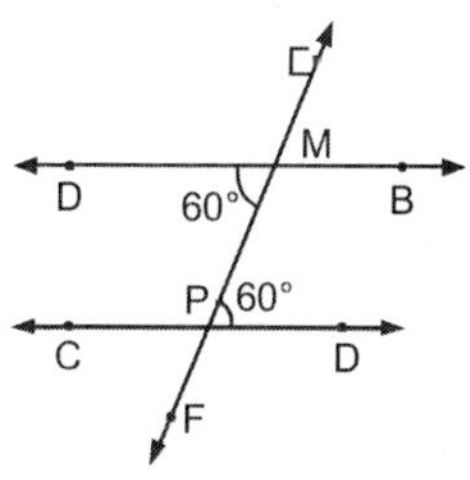

$\angle$ DMP = $\angle$ MPD = 60°
alternate angles

Fig. Alternate angles

Altitude ***(उन्नयन)*** **(1)** Altitude is another word for height. It is usually used to describe how high something is above sea level .

(2) Altitude in geometry is a line drawn downwards from a vertex that is perpendicular to the opposite side or face of a shape. (1) ऊँचाई के लिये उपयुक्त एक शब्द जिसके द्वारा किसी स्थान को समुद्र तल से ऊपर प्रदर्शित किया जाता है। (2) ज्यामिती में किसी रेखा के लम्बवत् ऊँचाई को प्रदर्शित करता है।

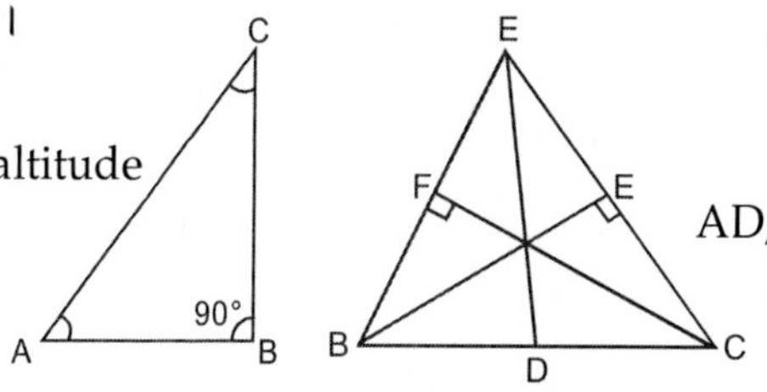

Fig. Altitude

Amount ***(मिश्रधन)*** The total money paid by borrower to the lender at the end of the specified period is called the amount. Amount = principal + interest. कुछ निश्चित अवधि के पश्चात ब्याज सहित लौटाई जाने वाली राशि को मिश्रधन कहते हैं। मिश्रिधन = मूलधन + ब्याज।

Amplitude ***(मध्य भाग)*** Half the distance from the highest point to the lowest point, the amplitude of a normal sine curve is 1, since the distance between top and bottom is 2. न्यूनतम तथा उच्चतम बिन्दु के बीच की दूरी का आधा भाग। जैसे-यदि किसी सामान्य वक्र की त्रिज्या का मध्य भाग '1' है तो न्यूनतम और उच्चतम बिन्दु की दूरी '2' होगी।

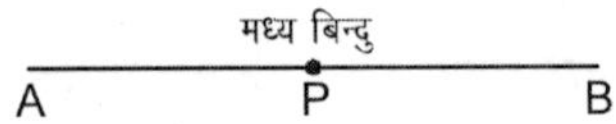

Fig. Amplitude (मध्य भाग)

Analysis ***(विश्लेषण)*** In business, analysis means studying a company's accounts to decide how healthy it is in financial terms. व्यवसायिक सन्दर्भ में किसी कम्पनी के समृद्धि का अध्ययन करना है।

Angle ***(कोण)*** An angle is the point where two lines or surfaces meet. The angle between two lines measures how much the line turns away from the other Angles are measured in degrees with a protractor. कोण वह बिन्दु है जो दो रेखाओं अथवा सतहों से निर्मित होता है तथा यह प्रदर्शित करता है कि एक रेखा दूसरी रेखा से कितनी दूर है। इसे चाँदे से डिगरी (°) में मापा जाता है। यह निम्न प्रकार का हो सकता है।

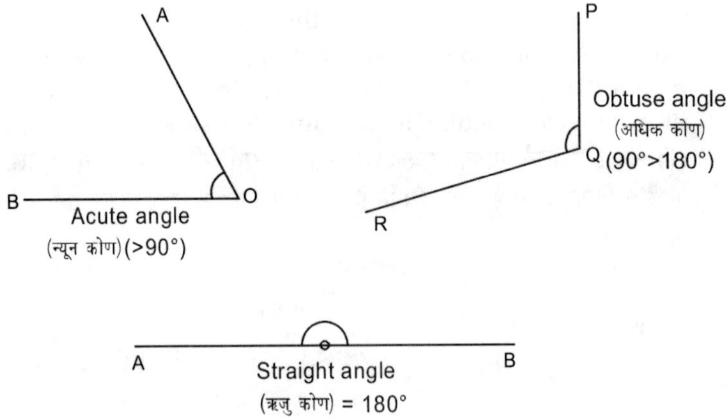

Fig. Angle

- **Angle between two straight lines** ***(दो सीधी रेखाओं के बीच का कोण)***

  (*i*) $\tan\theta = \left|\frac{m_1 - m_2}{1 + m_1 m_2}\right|$

  (*ii*) Two lines are parallel if $m_1 = m_2$

  (*iii*) Two lines are perpendicular it, $m_1 m_2 = -1$

- **Angle at the centre and a circle** ***(वृत्त के केन्द्र में निर्मित कोण)*** **Angle between any two ratio of circle:** The size of the angle at the centre is directly proportional to the length of the arc. वृत्त के केन्द्र में निर्मित कोण चाप के समानुपाती होता है। In a circle the angle at the centre is twice the angle at the circumference when both are subtended by a common chord AB. किसी वृत्त की जीवा से निर्मित केन्द्रीय कोण उसी जीवा द्वारा वृत्त के परिधि पर निर्मित कोण का दुगना होता है।

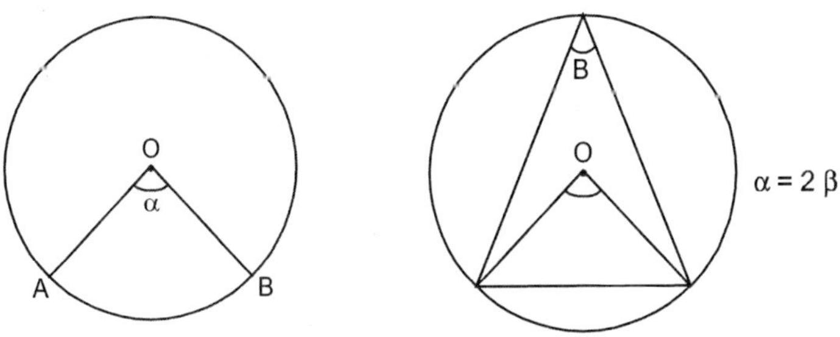

Fig. Angle at the centre and a circle

- **Angle at the circumference of a circle** ***(वृत्त के परिधि में निर्मित कोण)*** The angle between any two chords of a circle which have a common point on the circumference of a circle. एक ही जीवा द्वारा निर्मित कोण परस्पर बराबर होते है।

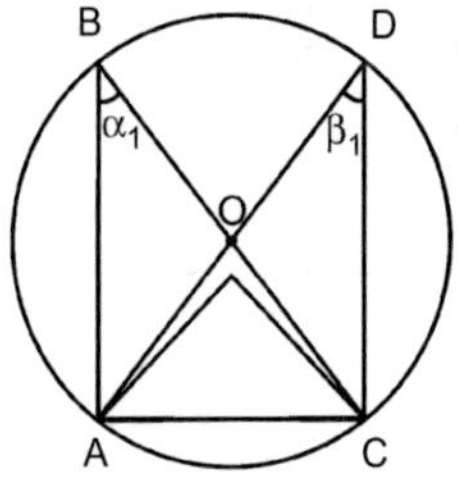

यदि O केन्द्र है; AB, CD जीवा है तो,

$\alpha_1 = \beta_2$

Fig. Angle at the circumference of a circle

- **Angle of depression** ***(अवनमन कोण)*** The angle of depression is the angle between a horizontal line and a line to a point below the horizontal line. किसी क्षैतिज रेखा के नीचे किसी दूसरी क्षैतिज रेखा के किसी बिन्दु से निर्मित कोण अवनमण कोण कहलाता है।

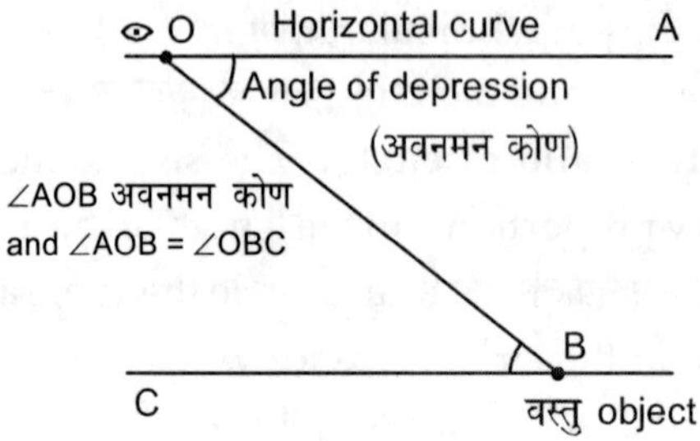

Fig. Angle of depression

- **Angle of elevation** ***(उन्नयन कोण)*** The angle of elevation is the angle between a horizontal line and a line to a point above the horizontal line. क्षैतिज रेखा के ऊपर किसी दूसरी क्षैतिज रेखा के किसी बिन्दु से निर्मित कोण उन्नयन कोण कहलाता है।

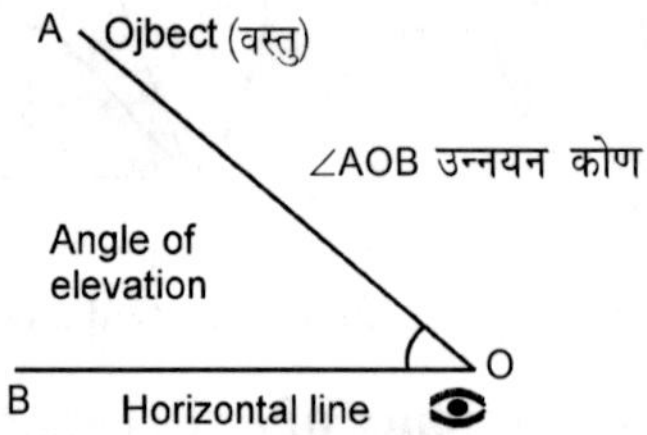

Fig. Angle of elevation

- **Angle in semi circle** ***(अर्धवृत्त में स्थित कोण)*** The angle in a semicircle is always a right angle. अर्धवृत्त में स्थित कोण समकोण होता है।

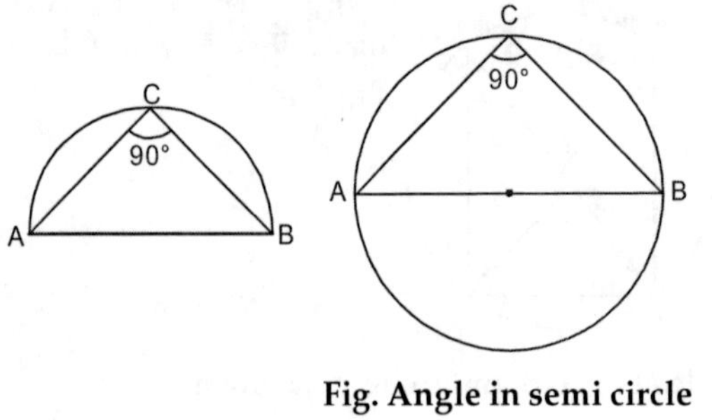

AB is diameter
then $\angle ACB = 90°$

Fig. Angle in semi circle

- **Angular displacement** ***(कोणीय विस्थापन)*** The angle of rotation measured from direction. यह किसी निश्चित दिशा से कोणीय चक्रण को दर्शाता है, घड़ी की सूई के विपरीत घुमाव पर यह धनात्मक होता है।
- **Angular velocity** ***(कोणीय वेग)*** It is the rate and change of angular distance denoted by ω or $\frac{d\theta}{dt}$. यह कोणीय विस्थापना के परिवर्तन की दर है इसे ω या $\frac{d\theta}{dt}$ से दर्शाते हैं।

Annulus : The region enclosed by two concentric circles. यह दो संकेन्द्री वृत्त के परिधि का मध्य भाग है।

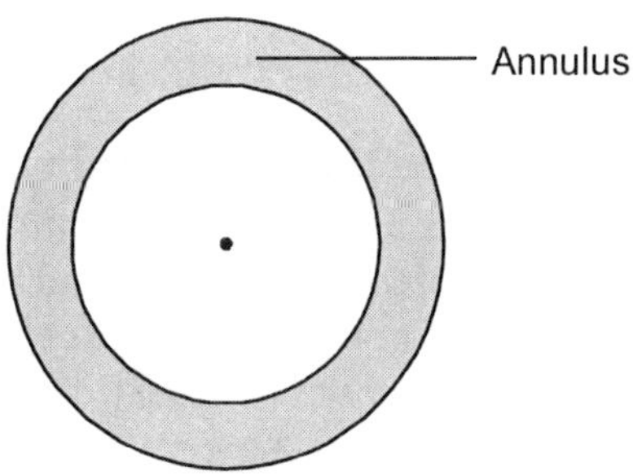

Fig. Annulus

Antecedent ***(वृत्तांत या पूर्वत्व)*** The hypothesis of conditional statement. The 'If' part of an 'if, then' statement. यह परिस्थितीय परिकल्पना है यदि ऐसा होता तब क्या होगा।

Anti-Logarithms ***(प्रतिलघुगुणक)*** It is the inverse of logarithm e.g. $\log_{10} 1000 = 3$ its antilog $\frac{3}{10} = 1000$. यह लघुगुणक का व्युत्पन्न होता है।

Apex ***(शीर्ष)*** It is the highest point of a solid or place figure with respect to a line or plane chosen as base. यह किसी आकृति के आधार बिन्दु से उच्चतम बिन्दु को दर्शाता है।

Apparent weight ***(आभाशी भार)***
In a lift when in motion

When lift moves upwards (जब लिफ्ट ऊपर को जाती है।) $m(g+f)$

When lift moves downwards (जब लिफ्ट नीचे को आती है।) $m(g-f)$

Arc *(चाप)* An arc is a section of the circumference of a circle, or part of a curve . A pair of compasses can be used to draw regular arcs. यह किसी वृत के परिधि का एक भाग या वक्रक होता है। इसे किसी परकार द्वारा निर्मित किया जा सकता है।

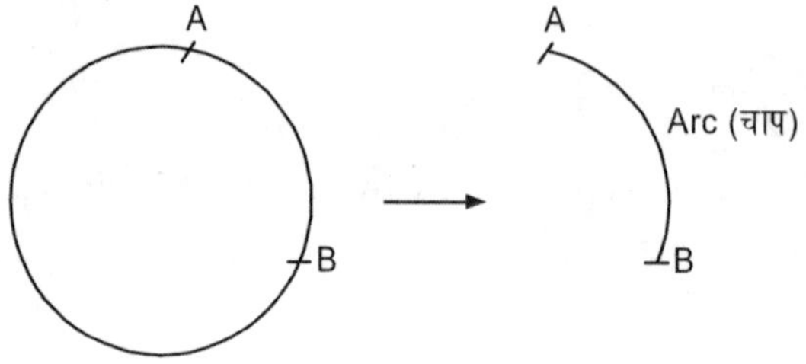

Fig. Arc

Archimedes Principle *(आर्किमीडिज का सिद्धान्त)* When a body is partly or wholly immersed in a liquid it experiences an upward thrust equal to the weight of the liquid displaced by the body and it acts through the centre of gravity of the space occupied originally by the displaced liquid. जब कोई ठोस अंशतः अथवा पूर्णत किसी द्रव में डुबोया जाता है तो उसके भार में कमी प्रतीत होती है, यह अभासी कमी ठोस द्वारा हटाये हुए द्रव के भार के बराबर होती है।

Area *(क्षेत्रफल)* Area is the amount of that spare something takes up on a surface. Area is measured in square metres or square yards. कोई वस्तु सतह पर जितना स्थान घेरती है वह उसका क्षेत्रफल कहलाता है। इसे वर्ग में नापा जाता है। जैसे–मी^{2}

- **Area between two curves** *(दो वक्रों के बीच का क्षेत्रफल)*

(*i*) When two curves intersect at two point (जब दो वक्र अलग-अलग बिंदु पर काटते हैं–

Common area = $\int_{A}^{b} (y_1 - y_2)\, dx$

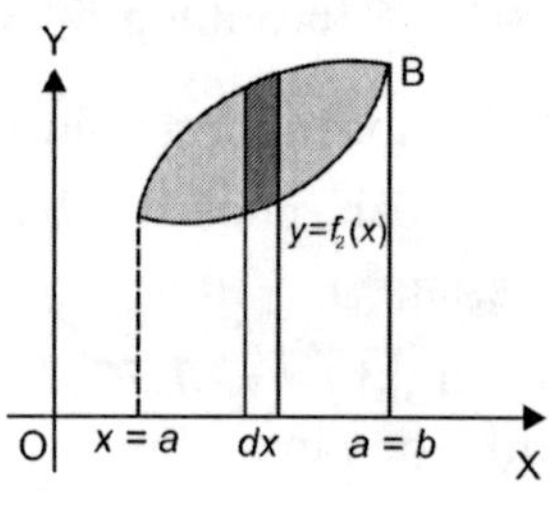

(*ii*) When two intersect at a point जब दोनों एक बिंदु पर काटते हैं–

$$\text{area} = \int_a^b f_1(x)\,dx + \int_\alpha^b f_2(x)\,dx$$

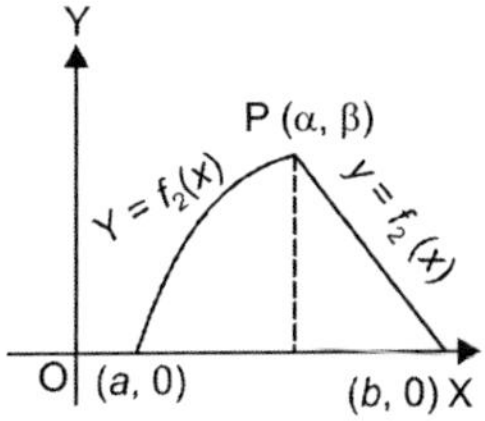

- **Area bounded by a curve** *(वक्र से घिरा क्षेत्रफल)*

(*i*) The area bounded by a cartesian curve $y = f(x)$, x–axis and abscissa $x = a$ and $x = b$ is given by, जब वक्र $y = f(x)$ है–

$$\text{Area} = \int_a^b y\,dx = \int_a^b f(x)\,dx$$

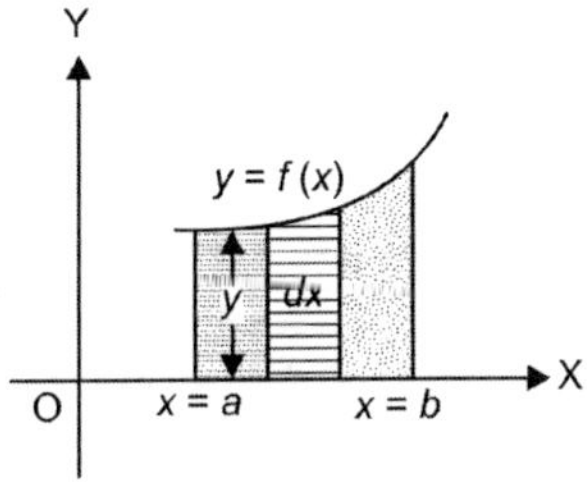

(*ii*) The area bounded by a cartesian curve $x = f(y)$, y - axis and ordinates $y = c$ and $y = d$
जब वक्र, $u = f(x)$ है

$$\text{Area} = \int_c^d x\,dy = \int_c^d f(y)\,dy$$

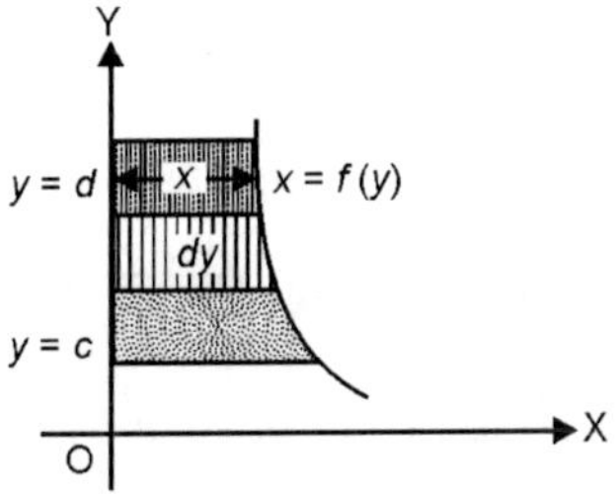

(*iii*) If the equation of a curve is in parametric form, say x = $f(t)$, $y = g(t)$, then the area प्राचलिक रूप में वक्र का क्षेत्रफल

$$= \int_A^b y\,dx = \int_{t_1}^{t_2} g(t)f'(t)dt$$

Where t_1 and t_2 are the values of t respectively correspoding to the values of a & b of x.
जहाँ t_1 व t_2 a व b के अनुसार परिवर्तित मान है।

- **Area of Circle *(वृत्त का क्षेत्रफल)*** Area = $\pi r^2 = \dfrac{\pi d^2}{4}$

where r = radius and d = diameter

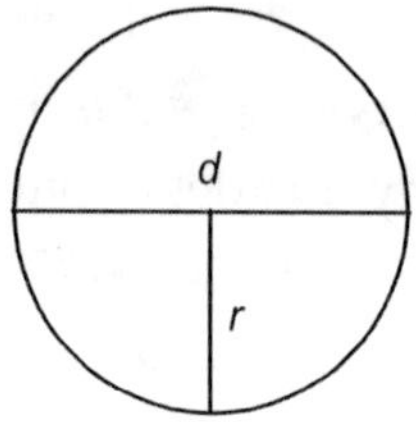

Area of Circle

- **Area of ellipse *(अण्ड वृत्त का क्षेत्रफल)* Area = π.ab**

π = Constant (3. 14) = 22/7
a = Major axis of ellipse
b = Minor axis of ellipse

- **Area of parallelogram *(समचतुर्भुज का क्षेत्रफल)*** Area = $b \times h$

(*i*) If a and b are two adjacent sides of a parallelogram then the (जब a और b दो बगल की भुजाए हैं।)

$$\text{area} = |a \times b|$$

(*ii*) If a and b represent two diagonasls of a parallelogram then the

(जब a and b समचतुर्भुज के विकर्ण हैं) area = $\dfrac{1}{2}\,|a \times b|$

- **Area of quadrilateral *(चतुर्भुज का क्षेत्रफल)***

$$= \frac{1}{2}\,[x_1y_2 - x_2y_1) + (x_2y_3 - x_3y_2) + (x_3y_4 - x_4y_3) + (x_4y_1 - x_1y_4)]$$

(*i*) Area of triangle ABC = $\dfrac{1}{2}$ [AB$\left|\vec{AB} \times \vec{AC}\right|$

(*ii*) If a, b, c are position vectors of vertices of a ΔABC then its

$$\text{Area} = \frac{1}{2}\,[(a + b) + (b \times c) + (c \times a)]$$

- **Area of a Sector of a Circle** *(वृत्त के त्रिज्यखण्ड का क्षेत्रफल)*

  Area = $\pi r^2\left(\frac{\theta}{360}\right)$

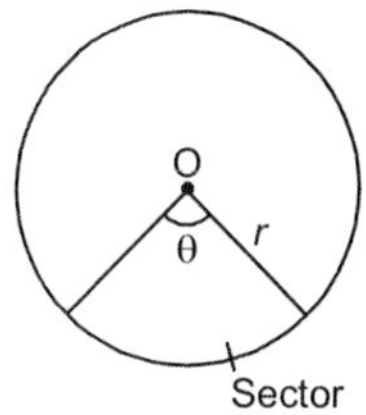

Area and Sector of a Circle

- **Area of a segment ACB :** *(वृत्त खण्ड का क्षेत्रफल)*

$$= \text{Area of sector OAB} - \text{Area of } \Delta OAB$$

$$= \pi r^2\left(\frac{\theta}{360}\right) - \frac{1}{2}r^2 \sin\theta$$

- **Area of ΔOAB**

$$= \frac{1}{2}r^2 \sin\theta.$$

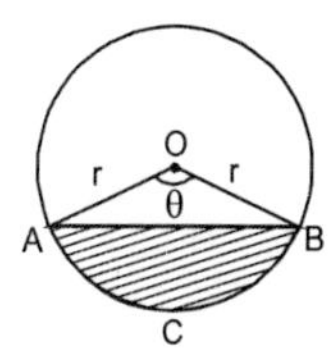

- **Area of Rectangle** *(आयत का क्षेत्रफल)* Area = $b \times h$

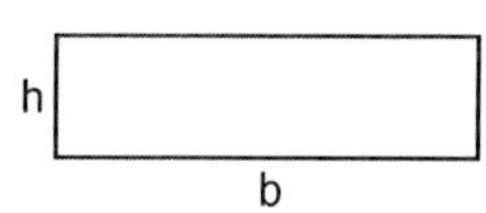

Fig. Area of Rectangle

- **Area of trapezium** *(समलम्ब चतुर्भुज का क्षेत्रफल)* Area = $\frac{a+b}{2} \times h$

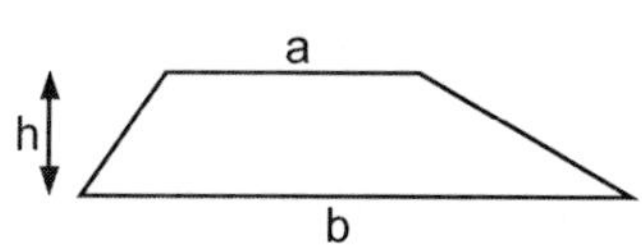

Area and trapezium

- **Area of a triangle** *(त्रिभुज का क्षेत्रफल)* Area = $\frac{b \times h}{2}$

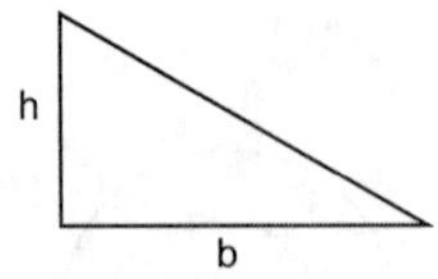

Area of a triangle

- **Area of triangle** *(त्रिभुज का क्षेत्रफल)*

$$\frac{\sin A}{a} = \frac{\sin B}{b} = \frac{\sin C}{c} = \frac{2\Delta}{abc}$$

The area of ΔABC is given by

(*i*) $\Delta = \frac{1}{2} bc \sin A$

(*ii*) $\Delta = \frac{1}{2} ba \sin B$

(*iii*) $\Delta = \frac{1}{2} ab \sin C$

B

Ball ***(गेंद)*** A sphere togather with its interior. गोले का आंतरिक भाग।

Band Matrix ***(बैंड आव्यूह)*** A matrix whose only non-zero entries lie or a band around the leading diagonal. आव्यूह जिसमें शून्य रहित आकड़ें बैंड पर अंकित होते हैं।

Bar ***(बार)*** It is a unit of pressure in C.G.S. system.
$1 \text{ Bar} = 10^6 \text{ dynes/ cm}^2$ सी.जी.एस पद्धति में दाब मात्रक है।

Bar graph ***(स्तम्भ आलेख)*** In this statistical data is presents by vertical bars of equal widths and their lengths depend on frequencies. इसमें सांख्यिक आंकड़ों को एक समान चौड़ाई वाले ऊर्ध्वाधर खीचें गए दंडों द्वारा व्यक्त किया जाता है। इसकी लम्बाई आवृत्ति पर निर्भर करती है।

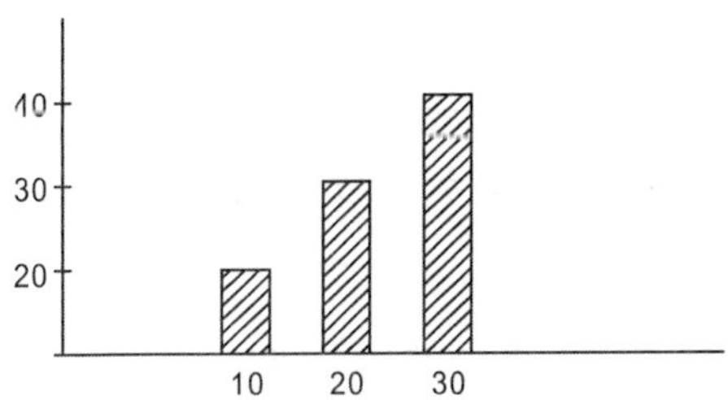

Fig. Bar Graph

Base ***(आधार रेखा)*** Base is a line on which figure stands. वह रेखा जिस पर कोई आकृति स्थिर होती है।

Basic proportionality theorem (BPT) ***(आधारभूत समानुपातिकता प्रमेय)*** If a line drawn parallel to one side of a triangle intersecting the other two sides then it divides these sides in the same ration. यदि एक त्रिभुज की किसी एक भुजा के समान्तर दो अन्य भुजाओं को प्रतिच्छेद करती हुई रेखा खींची जाय जो दो अन्य भुजाओं को समान अनुपात में बाँटती है। तब

Here $BC \parallel DE$

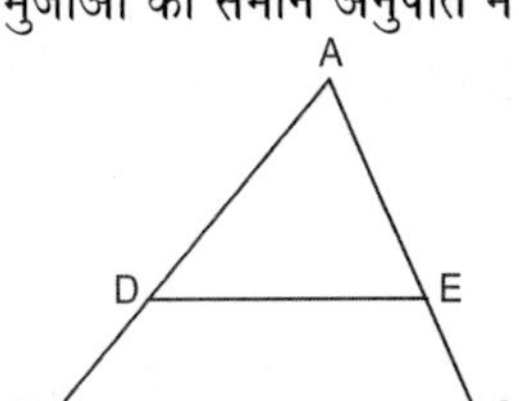

$$\therefore \frac{AD}{BD} = \frac{AE}{EC}$$

Fig. Basic proportionality theorem

Baye's Rule *(बॉयस नियम)* A rule for finding conditional probability. वह नियम जो परिस्थितिक संभावनाओं को व्यक्त करता है।

Bearing *(व्यवहारिक स्थिति)* A bearing is a direction measured in degree. It is always the measurement of the angle between line running north to south and a second line. किसी रेखा की स्थिति को उत्तर से दक्षिण की दिशा में हुई गति को अंश में व्यक्त किया जाता है।

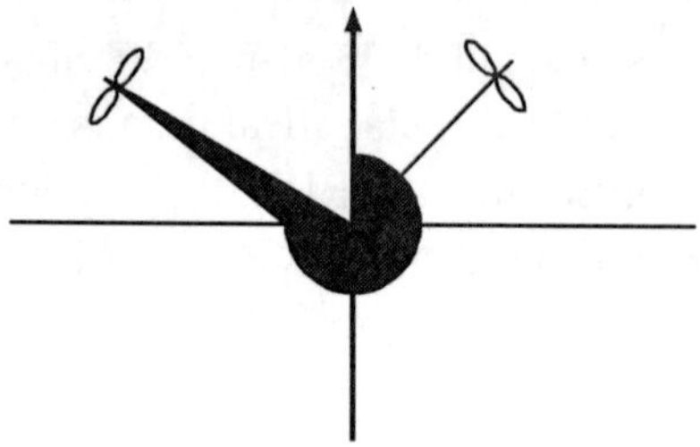

Fig. Bearing

Bernoulli equation *(बरनौली समीकरण)* It is a differential equation of the form as given below

$$\frac{dy}{dx} + yf(x) = yg(x)$$

यह एक अवकलन समीकरण है।

Bias *(प्रवृत्त (पसँघा)* The bias is the average difference between the measurement and truth. यह यथार्थ तथा मापी गयी मात्रा के बीच के अन्तर को व्यक्त करता है।

Bi-conditional statement *(द्विआश्रित कथन)* A compound statement that says one sentence is true if and only if the other sentence is true. वह संयुक्त कथन जिसमें यदि दूसरा कथन सत्य है तभी पहला सत्य होगा।

Billion *(दस अरब)* It is equal to a million. यह मिलियन के बराबर होता है। In Britain and Germany 1 billion = 10^{12} and France 1 billion = 10^9.

Bimodal *(द्विमॉडल)* A data having two modes. वह स्थिति जिसमें दो मॉडल हों।

Binary number *(द्विगुण संख्या)* A number written to base 2. वह संख्या जो आधार 2 पर व्यक्त की जाती है।

Binary number system *(द्विगुण संख्या पद्धति)* The number system that uses only 0's and 1's. The places in the binary numbers are ...

$2^n.....2^5 = 32, 2^3 = 8, 2^1 = 2, 2^0 = 1$. वह पद्धति जिसमें केवल दो संख्या (0 तथा 1) होता है।

Binary operation ***(द्विगुण सरलीकरण)*** A binary operation is an operation that involves two operands. For example, addition and subtraction are binary operation. वह सरलीकरण जिसमें दो विपरित विद्या को सरल किया जाता है।

Binomial ***(द्विपद)*** Any Polynomial that contains only two terms. ऐसा d kbZc gqin ft l esnkO; ksd gkst \$ s $(6x + 2y)$.

Binomial coefficients & their properties ***(द्विपदीप गुणक और उसके गुण)*** In the expansion of $(1 + x)^n = C_0 + C_1x + C_2x_2 + ... + C_rx_r + ... + C_nx^n$

Where $C_0 = 1, = n, C_2 = \dfrac{n(n+1)}{2!}$

(*i*) $C_0 + C_1 + C_2 + ... + C_n = 2^n$

(*ii*) $C_0 - C_1 + C_2 - C_3 + ... = 0$

(*iii*) $C_0 - C_2 + ... = C_1 + C_3 + ... = 2^{n-1}$

(*iv*) $C_0^2 - C_1^2 + C_2^2 + ... + C_n^2 = \dfrac{2n!}{n!n!}$

(*v*) $C_0 - 2C_1 + 3C_2 + ... + (n+1)C_n = 2^{n-1}(n+2)$

(*vi*) $C_0 + \dfrac{C_1}{2} + \dfrac{C_2}{3} + ... + \dfrac{C_n}{n+1} = \dfrac{2^{n+1}-1}{n+1}$

Binomial Expression ***(द्विपद व्यंजक)*** An algebraic expression containing two terms is called a binomial expression. ऐसा व्यंजक जिसमें दो पद, बीजीय संकेतांक्षरों '+' अथवा '–' से जुड़े होते हैं। द्विपद व्यंजक कहलाते हैं। जैसे– $x + y, a + b, 2n - 3y$ etc.

Binomial surd ***(द्विपदीय करणी)*** An expression consisting of the sum or difference of two monomial surds or the sum of a monomial surd and a rafional number is called a binomial surd. वह करणी जिसमें दो एकपदी करणीयाँ या एकपदी करणी और दूसरी कोई परिमेय संख्या होती है, द्विपदी करणी कहलाती है जैसे– $2+\sqrt{3}$, $\sqrt{3}-2$, $\sqrt{3+\sqrt{5}}$.

Binomial theorem ***(द्विपद प्रमेय)*** If n is a +ve integer then

$$(x+a)^n = n\,c_0\;x^n + n\,c_1 x^{n-1} + nc_2 x^{n-2} + \ldots$$

where x and a are any numbers.

ऐसा सिद्धान्त जिसकी सहायता से किसी भी घातांक के लिये द्विपद प्रमेय का विस्तार किया जा सकता है, द्विपद प्रमेय कहलाता है।

Bisect *(समद्विभाजित)* To cut or divide something in half. किसी चीज को दो बराबर भागों में बाँटना।

Line BD bisects angle ABC

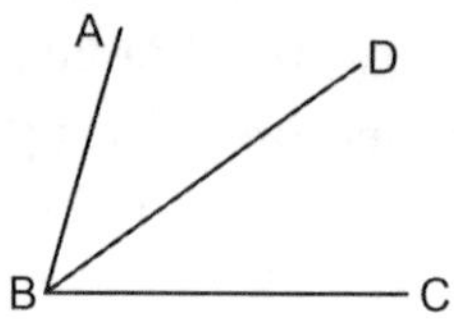

Fig. Bisect

Bisectors of angles between two lines *(दो रेखाओं के बीच के कोण का समद्विविभाजक)*

$$\frac{a_1x + b_1y + c_1}{\sqrt{a_1^2 + b_1^2}} = \frac{a_2x + b_2y + c_2}{\sqrt{a_2^2 + b_2^2}}$$

Boolean Algebra *(बूलिन बीजगणित)* The set of rules permitting logical statements to be written in algebraic form using symbols and set theory. It is possible to represent the results of such statements in a truth table. बीजगणित के तार्किक नियमों का संग्रह जिससे यर्थाथ सारणी बनाते हैं।

Boundary *(सीमा)* The boundary of a figure is the curve or curves which define outer edges of the figure. वह वक्र जो आकृति की बाह्य परिधि को व्यक्त करता है।

Brackets *(कोष्ठक)* Brackets are used for indicating the order in which mathematical operation are to the carried out e.g.

$$9 + (3 \times 4) = 9 + 12 = 21$$

कोष्ठक से सरलीकरण की विधि व्यक्त की जाती है।

Breakdown point *(ब्रेकडाउन बिन्दु)* The breakdown point of an estimator is the smallest fraction of observation one must corrupt to make the estimator take any value one wants. वह न्यूनतम अंश जिससे आकलन प्रभावित होता है।

C

Calculation *(गणना)* A calculating is a way of solving a number problem. Calculation can use addition, subtraction, multiplication and division to produce an answer. संख्याओं को सरल करने की एक विद्या जिसमें संख्याओं का जोड़ घटाव, गुणा या भाग किया जाता है।

Calculator *(कॉल्क्युलेटर)* A calculator is a machine that can do arithmetical operation and logical operations.यह अंकगणतीय गणना या सरल करने वाला एक यंत्र है।

Calculus *(काल्कुलस)* (1) A branch of mathematics concerned with rate of change, gradients of curves, maximum and minimum value of function and the calculation of lengths, areas, volumes. It involves determining areas (integration) and tangents (differentiation) which are mutually inverse. गणित की वह शाखा जो परिवर्तन की दर, वक्र का झुकाव, महत्तम, न्यूनतम, फलन का मान, गणना, लम्बाई, क्षेत्रफल, आयतन, आवकलन तथा समाकलन आदि का ज्ञान कराती है।

(*ii*) Calculus is a way of calculating in mathematics. If often involves the use of symbols from algebra to solve problems concerned with statistics and changing quantities or amounts. गणना करने की एक विशेष विधि जिसमें संख्याओं या मात्राओं को बीजगणतीय विधि द्वारा किया जाता है।

Calories *(कैलोरी)* It is the amount of heat energy needed to increase the temperature of 1g of water through 1 ic (14.5°C to 15. 5 °C)

1 Calorie = 4.1840 joules

एक ग्राम जल का तापमान 1°C बढ़ाने के लिये (14.5°C–15.5°C) आावश्यक उष्मा की मात्रा को कैलोरी कहते हैं।

Cancel *(सरल करना)* To cancel is to simplify a fraction down to its lowest form in cancelling both the numerator and denominator are divided by the same number. किसी भिन्न के अंश और हर में किसी एक संख्या द्वारा विभाजित करके लघुतम रूप में व्यक्त करना।

Cancellation *(सरलीकरण)* Cancellation is the process that is used for producing on equivalent fraction, from a given fraction. In it numerator and denominator are divided by same common factor e.g. $\frac{20}{35} = \frac{4}{7}$. किसी दिये गये भिन्न के समतुल्य भिन्न प्राप्त करने की विधि जिसमें समान संख्या से अंश और हर को विभाजित किया जाता है।

Capacity ***(क्षमता)*** Capacity is the amount of space or volume that something which can be poured takes up. The main metric unit of capacity is the litre. किसी वस्तु द्वारा घेरने वाला स्थान या धारण की मात्रा जब इसमें कोई वस्तु रखी जाती है। क्षमता की मुख्य मैट्रिक इकाई लीटर है।

Capital ***(मूलधन)*** The capital of business is the amount of money invested in the business. The money is spent to buy the things the business needs to carry on its trade. किसी व्यापार में खर्च की जाने वाली राशि या उधार लिये गए धन को जिससे व्यापार चलाया जाता है।

Carat ***(कैरेट)*** A unit of mans used for precious stones or metals. कीमती धातु या पत्थर की मात्रा व्यक्त करने का मात्रक कैरेट कहलाता है।

Cardinal number ***(समपदी संख्या)*** It is a whole number that represents the number of elements present in a set. वह सम्पूर्ण संख्या जो किसी समुच्चय में व्यक्त संख्या को दर्शाता है।

Carnot's Theorem ***(कैरनाट की प्रमेय)***

$$a^2 = b^2 + c^2 - 2bc \cos A$$

$$b^2 = a^2 + c^2 - 2ac \cos B$$

$$c^2 = a^2 + b^2 - 2ab \cos C$$

Cartesian co-ordinates ***(कारटेशियन समपद)*** A method of defining the position of a point by its distance from a fixed point, called origin, in the direction of two or more straight lines. In a plane the two straight lines are known as x- axis and y - axis and they form the basis of two dimensional coordinate system. The origin is the point of intersection of two axis.

यह किसी तल में x-अक्ष तथा y-अक्ष में स्थित किसी बिन्दु की स्थिति को नियत बिन्दु से दूरी प्रदर्शित करने वाली समपद संख्या है।

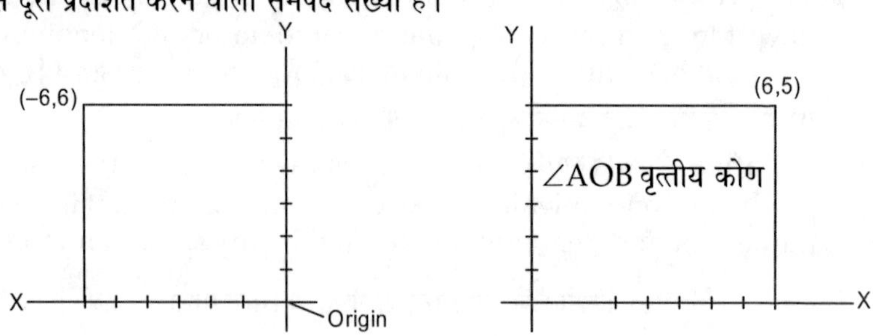

Fig. Cartesian co-ordinates

Cash *(नगद)* Cash is money in the form of notes and coins. Money held in a bank account is also referred to as cash. वह नगदी जो सिक्कों तथा नोटों में होती है। किसी बैंक खाता में जमा रकम भी नगदी की श्रेणी में रखी जाती है।

Cash card *(कैस कार्ड)* A cash card is a small plastic card which is used to draw money from a cash dispenser. यह प्लास्टिक का एक कार्ड है जिसके द्वारा एक विशेष प्रकार की मशीन से नगद निकाला जाता है।

Casting out nines *(9 द्वारा सत्यता जाँचना)* It is a way of checking the accuracy of an operation (basic arithmetic operation i.e. addition, subtraction, multiplication, division), the numbers are written in modulo 9 number system. The remainder left when the number is divided by 9 is called excess of nine

Addition = 639 + 271 = 910

The sum of digits (18) + (10) = (10)

in modulo 9 excess of nine 9 + 1 = 10 = 1

(1) – (1)

इसमें किसी संख्याओं की गणना की जाँच अंक 9 की संहायता से की जाती है जैसा कि ऊपर समझाया गया है।

Census *(जनगणना)* The count of a population . जनसंख्या की गिनती व गणना करना।

Centimetre *(सेन्टीमीटर)* A centimetre is a measure of length in the metrisystem. There are 100 centimetres in a metre. The short from centimetres is cm. लम्बाई को मापने की एक ईकाई जिसे सेन्टीमीटर कहते हैं। 1 मीटर में 100 सेन्टीमीटर होते हैं। इसे cm से दर्शाया जाता है।

Central angle *(वृत्तीय कोण)* An angle that has its vertex at the centre of a circle. Here $\angle AOB$ is central angle. केन्द्र पर बना कोण वृत्त का वृत्तीय कोण कहलाता है।

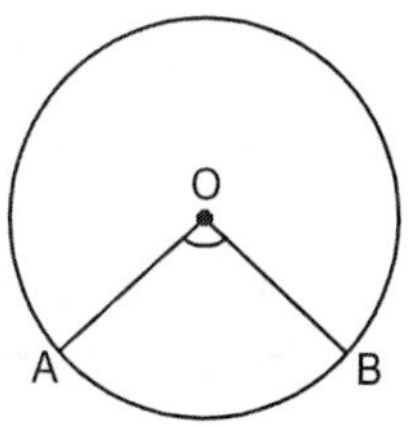

Fig. Central angle

Centres of triangle *(वृत्त का केन्द्र)*

If A(x_1, y_1); (x_2, y_2) and C (x_3, y_3) are vertices of a triangle ABC, then

(*i*) Co-ordinates of centroid G $\left(\frac{x_1+x_2+x_3}{3}, \frac{y_1+y_2+y_3}{3}\right)$ (केन्द्रक के निर्देशांक)

(*ii*) Co-ordinates of incentre $\left(\frac{ax_1+bx_2+cx_3}{a+b+c}, \frac{ay_1+by_2+cy_3}{a+b+c}\right)$ अंतः केन्द्र के निर्देशांक

(*iii*) **Circumcentre :** The coordinates of circumcentre O(x,y) are obtained by solving the equations given by $OA^2 = OB^2 = OC^2$

(*iv*) **Orthocentre :** It can be obtained by solving the equation of any two altitudes.

Congruent triangles *(सर्वांगसम त्रिभुज)*

1. Two triangles are curgruent, if in a matching of their vertices, the three sides and the three angles of one triangles are respectively equal to the corresponding parts of the other. (AAA congruency)
2. Two sides and induded angle are equales to the other two sides and induded angles. (SAS congruency)
3. Two angles and included side are equales to the other two sides and induded angles. (ASA congruency)
4. Three sides are equal to other two sides. (SSS congruency)
5. Right angle, hypotenuse and one side are equal to other right and hypotenuse and one sides. (RHS congruency)

1. दो त्रिभुज सर्वांगसम होते हैं, यदि उनके शीर्षों के एक सुमेलन के अंतर्गत एक त्रिभुज की तीनों भुजाएँ और तीनों कोण क्रमशः दूसरे त्रिभुज की संगत भुजाओं और कोणों के बराबर हैं।
2. दो त्रिभुज सर्वांगसम होते हैं, यदि एक त्रिभुज की दो भुजाएँ और उनके बीच का कोण क्रमशः दूसरे त्रिभुज की दो भुजाओं और उनके बीच के कोण के बराबर हैं **(SAS सर्वांगसमता प्रतिबंध)**।
3. दो त्रिभुज सर्वांगसम होते हैं, यदि एक त्रिभुज के दो कोण और उनके बीच की भुजा क्रमशः दूसरे त्रिभुज के दो कोणों और उनके बीच की भुजा के बराबर हैं **(ASA सर्वांगसमता प्रतिबंध)**।
4. दो त्रिभुज सर्वांगसम होते हैं, यदि एक त्रिभुज की तीनों भुजाएँ क्रमशः दूसरे त्रिभुज की तीनों भुजाओं के बराबर हैं **(SSS सर्वांगसमता प्रतिबंध)**।
5. दो समकोण त्रिभुज सर्वांगसम होते हैं, यदि एक त्रिभुज का कर्ण और कोई एक भुजा क्रमशः दूसरे त्रिभुज के कर्ण और एक भुजा के बराबर हैं **(RHS सर्वांगसमता प्रतिबंध)**।

Centroid *(केन्द्रक)* The centre of mass of an object is that point where the would balance if supported by a single support. The point in a triangle where the three medians intersect . Here G is centroid of the triangle. किसी भी वस्तु का मध्य बिन्दु, त्रिभुज की माध्यिकाओं के मिलने का स्थान त्रिभुज का केन्द्रक कहलाता है, चित्र में G केन्द्रक है।

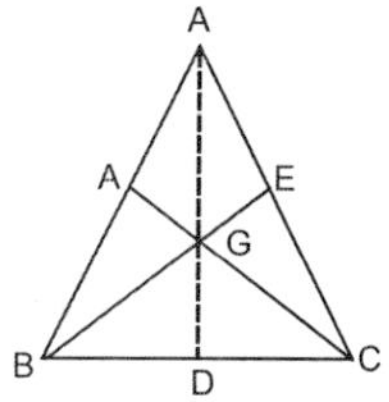

Fig. Centroid

Century *(शताब्दी)* A Century means 100 years. The name 'century' comes from the word 'centura' which means a hundred. इसकी उत्पत्ति लैटिन भाषा के 'सेन्चुरा' शब्द से हुई है। जिसका अर्थ 100 वर्ष का काल होता है।

Chain *(चेन)* It is an instrument used for surrey. Its standard lenght is 66 feet (22 yards) 1 acre = 10 square chain = 4840 square yards. सर्वे करने का एक यंत्र जिसकी परिमाणिक लम्बाई 66 फीट होती है।

Chance *(क्रमहीनता)* Chance is the way something seem to happen without a reason. The word chance is also sometimes used to mean probability. वह क्रम जो बिना किसी कारण के होता है, इसका अर्थ कभी-कभी संभावनाओं से भी होता है।

Cheque *(चेक)* A Cheque is a printed piece of paper which orders bank to pay out money from on account held by the owner of the cheque. किसी बैंक द्वारा मुद्रित कागज की स्लिप जिसका उपयोग बैंक से नगदी निकालने में किया जाता है।

Chord *(जीवा)* A chord is a straight line that joins two points on the circumference of a circle. If does not pass through the centre of the circle. वृत्त की परिधि पर स्थित दो बिन्दुओं से निर्मित रेखाखण्ड जो वृत्त के केन्द्र से होकर न गुजरती है।

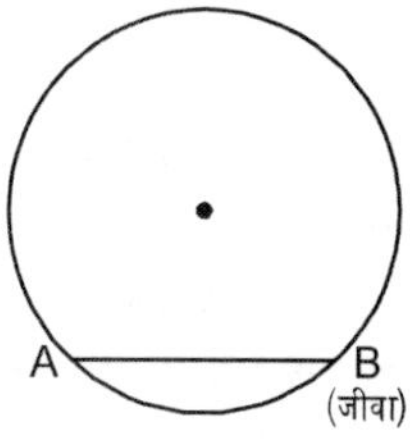

Fig. Chord

Chord of a circle ***(वृत्त की जीवा)*** A line segment with its end points, lying on a circle is called a chord of the circle. Here AB, CD are chord of the circle, Diameter is the longest chord of the circle. वह रेखाखण्ड जिसके दोनों सिरे वृत्त की परिधि पर वृत्त की जीवा कहलाती है व्यास वृत्त की सबसे बड़ी जीवा होती है। AB और CD वृत्त की जीवा है।

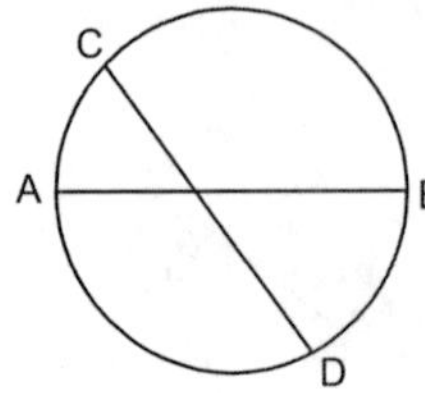

Fig. Chord of a circle

Circle ***(वृत्त)*** (*i*) A circle is a round shape. The edge or circumference of a circle is always the same distance from the centre point. वृत्त तल में बनी एक बन्द आकृति है जो तल मे स्थित उन सभी बिन्दुओं से मिलकर बनती है, जो तल में स्थित एक निश्चित बिन्दु (केन्द्र) से आचर दूरी पर होते हैं।

(*ii*) Circle is a set of those points in a plane which are at the constant distance from the fixed point, the fixed point is said to be the centre and constant distance is its radius. बिन्दुओं के निश्चित दूरी बनायें रखने का एक पथ जो किसी बिन्दु से हो, उस बिन्दु को केन्द्र तथा निश्चित दूरी को त्रिज्या कहते हैं।

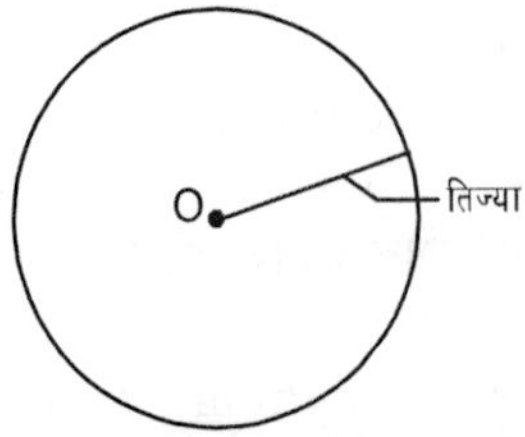

Fig. Circle

- **Circle** ***वृत्त, (तथ्य)***

1. The region bounded by an are of the circle and the chord of the are is called a segment of the circle.
2. Angles in a semicircle is a right angle.
3. Angle formed in the same segment are equal
4. Two equal chords are equidistant from the centre

1. एक वृत्त के चाप तथा चाप की संगत जीवा से परिबद्ध क्षेत्र वृत्तखंड कहलाता है।
2. अर्धवृत्त में बना कोण एक समकोण होता है।
3. एक ही वृत्तखंड में बने कोण बराबर होते हैं।
4. समान लम्बाई की जीवा केन्द्र से समान दूरी पर स्थित होती है।

Circular region ***(वृत्तीय क्षेत्र)*** The interior of a circle together with the circle itself is called is called the circular region. वृत्त का आन्तरिक भाग वृत्तीय क्षेत्र कहलाता है।

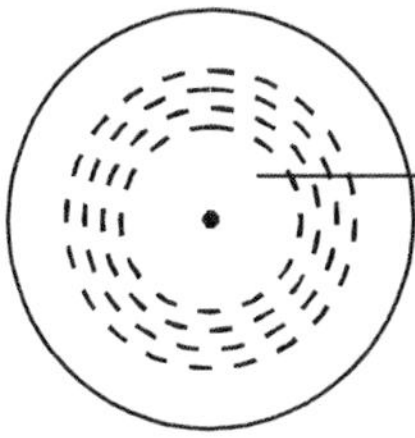

Fig. Circular region

Circumference ***(परिधि)*** The circumference of a circle is the distance measured around its edge if the circumference of circle is divided by the diameter, the answer is always the same. This number is called pi and written as π,

$$\pi = \frac{\text{circunference of cirde}}{\text{diameter of a cirde}}$$

$$\pi = 3.14 \text{ or } \frac{22}{7}$$

किसी वृत्त की परिधि वह लम्बाई है जिसके द्वारा वृत्त घिरा रहता है, यदि वृत्त की परिधि को इसके व्यास से विभाजित किया जाए तो एक निश्चित मान प्राप्त होता है। जिसे पाई (π) कहते हैं। इसका मूल्य 3.14 $\frac{22}{7}$ होता है।

Circumcircle of a triangle and its radius ***(त्रिभुज का अन्तवृत्त और उसकी त्रिज्या)***

(*i*) $R = \frac{a}{2\sin A} = \frac{b}{2\sin B} = \frac{c}{2\sin C}$

(*ii*) $R = \frac{abc}{4\Delta}$

(*iii*) $R = \frac{\sin A}{a} = \frac{\sin B}{b} = \frac{\sin C}{c} = \frac{1}{2R}$

Clock ***(घड़ी)*** A clock is an instrument for measuring time, there are two main types of clock. Some have pointers called hands, which turn slowly and point to numbers around the outside of a circular face. Other known as digital clocks, show a set of numbers on a screen or read out that change every minute or second. समय मापने का एक यंत्र, यह दो प्रकार का होता है। एक में समय सूईयों के द्वारा ज्ञात किया जाता है जबकि दूसरे प्रकार में समय स्क्रीन पर अंकित होता रहता है।

Closure property ***(संवरक गुणधर्म)*** If the result of doing an operation an any two elements of set is always an element of the set , then the set is set is closed under the operation. किसी समुच्चय के दो अवयव हमेशा उसी के अवयव होगें।

Coin ***(सिक्का)*** A coin is an item of money made of metal. It is usually of small value only. धातु की बनी मुद्रा, इसे प्रायः कम मूल्य के लिये बनाया जाता है।

Coincident lines ***(अनुरूप रेखाएँ)***

Two lines $a_1x + b_1y + c_1 = 0$ and $a_2x + b_2y + c_2 = 0$ are coincident only and only if (दो रेखाओं एक-दूसरे के अनुरूप होंगी जब)

$$\Rightarrow \frac{a_1}{a_2} = \frac{b_1}{b_2} = \frac{c_1}{c_2}$$

Condition of concurrency ***(सर्वांगसमता की दशा)***

$$\begin{vmatrix} a_1 & b_1 & c_1 \\ a_2 & b_2 & c_2 \\ a_3 & b_3 & c_3 \end{vmatrix} = 0$$

Collinear points ***(एकरेखीय बिन्दु)*** Three or more points are known as collinear if there is a line which contain all.

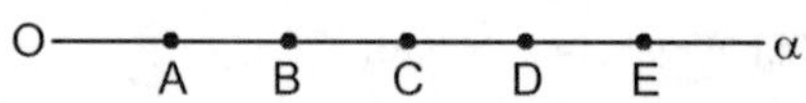

Fig. Collinear points

तीन या तीन से अधिक बिन्दु जो एक रेखा पर स्थित होते हैं।

Column Matrix ***(स्तम्भ आव्यूह)*** A single column matrix is called a column or a column vector e.g the matrix $\begin{vmatrix} a_1 \\ a_2 \\ a_3 \end{vmatrix}$. जिस आव्यूह में केवल एक स्तम्भ होता है उसे स्तम्भ आव्यूह कहते हैं। जैसे $\begin{vmatrix} 7 \\ 8 \\ 9 \end{vmatrix}$ एक स्तम्भ आव्यूह है।

Common denominator ***(सम-हर)*** A common denominator is a denominator that is the same for every fraction in a group of fraction. In order to be able to add or subtract a group of fraction they must all have a common denominator.

$$\frac{1}{4}+\frac{1}{3}=\frac{3}{12}+\frac{4}{12}, 12 \text{ is the common denominator.}$$

ऐसे भिन्न जिनका हर समान होता है, यदि हर समान न हो तो हर को समान ही जोड़ा या घटाया जाता है।

Common-factor ***(समगुणनखण्ड)*** Any number or an expression which divides two or more given numbers or expression is called a common factor. वह संख्या या पद जो दो या अधिक संख्याओं या पदों को विभाजित कर सकता है।

Common multiple ***(समगुणक)*** Any whole number which is a multiple of a group of numbers e.g. 100 is common multiple of 4, 5, 10 , 20 , 25. वह पूर्ण संख्या जो एक समूह संख्याओं का गुणक होता है जैसे– 100 के समगुणक 5, 10, 20, 25 हैं।

Compass ***(चुम्बकीय सूई)*** (*i*) A compass is a device used to locate the north pole. It has a circular face with north, east and west marked on it and a magnetic needle that always points to the magnetic north pole. एक चुम्बकीय सूई जिसकी सूई हमेशा उत्तरी ध्रुव की तरफ स्थिर होती है जिस पर चारों दिशाओं के संकेत अंकित होते हैं।

(*ii*) ***(गोलाप्रकार)*** A tool used to draw a circle or measure small distance. एक प्रकार का यंत्र जिससे गोला बनाया जाता है या छोटी दूरी नापी जाती है।

Combination ***(संचय)*** Each of the different selections made by taking some or all of a number to objects, irrespective of their arrangements is called a combination.

Here the different combinations formed by three letters A, B, C at time are AB, BC, AC. यदि कुछ दी गई वस्तुओं में से कुछ अथवा सभी को साथ लेकर विभिन्न प्रकार के समुदाय या विन्यास उनके क्रम को ध्यान में न रखते हुए बनाये जाएँ तो उनमें से प्रत्येक समुदाय को संचय कहते हैं।

Example—तीन अक्षरों a, b, c मे से दो अक्षर एक साथ लेकर तथा क्रम का ध्यान रखते हुए विभिन्न संचय ab, ac, bc बनेंगे।

Complementary Combination ***(पूरक संचय)*** दी हुई n वस्तुओं में से r वस्तुओं को

लाने पर प्राप्त संचयों की संख्या उन्हीं n वस्तुओं में से $(n-r)$ वस्तुओं को लाने पर प्राप्त संचयों की संख्या के बराबर होता है।

$$^nC_r = {^nC_{n-r}}$$

$\therefore$ n वस्तुओं में से r वस्तुओं लेने पर संचयों की संख्या

$$^nC_r = \frac{n!}{r! \times (n-r)}!$$

Complement ***(परिपूरक)*** (*i*) A complement is the collection of all the things in a subset that are not part of a universal set. किसी उपसमुच्चय में एकत्रित समस्त वस्तु जो सार्वभौमिक समुच्चय में नहीं होते हैं।
(*ii*) The complement of a subset of a given set is the collection of all elements of the set that are not elements of the subset. सम्पूर्ण अवयव का समूह उस समुच्चय का पूरक समुच्चय होता है।

Complementary angles ***(पूरक कोण)*** Complementary angles are two angles that add to 90°, Angles 60° and 30° are complementary.

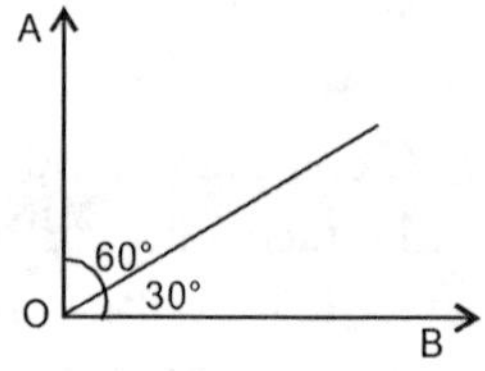

Fig. Complementary angles

यदि दो कोणों के मापों का योगफल 90° हो तो उन्हें पूरक कोण कहते हैं।

Compound angles ***(संयुक्त कोण)*** Sum or difference of two or more angles. दो कोणों के योग या अन्तर को संयुक्त कोण कहते हैं।

Composite number ***(भाज्य संख्याएं)*** Any integer which is not a prime number, i.e., evenly divisible by numbers other than 1 and itself or a number which has more than two factors are called composite number least composite no is 4. ऐसी संख्याएं जिनके दो से अधिक गुणनखण्ड हों।

Compound interest ***(चक्रवृद्धि ब्याज)*** Compound interest is interest calculated on the amount of the original sum of money borrowed, plus any interest which has been added to this sum. मूलधन में अर्जित ब्याज जोड़ने से प्राप्त मूलधन पर प्राप्त ब्याज को चक्रवृद्धि ब्याज कहते हैं।

$$CI = P\left[1+\frac{r}{100}\right]^4 - 1 \text{ or } CI = A - P.$$

Computer *(कम्प्यूटर)* Computer is an electronic machine that can analyses and store information and make calculation. एक इलेक्ट्रानिक मशीन जो ऑकडों का विश्लेषण व उनको एकत्रित करता है। इससे ऑकडों की गणना भी की जा सकती है।

Concentric *(संकेन्द्री)* Concentric means to have the same centre. A group of circles which share the same centre are called concentric circles. ऐसे वृत्त जिनका केन्द्र एक ही होता है।

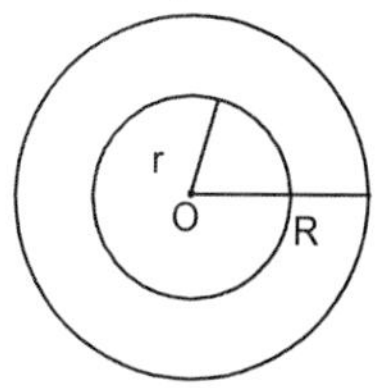

Fig. Concentric

Concurrent lines *(संरेख रेखाएँ)* Three or more straight lines are said to be concurrent lines if they meet in a point. तीन या तीन से अधिक रेखाएँ संरेख होंगी यदि वे किसी एक ही बिन्दु से गुजरती हो।

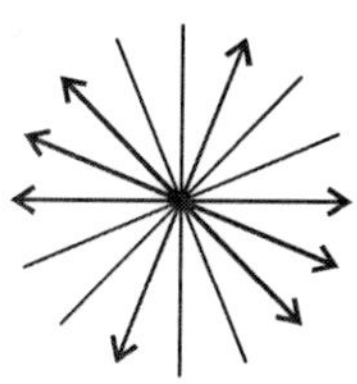

Fig. Concurrent lines

Cone *(शंकु)* A cone is a kind of said shape or polyhedron. It has a flat circular bottom and sloping sides. The sides rise up from the base and meet at a point at the top, called the vertex.

Fig. Cone

एक नोकदार आकृति जिसकी सतह गोल होती है तथा दूसरी सिरा नुकीला होता है।

Congruence ***(सर्वांग समता)*** The state of having the same size and shape. एक ही नाप व आकार के चिन्ह।

Congruent ***(सर्वांगसम)*** Two shapes in the plane or in space are congruent if there is a rigid motion that identifies one with the other. दो चित्र एक दूसरे के ठीक समान हो जैसे–

$\Delta ABC \cong \Delta DEF$

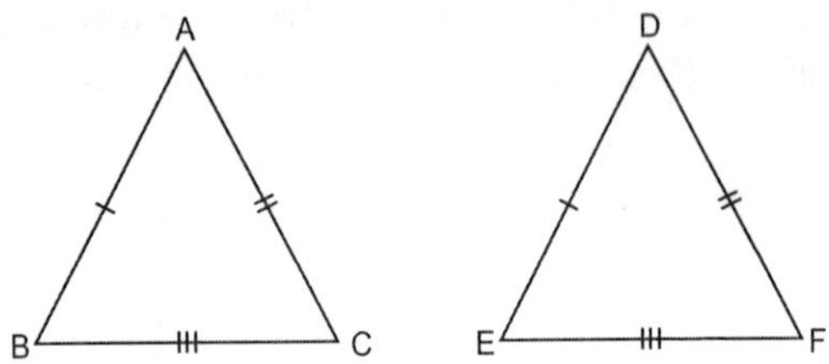

Fig. Congruent

Conjugate (of a complex no) ***(युगल मिश्रित संख्याएँ)*** The conjugate of a complex number is formed by reversing the sign on the imaginary part of a number the conjugate of $a + bi$ is $a - bi$. अल्पनिक भाग के चिन्ह को बदलने पर युगल मिश्रित संख्या प्राप्त होती है।

Conjugated surds ***(संयुग्मी करणी)*** Two binominal surds which differ only in sign (+ or –) between in terms connecting them are called conjugated surds e.g. $a+\sqrt{5}$ and $a-\sqrt{5}$ are conjugated surds. दो द्विपदी करणी जो केवल चिहनों (+, –) में अलग होते हैं।

Coordinate ***(निर्देशांक)*** (1) A set of numbers which gives the location of certain point or object. (2) A set of numbers that locates the position of a point usually represented by (x, y) values. किसी बिन्दु या वस्तु की स्थिति का बोध अंकों द्वारा या अक्षरों द्वारा ज्ञात किया जाए।

Coordinate axis ***(निर्देशांक अक्ष)*** The two perpendicular lines that form the x and y-axis and create four quadrants. दो लम्बवत रेखाएं (x अक्ष और y अक्ष) चार बराबर भाग बनाती हैं। दोनों लम्बवत रेखाएं निर्देशांक अक्ष कहलाती हैं। क्षैतिज रेखा x-अक्ष या उर्ध्वाधर रेखा y-अक्ष कहलाती हैं।

D

Data *(डाटा)* Information, often numerical, that is usually organized in graphs or charts to show relationships. किसी आलेखन चार्ट द्वारा जो अंकीय सूचना या सम्बन्ध प्रदर्शित करता हो।

Decagon *(दशभुज)* A polygon with 10 sides. वह बहुभुज जिसमें 10 भुजाऐं हो।

Fig. Decagon

Decameter *(डेकामीटर)* A term used in metric system, 10 metres or approximately 32.808 feet. 1 डेकामीटर = 10 मीटर

Decimal *(दशमलव)* A fraction having a power of ten as denominator, such as 0.34 = 34/100 or 0.344 = 344/1000. वह भिन्न जिसका हर अंश दश की घात में हो।

$$0.34 = \frac{34}{100} = \frac{34}{10^2}$$

$$\text{or } 0.344 = \frac{344}{1000} = \frac{344}{10^3}$$

Decimal (Decimal number) *(दशमलव अंक)* A number written using base ten; a number containing a decimal point. वह संख्या जिसका आधार दस हो।

Decimetre *(डेसीमीटर)* One-tenth of a metre approximately 3.937 inches. एक मीटर का दशवाँ भाग 1 डेसीमीटर होता है।

1 डेसीमीटर $= \frac{1}{10}$ मीटर या 1 मी. = 10 डेसीमीटर

Decimal point *(दशमलव बिन्दु)* A dot separating the ones and the tenths places in a decimal number. एक बिन्दु जो इकाई और दशवाँ भाग के बीच में स्थित हो।

Definite Integral ***(समाकलन)*** Definite integral as limit of sum. सीमाओं के जोड़ को समाकलन कहते हैं।

$$\int_a^b f(x)\,dx = (b-a)\lim \frac{1}{x}[f(a)+(a+b)+f(an-\delta h)]$$

In the expression $\int_a^b f(x)\,dx\,dx$ a and b known as. $\int_a^b f(x)\,dx\,dx$ में a और b समाकलन की सीमाऐं हैं। तथा $f(x)$ फलन है। और x समाकलन का (परिवर्तनीय) है।

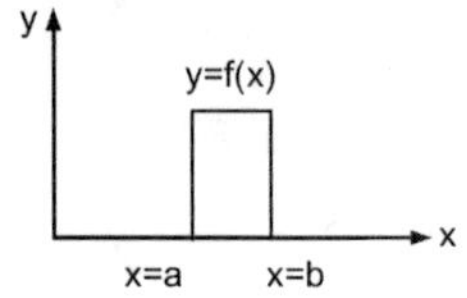

Fig. Definite Integral

- **Limits of integration** $f(x)$ is integrand and x known as variable of integration
- **Properties of definite integrals.** ***(समाकलन के गुण)***

(i) $\int_a^b f(x)dx = \int_b^a f(x)\,dx$

(ii) $\int_a^b f(x)dx = \int_0^a (x)\,dx + \int_a^b f(x)dx,\ a<c<b$

(iii) $\int_a^b f(x)\,dx = 0$

(iv) $\int_a^b f(x)\,dx = \int_a^b f(a-x)\,dx$

(v) $\int_{-a}^a f(x)\,dx = 2\int_a^a f\,(x)\,dx$, if $f(x)$ is an even function

$= 0$, if (x) is an odd function

$f(x)$ समफलन

$= 0$ यदि $f(x)$ विषम फलन हो।

Degree ***(डिग्री)*** A unit of angular measure. कोण को मापने की इकाई।

Denominator ***(हर)*** The term below the line in a fraction the term that divides the numerat or e.g. the deminator of $\frac{2}{3}$ is 3. भिन्न के नीचे का

भाग या अंश को विभाजित करने वाला जैसे $\frac{2}{3}$ में 3 हर है।

De Moivre Theorem ***(डी मोवरी प्रमेय)***

(*i*) If n is any integer (positive or negative) then, यदि ON कोई धनात्मक ऋणात्मक पूर्णाक है। $(\cos\theta + i\sin\theta)^n = \cos n\theta + i\sin n\theta$

(*ii*) If n is a rational number then one of the values of $(\cos\theta + i\sin\theta)$ यदि n यदि परिमेय संख्या तब $(\cos\theta + i\sin\theta)^n$ का एक मूल्य $(\cos n\theta + i\sin\theta)$ है।

✤ **De Moivre's Theorem:** ***(डी मोवरी प्रमेय)***

$$[\cos\theta + \sin\theta]^n = \cos n\theta + \sin n\theta, \text{ for}$$

$$n = \pm 1, \pm 2, \pm 3...$$

$$[\cos\theta + \sin\theta]^{-1} = \cos(-\theta) + i\sin(-\theta)$$

$$= \cos\theta - i\sin\theta$$

If 'a' is a complex number = $p(\cos\theta + i\sin\theta)$

$$\text{then } a^{\frac{1}{n}} = z = \sqrt[n]{p}\left[\cos\left(\frac{\theta}{n} + k\times\frac{2\pi}{n}\right) + i\sin\left(\frac{\theta}{n} + k.\frac{2\pi}{n}\right)\right]$$

where $k = 0, 1, 2......(n-1)$

(दिमातर प्रमेय)

$$[\cos\theta + \sin\theta]^n = \cos n\theta + \sin n\theta, \text{ तब}$$

$$n = \pm 1, \pm 2, \pm 3...$$

$$[\cos\theta + \sin\theta]^{-1} = \cos(-\theta) + i\sin(-\theta)$$

$$= \cos\theta - i\sin\theta$$

यदि a मिश्रित संख्या है = $p(\cos\theta + i\sin\theta)$

$$\text{तब } a^{\frac{1}{n}} = z = n\sqrt{p}\left[\cos\left(\frac{\theta}{n} + k\times\frac{2\pi}{n}\right) + i\sin\left(\frac{\theta}{n} + k.\frac{2\pi}{n}\right)\right]$$

जहाँ $k = 0, 1, 2......(n-1)$

Derivative ***(निगमन)*** For a function $f = (x)$, the derivative $\frac{dy}{dx}$ at a is the rate of change of function with respect to x at a. It is found by differentiation

$$f(x) = x^3$$

$$f'(x) = 3x^2$$

thus rate of change of x^3 at $x = 4$ is $3 \times 4^2 = 48$

for any real function its derivative is given by

$$\lim_{\Delta x \to x} \frac{f(x + \Delta x) - f(x)}{\Delta x}$$

the function can be expressed as $y = f(x)$

$$\frac{dy}{dx} = \lim_{\Delta x \to 0.} \frac{\Delta y}{\Delta x}$$

a फलन $y = f(x)$ का निगमन $\left(\frac{dy}{dx}\right)$ यहाँ a, x के साथ बदल रही है। इसका अवकलन

$$f(x) = x^3$$

$$f'(x) = 3x^2$$

इस प्रकार बदलती है। $x = 4$

$$3 \times 4^2 = 48$$

इसका वास्तविक निगमन

$$\lim_{\Delta x \to x} \frac{f(x + \Delta x) - f(x)}{\Delta x}$$

फलन $y = f(x)$

$$\frac{dy}{dx} = \lim_{\Delta x \to 0.} \frac{\Delta y}{\Delta x}$$

Derivatives of some important functions *(निगमन के कुछ सूत्र)*

$$\frac{d}{dx}(x^n) = n.x^{n-1} \qquad \frac{d}{dx}(a^x) = a^x \log a$$

$$\frac{d}{dx}(\sin x) = \cos x \qquad \frac{d}{dx} + (e^x)$$

$\frac{d}{dx}(\sin x) = -\sin x$ $\qquad$ $\frac{d}{dx}(\log x) = \frac{1}{x}$

$\frac{d}{dx}(\tan x) = \sec^2 x$ $\qquad$ $\frac{d}{dx}(\sin^{-1} x) = \frac{1}{\sqrt{1-x^2}}$

$\frac{d}{dx}(\cot x) = -\text{cosec}^2 x$ $\qquad$ $\frac{d}{dx}(\cos^{-1} x) = \frac{-1}{\sqrt{1-x^2}}$

$\frac{d}{dx}(\sec x) = \sec x \tan x$ $\qquad$ $\frac{d}{dx}(\tan^{-1} x) = \frac{-1}{1-x^2}$

$\frac{d}{dx}(\text{cosec } c) = -\text{cosec } x \cot x$ $\qquad$ $\frac{d}{dx}(\cot^{-1} x) = \frac{-1}{1+x^2}$

$\frac{d}{dx}(\sqrt{x}) - \frac{1}{2\sqrt{x}}$ $\qquad$ $\frac{d}{dx}(\sec^{-1} x) = \frac{1}{x\sqrt{x^2-1}}$

$\frac{d}{dx}(\log_a^x) = \frac{1}{x}. \log a$ $\qquad$ $\frac{d}{dx}(\text{cosec}^{-1} x) = \frac{-1}{x\sqrt{x^2-1}}$

- **n^{th} Derivatives of some standard functions** *(कुछ फलनों के n^{th} निगमन)*

(*i*) $\frac{d^n}{dx^n} \sin(ax+b) = a^n \sin\left(\frac{n\pi}{2} + ax + b\right)$

(*ii*) $\frac{d^n}{dx^n} \cos(ax+b) = a^n \cos\left(\frac{n\pi}{2} + ax + b\right)$

(*iii*) $\frac{d^n}{dx^n}(ax+b) = \frac{m!}{(m-n)!} a^n (ax+b)^{m-n}$, where $m > n$

(*iv*) $\frac{d^n}{dx^n}(\log(ax+b)) = \frac{(-1)^{n-1}(n-1)!a^n}{(ax+b)^n}$

(*v*) $\frac{d^n}{dx^n}(e^{ax}) = a^n e^{ax}$

(*vi*) $\frac{d^n(a^x)}{dx^n} = a^x (\log a)^n$

(vii) $\frac{d^n}{dx^n}(e^{ax}\sin(bx+c)) = r^n e^{ax}\sin(bx+c+n\phi\tilde{)}$

Where $r = \sqrt{a^2+b^2};\ \phi = \tan^{-1}\frac{b}{a}$

(viii) $\frac{d^n}{dx^n}e^{ax}\cos(bx+c) = r^n e^{ax}\cos(bx+c+n\phi)$

Determinant ***(सारणिक)*** Every square matrix can be associated to can expression or a number which is know as its determinant, it $A = [a_{ij}]$ is a square matrix of order n, then the determinant of A is denoted by det A or $|A|$. कुछ पंक्तियों तथा उनके ही स्तम्भों के रूप में किसी निश्चित ढंग से क्रमबद्ध संख्याओं के विन्यास को जिनको एक निश्चित सारणिक कहते हैं। जो उन पंक्तियों अथवा स्तम्भों की संख्या है। सारणिक में क्षैतिज रेखा उसकी पंक्तियां (R) तथा उर्ध्वाधर रेखा स्तम्भ (C) कहलाती है।

$$\begin{vmatrix} a_{11} & a_{12} & a_{ij} & a_{1n} \\ a_{21} & a_{22} & a_{2j} & a_{2h} \\ \cdots & \cdots & \cdots & \cdots \\ \cdots & \cdots & \cdots & \cdots \\ a_{i1} & a_{i2} & a_{ij} & a_{in} \\ a_{n1} & a_{n2} & a_{nj} & a_{n2} \end{vmatrix}$$

Determination of the distance from the centre of a circle to a straight line ***(किसी वृत्त के केन्द्र से किसी सीधी रेखा पर डाले गये लम्ब की दूरी)*** Given the point $P(x_1, y_1)$ and the straight $ax + by + c = 0$, the distance of point P from the straight line is given by

$$d = \frac{ax_1 + by_1 + c}{\sqrt{a^2+b^2}}$$

if $d < R$, the straight line is secant. (सीधी रेखा प्रतिच्छेदी रेखा है)

$d = R$, the straight line is tangent. (सीधी रेखा स्पर्श रेखा है)

$d > R$, the straight line is external. (सीधी रेखा बाह्य रेखा है)

केन्द्र पर दिये गये बिन्दु (x_1, y_1) और सीधी रेखा $ax + by + c = 0$, हो तब केन्द्र P से रेखा तक की दूरी

$$d = \frac{ax_1 + by_1 + c}{\sqrt{a^2 + b^2}}$$

Diagonal ***(विकर्ण)*** In a polygon the line segment joining a vertex with another (non-adjacent) vertex is called a diagonal. किसी बहुभुज के एक सिरे को दूसरे सिरे से मिलाने वाली रेखा विकर्ण कहलाती है। चित्र में AC विकर्ण है।

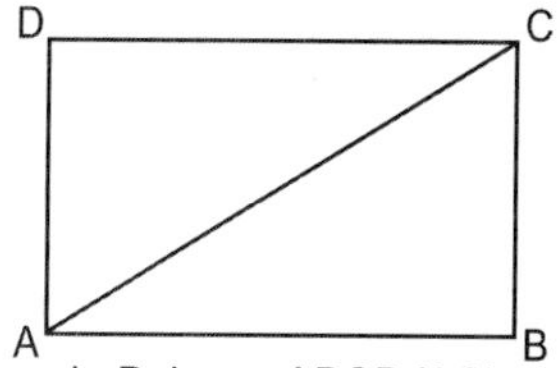

In Polygon ABCD 'AC' is diagonal

Fig. Diagonal

Diameter ***(व्यास)*** The longest chord of a figure. In a circle, a diameter is a chord that passes through the centre of the circle. वृत्त की सबसे बड़ी जीवा जो वृत्त के केन्द्र से जाती हो। चित्र में AC वृत्त की व्यास है।

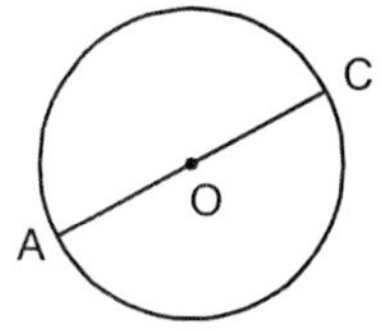

Here 'AC' is the diameter on the circle with centre 'O'

Fig. Diameter

Here 'AC' is the diameter of the circle with centre 'O'.

- **Diameter from of the equation of a circle** ***(वृत्त समीकरण से व्यास)*** The equation of the circle, the coordinates of the extremities of whose diameter are (x_1, y_1) and (x_2, y_2) is given by

$$(x - x_1)(x - x_2) + (y - y_1)(y - y_2) = 0$$

किसी वृत्त में व्यास के दोनों सिरों के निर्देशांक (x_1, y_1) और (x_2, y_2) हो तो उस वृत्त का समीकरण–

$$(x - x_1)(x - x_2) + (y - y_1)(y - y_2) = 0$$

Difference ***(अन्तर)*** The amount that remains after one quantity is subtracted from another. एक राशि को दूसरी राशि से घटाने पर जो बचता है।

Differential calculus *(अवकलन गणित)* Differentiation is concerned with rates of change and calculating the gradient at any point from the equation of the curve, $y = f(x)$.

Differential coefficient of some standard function
(सरलतम फलन का अवकलन गुणांक)

(i) $\frac{d}{dx}(\text{constant}) = 0$

(ii) $\frac{d}{dx}(\text{ax}) = a$

(iii) $\frac{d}{dx}(x^n) = nx^{n-1}$

(iv) $\frac{d}{dx}(e^x) = e^x$

(v) $\frac{d}{dx}(a^x) = a^x = \log_e a$

(vi) $\frac{d}{dx}(\log_e x) = 1/x$

(vii) $\frac{d}{dx}(\log_a x) = \frac{1}{x \log a}$

(viii) $\frac{d}{dx}(\sin x) = \cos x$

(ix) $\frac{d}{dx}(\cos x) = -\sin x$

(x) $\frac{d}{dx}(\tan x) = \sec^2 x$

(xi) $\frac{d}{dx}(\cot x) = co\sec^2 x$

(xii) $\frac{d}{dx}(\text{cosec } x) = -co\sec x \cot x$

(xiv) $\frac{d}{dx}(\sin^{-1} x) = \frac{1}{\sqrt{1-x^2}}, -1 < \text{x} < 1$

(xv) $\frac{d}{dx}(\cos^{-1} x) = \frac{1}{\sqrt{1-x^2}}, -1 < \text{x} < 1$

(xvi) $\frac{d}{dx}(\tan^{-1}x) = \frac{1}{\sqrt{1+x^2}}$,

(xvii) $\frac{d}{dx}(\cot^{-1}x) = -\frac{1}{1+x^2}$

(xviii) $\frac{d}{dx}(\sec^{-1}x) = -\frac{1}{x\sqrt{x^2-1}}, |x| > 1$

(xix) $\frac{d}{dx}(\operatorname{cosec}^{-1}x) = -\frac{1}{x\sqrt{x^2-1}}$

(xx) $\frac{d}{dx}(\sinh x) = \cosh x$

(xxi) $\frac{d}{dx}(\cosh x) = \operatorname{sinn} x$

(xxii) $\frac{d}{dx}(\tanh x) = \operatorname{sech}^2 x$

(xxiii) $\frac{d}{dx}(\coth x) = -\operatorname{cosech}^2 x$

(xxiv) $\frac{d}{dx}(\operatorname{sech} x) = -\operatorname{sech} x \tanh x$

(xxv) $\frac{d}{dx}(\operatorname{cosech} x) = -\operatorname{cosech} x \coth x$

(xxvi) $\frac{d}{dx}(\sinh^{-1}x) = \frac{1}{\sqrt{1+x^2}}$

(xxvii) $\frac{d}{dx}(\cosh^{-1}x) = \frac{1}{\sqrt{x^2-1}}, x > 1$

(xxviii) $\frac{d}{dx}(\tanh^{-1}x) = \frac{1}{1-x^2}$

(xxix) $\frac{d}{dx}(\coth^{-1}x) = \frac{1}{\sqrt{x^2-1}}, |x| > 1$

(xxx) $\frac{d}{dx}(\operatorname{sech}^{-1}x) = \frac{1}{x\sqrt{1-x^2}}, (0 < x < 1)$

(xxxi) $\frac{d}{dx}(\operatorname{cosech}^{-1}x) = \frac{1}{|x|\sqrt{x^2+1}}, x \neq 0$

(xxxii) $\frac{d}{dx}(e^{ax}\sin bx) = e^{ax}(a \sin b\,x + b \cos bx)$

$$= \sqrt{a^2 + b^2} e^{ax} \sin (bx + \tan^{-1} b/a)$$

(*xxxiii*) $\frac{d}{dx}(e^{ax} \cos b x) = e^{ax} (a \cos b\ x - b \sin b x)$

$$= \sqrt{a^2 + b^2} e^{ax} \cos (bx + \tan^{-1} b/a)$$

- **Some theorems on Differentiation** ***(अवकलन पर आधारित प्रमेय)***

Theorem I $\frac{d}{dx}[kf(x)] = k\, d/dx[f(x)]$, where k is aconstant

Theorem II $\frac{d}{dx}[f_1(x) \pm f_2(x) \pm f_3(x) \pm ...]$

$$= \frac{d}{dx}[f_1(x)] \pm \frac{d}{dx}[f_2(x) \pm \frac{d}{dx}[f_3(x)] + ...$$

Theorem III $\frac{d}{dx}[f(x).g(x)] = f(x)\frac{d}{dx}[g(x)] + g(x)\frac{d}{dx}[f(x)]$

Theorem IV $\frac{d}{dx}\left[\frac{f(x)}{g(x)}\right] = \frac{g(x)d/dx[f(x)] - f(x)d/dx[g(x)]}{[g(x)]^2}$

Differential equation ***(अवकलन समीकरण)*** Equations involving total or partial differentiation coefficients and, about the rate of change; the difference between some quantity now. समीकरण पूर्ण व आंशिक अवकलन गुणांक पर आधारित है।

- **Differentiation of infinite Series** ***(अनंत सारिणी का अवकलन)***

(*i*) If $y = \sqrt{f(x) + \sqrt{f(x) + \sqrt{f(x) + ...\infty}}}$ then

$$\Rightarrow \quad y = \sqrt{f(x) + y}$$

$$\Rightarrow \quad y^2 = f(x) + y$$

$$2y\frac{dy}{dx} = f'(x) + dy/dx$$

$$\therefore \quad \frac{dy}{dx} = \frac{f'(x)}{2y - 1}$$

(*ii*) If $y = f(x)^{f(x)f(x)....}$, then $y = f(x)\,y$.

$$\therefore \quad \log y = y \log [f(x)]$$

$$\frac{1}{y}\frac{dy}{dx} = \frac{y.f'(x)}{f(x)} + \log f(x).\left(\frac{dy}{dx}\right)$$

$$\therefore \quad \frac{dy}{dx} = \frac{y2f'(x)}{f(x)[1 - y\log f(x)]}$$

(*iii*) If $y = f(x)_{+\frac{1}{f(x)_{+\frac{1}{f(x)_{+\frac{1}{f(x)}}}}}}$

Then $$\frac{dy}{dx} = \frac{yf'(x)}{2y - f(x)}$$

Digit ***(अंक)*** Any one of following ten symbols { 0, 1, 2, 3, 4, 5, 6, 7, 8, 9, }. शून्य से 9 तक की कोई भी गिनती अंक कहलाती है।

Diameter of a circle ***(वृत्त का व्यास)***

The diameter of a circle $x_2 + y_2 = r_2$ corresponding to the system of parallel chords $= mx + c$ is $x + my = 0$

Dimension ***(आकार)*** Either the length and / or width of a surface (two-dimensional) or height, of a solid (three-dimensional). जिसमें लम्बाई और चौड़ाई हों उसे अथवा द्विविमीय तथा जिसमें लम्बाई चौड़ाई तथा ऊचाई तीनों हो उसे ठोस अथवा त्रिविमीय कहते है।

Direct Variation ***(अनुक्रमानुपाती विचरण)***

- Two quantities x and y vary directly if the ratio $\frac{x}{y}$ remains constant. In other words, x and y are said to vary directly if $\frac{x}{y}$ = k, where is a positive constant.
- दो राशियों x और y को एक दूसरे के साथ अनुक्रमानुपाती विचरण में कहते हैं, यदि वे इस प्रकार एक साथ बढ़ें (घटें) कि इनके संगत मानों का अनुपात अचर रहे। दूसरे शब्दों में, x और y का विचरण अनुक्रमानुपाती होता है, यदि $\frac{x}{y} = k$ हो, जहाँ k कोई धनात्मक अचर संख्या है।

Directly proportional ***(अनुलोम अनुपात)*** y is directly proportional to x if $y = kx$. x के साथ-साथ y का भी बढ़ना या घटना एक साथ निश्चित हो।

Directrice of the hyperbole ***(अतिपरवलय की नियताएं)***

We have $\frac{PF_1}{PD_1} = \frac{PF_2}{PD_2} = e$

Each of the line $x = \frac{a}{e}$

and $x \equiv \frac{-a}{e}$

is called the directrix of the hyperbola.

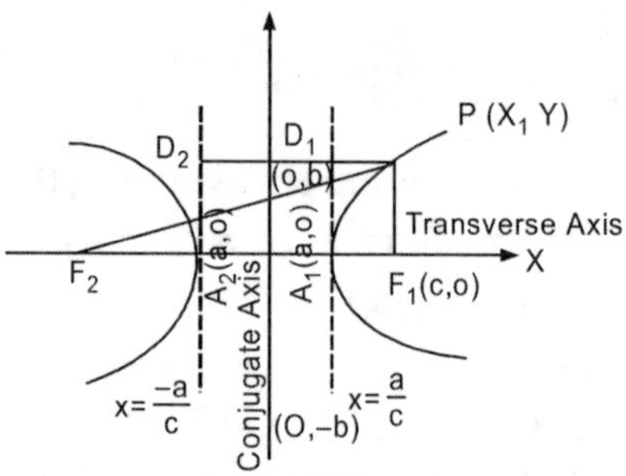

Fig. Directrice of the hyperbole

हम जानते है $\frac{PF_1}{PD_1} = \frac{PF_2}{PD_2} = e$

प्रत्येक रेखा $x = \frac{a}{e}$

और $x \equiv \frac{-a}{e}$

यह अतिपरवलय की नियता कहलाती है।

Directed ***(सीधी रेखा)*** A directed line is one whose direction is fixed i.e. it has one positive direction and the other a negative direction. वह रेखा जिसकी दिशा निश्चित हो। सीधी रेखा कहलाती है।

Direction ***(दिशा)*** A property of vector quantities, usually defined in reference to a fixed origin and axes. The direction of a point is the angle from the x axis to the tangent at the point. सदिश राशि का वह गुण किसी निश्चित बिन्दु और अक्षों पर प्रदर्शित किया जाए तो x अक्ष पर जो tangent angle बनाती है दिशा कहलाती है।

Direction angles ***(कोणों की दिशा)*** The angles made by a line with the positive direction of x axis, y-axis and z- axis. धनात्मक x-अक्ष y-अक्ष पर किसी रेखा द्वारा बनाऐ कोणों की दिशा को कोणों की दिशा कहते हैं।

Direction cosines of a line *(रेखा की दिक्कोज्याओं की दिशा)* The cosines of the angles which a line make with the positive directions of the coordinates axes are called the direction cosines of the line. रेखा द्वारा धनात्मक निर्देशांक अक्ष पर बनायें गये दिक्कोज्या कोणों को रेखा की दिक्कोज्या की दिशा कहते हैं।

If α, β, λ are the angles then directions cosines l, m, n will be given by $l = \cos\alpha$, $m = \cos\beta$, $n = \cos\lambda$.

Direction ratios of a line *(रेखा का दिशा अनुपात)* A set of any three number a, b, c which are proportional to l, m, n are called the direction ratios of the line.

We have $\frac{1}{a} = \frac{m}{b} = \frac{n}{c}$

$$l = \pm\frac{a}{\sqrt{a^2+b^2+c^2}},\ m = \pm\frac{b}{\sqrt{a^2+b^2+c^2}}$$

$$n = \pm\frac{c}{\sqrt{a^2+b^2+c^2}}$$

and $l^2 + m^2 + n^2 = 1$

abc . l, m, n के समानुपाती हो तो इन्हें रेखा की दिशा का अनुपात कहेंगे।

Director circle *(नियामी वृत्त)* It is the locus of the point of intersection of a pair of tangents to a central conic which are at right angles to each other for the central conic (संकेन्द्र शांकव के लिये)

$$ax^2 + 2h\,xy + by^2 + 2gx + 2fy + c = 0$$

the equation of the director circle is (नियामी वृत्त का समीकरण)

$$(ab - h^2)(x^2 + y^2) - 2(hf - bg)\,x - 2\,(gh - af)y + c(a + b) - (f^2 + g^2) = 0$$

दीर्घ वृत्त की परस्पर लम्ब स्पर्शियों के प्रतिच्छेद बिन्दुओं का बिन्दुपथ, दीर्घ वृत्त का नियामी वृत्त कहलाता है।

Dirichlet theorem *(डिरिचलेट प्रमेय)* Every arithmetic progression a, $(a + b)$, $(a + 2b)$ in which a, b, are integers. No common divisor greater than unity contains an infinity of primes. प्रत्येक गणितीय श्रेणी $a, (a + b), (a + 2b)$ जिसमें b पूर्णांक है।

Discontinuity *(असत्तता)* A function is considered to possess a discontinuity at a point if is not continuous at that point. वह फलक जो किसी बिन्दु तक सतूत नहीं होता है।

Discount *(बट्टा)* The difference between the issue price of a stock or share and its nominal value when its issue is less than the normal value. अंकित मूल्य और विक्रय मूल्य के अन्तर को बट्टा कहते हैं।

Discriminant *(विविक्तिकर)* The discriminant of a quadratic equation $ax^2 + bx + c = 0$ is $b^2 - 4ac$. The discriminant tells how many roots there are for the equation and nature of the roots. वर्ग समीकरण या द्विघात समीकरण $ax^2 + bx + c = 0$ के $x = \dfrac{-b \pm \sqrt{b^2 - 4ac}}{2a}$ से प्राप्ति $b^2 - 4ac$ को विविक्तिकर कहते है।

Distance *(दूरी)* It is a measure of length of path between two points. If $P(x_1, y_1, z_1)$ and $Q(x_2, y_2, z_2)$ are the two points in space then. यदि किसी रेखा के सिरों के बिन्दु $P(x_1, y_1, z_1)$ और $Q(x_2, y_2, z_2)$ हो। उनके बीच की दूरी

$\vec{Q}$ की स्थिति − $\vec{P}$ की स्थिति

$\vec{PQ}$ = position vector two Q – position vector of P

$$= (x_2 - x_1)\vec{i} + (y_2 - y_1)\vec{j} + (z_2 - z_1)\vec{k}$$

The distance between two points is given by दो बिन्दुओं के बीच की दूरी

$$PQ = \sqrt{(x_2 - x_1)^2 + (y_2 - y_1)^2 + (z_2 - z_1)^2}$$

Distance of the point $P(x, y, z)$ from the origin $(0, 0, 0)$ is given by

$OP = \sqrt{x^2 + y^2 + z^2}$. (बिन्दु $P(x, y, z)$ और $(0, 0, 0)$ के बीद की दूरी OP)

E

• **e (1)** 2.718281828... The base of the natural logarithm function. I can be found from the series $2 + 1/2! + 1/3! + 1/4! + 1/5! + ...$ e की श्रेणी $2 + 1/2! + 1/3! + 1/4! + 1/5! + ...$

(2) Euler's number, equal to about 2.718 , used as the base in a natural logarithm. यूलर्स संख्या का मान 2.718 के बराबर होता है। इसका उपयोग प्राकृतिक लघुगुणक में होता है।

(3) Symbol for the base of natural logarithms. वह प्रतीक जिसका आधार प्राकृतिक लघुगुणक हो।

Eccentricity *(उत्केन्द्रता)* A number that indicates the shape of a conic section is eccentricity. शंकाव के आकार को प्रदर्शित करने वाला अक्षर (e) उत्केन्द्रता होता है।

The constant ratio is called the eccentricity of the conic and is denoted by e for a circle (वृत्त के लिये) $e = 0$

for a parabola $e = 1$ (परवलय के लिए)

for an ellipse $e < 1$ (दीर्घवृत्त के लिए)

$$e = \sqrt{1 - \left(\frac{\text{minor axis}}{\text{major axis}}\right)^2}$$

for a Hyperbola (अतिपरवलय के लिए)

$$e < 1$$

$$e = \sqrt{1 + \left(\frac{\text{conjugate axis}}{\text{transverse axis}}\right)}$$

Ellipse *(दीर्घवृत्त)* It is the locus of all points, the sum whose distances from two fixed points is constant (equal to the major axis of the ellipse).

The two fixed points(F_1 , F_2)are called the foci of the ellipse.
Assuming F_1 (c, o) , F_2 (–c , o)

$$F_1 F_2 = 2c$$

The x -axis is on the straight line F_1 F_2 and the mid point of the line segment F_1 F_2 Origin is the centre of the ellipse whose equations is

$$\frac{x^2}{a^2}+\frac{y^2}{b^2}=1 \text{ or } b^2x^2+a^2y^2=a^2b^2$$

in which $2a$ = major axis

$2b$ = minor axis

$b^2 = a^2 - c^2$

also $PF_1 + PF_2 = 2a$

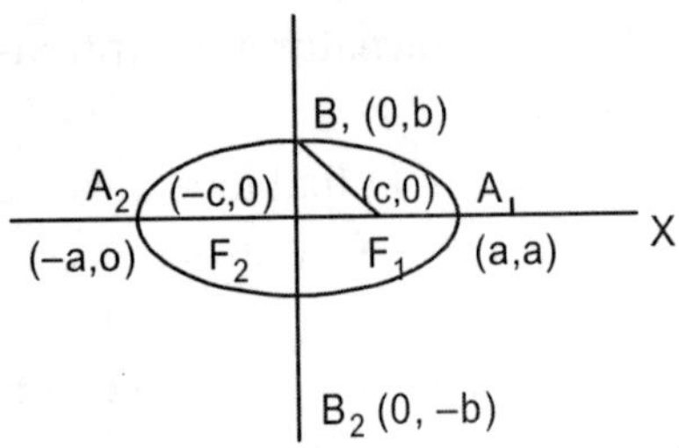

Fig. Ellipse

दीर्घवृत्त उस बिन्दु का पथ है जिसका दो निश्चित बिन्दुओं से दूरियों का योग नियताँक रहता है।
दो बिन्दु F_1, F_2 दीर्घवृत्त के नाभि कहलाते हैं।
तब $F_1(c, o)$ $F_2(-c, o)$

$F_1F_2 = 2c$

x अक्ष पर रेखा F_1F_2 तथा मध्य बिन्दु (0, 0) पर दीर्घवृत्त का समीकरण

$$\frac{x^2}{a^2}+\frac{y^2}{b^2}=1 \text{ or } b^2x^2+a^2y^2=a^2b^2$$

$2a$ = दीर्घाक्ष $2b$ = लघु अक्ष

$b^2 = a^2 - c^2$ $\boxed{PF_1 + PF_2 = 2a}$

Ellipsoid ***(दीर्घ वृत्ताज)*** Centre at the origin O (0, 0, 0) and semi - axis a, b, c can be represented as केन्द्र बिन्दु (0, 0, 0) और अर्ध अक्ष a, b, c हो तब समीकरण

$$\frac{x^2}{a^2}+\frac{y^2}{b^2}+\frac{z^2}{c^2}=1$$

Centred at $C(h, k, l)$ and semi axis a, b, c. जब केन्द्र बिन्दु $C(h, k, l)$ और अर्ध अक्षर a, b, c

$$\frac{(x-h)^2}{a^2}+\frac{(y-k)^2}{b^2}+\frac{(z-1)^2}{c^2}=1$$

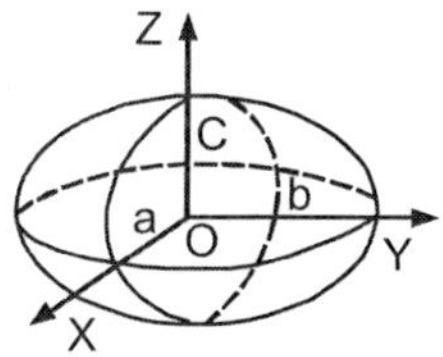

Fig. Ellipsoid

Empty Set ***(रिक्त समुच्चय)*** Such a set is denoted by ϕ and such a set contains no members. It is also known as a null set. ऐसा समुच्चय जिसमें कोई भी अवयव न हो, रिक्त समुच्चय कहते हैं। इसे ϕ से प्रदर्शित करते हैं। इसे नल समुच्चय के नाम से भी जाना जाता है।

Energy ***(ऊर्जा)*** It is the capacity to do work. कार्य करने की क्षमता को ऊर्जा कहते हैं।

Equation ***(समीकरण)*** An algebraic expression in which two values are shown as being equal: 4 = 2+ 2.

or Two expression connecting with equal sigh (=) as $2x + 3 = 5$. दो व्यंजक यदि बराबर (=) चिन्ह से जुड़े है। समीकरण कहलाता है।

Equation of circle ***(वृत्त का समीकरण)*** If γ is the radius and (h, k) is the centre then the equation of such a circle is

$$(x-h)^2+(y-k)^2=\gamma^2$$

or $\quad x^2+y^2+\alpha x+\beta y+\gamma=0$

in which

$$\alpha=-2h$$
$$\beta=-2k$$
$$\gamma=h^2+k^2-\gamma^2$$

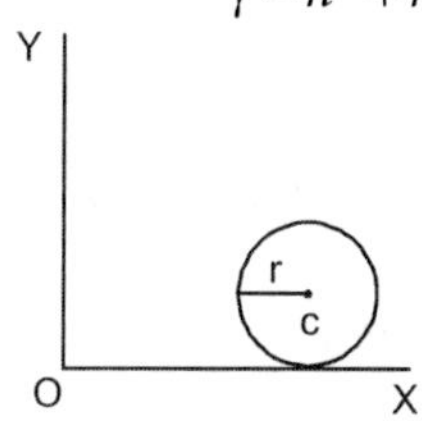

Fig. Equation of circle

यदि γ वृत्त की त्रिज्या और केन्द्र (h, k) हो तब वृत्त का समीकरण

$$(x-h)^2+(y-k)^2=\gamma^2$$

या $$x^2+y^2+\alpha x+\beta y+\gamma=0$$

जहाँ $$\alpha=-2h$$

$$\beta=-2k$$

$$\gamma=h^2+k^2-\gamma^2$$

- **Equation of the circle with radius γ and centre at the origin is (उस वृत्त का समीकरण जिसकी त्रिज्या γ तथा केन्द्र बिन्दु (0, 0) हो।)**

$$x^2+y^2=\gamma^2$$

- **Equation of circle in polar cordinates is** ***(वृत्त के ध्रुवीय निर्देशांक का समीकरण)***

$$r^2-2rr_0\cos(\theta-\theta_0)+r^2=R^2$$

- **Equation of hyperbola with transverse axis parallel to y-axis** ***उस अतिपरवलय का समीकरण जिसकी अनुप्रस्थ अक्ष y-अक्ष के समान्तर हो*** Equation of hyperbola becomes अतिपरवलय का समीकरण

$$\frac{y^2}{b^2}-\frac{x^2}{a^2}=1$$

- **Equation of hyperbola with centre C (h, k) and axis parallel to Cartesian axis** ***उस अतिपरवलय का समीकरण जिसका केन्द्र C (h, k) और अक्ष कार्टीजियन अक्ष के समान्तर हो।*** $(x \mid\mid a)$: In such a case the equation of hyperbola becomes

$$b^2(x-h)^2-a^2(y-k)=a^2b^2$$

or $$\frac{(x-h)^2}{a^2}-\frac{(y-k)^2}{b^2}=1$$

- **Equation of a straight line through two fixed points** ***(दो निश्चित बिन्दुओं से होकर जाने वाली रेखा का समीकरण)*** If A $(x_1, y_1\ z_1)$ B (x_2, y_2, x_2) are the fixed point on the line and they have position vectors $\vec{a}$ and $\vec{b}$ respectively. Then the equation of line is given by

$$\vec{r}=\vec{a}+\lambda(\vec{b}-\vec{a})$$

In Cartesian form the equation will be

$$\frac{x-x_1}{x_2-x_1}=\frac{y-y_1}{y_2-y_1}=\frac{z-z_1}{z_2-z_1}$$

यदि किसी रेखा पर दो बिन्दु A $(x_1, y_1\ z_1)$ तथा B (x_2, y_2, x_2) तथा स्थिति सदिश $\vec{a}$ और $\vec{b}$ हो, तब रेखा समीकरण कार्टीजियन अवस्था में समीकरण

$$\frac{x-x_1}{x_2-x_1}=\frac{y-y_1}{y_2-y_1}=\frac{z-z_1}{z_2-z_1}$$

- **Equation of motion** ***(गति का समीकरण)*** Equations that describes the motion of an object with constant acceleration (a). They relate the velocity v_1 of the start of timing to its velocity v_2 at some later time t, and the object displacement (s) they are: किसी पिण्ड का निश्चित त्वरस (a) तथा वेग v_1 हो तो t समय बाद वेग v_2 तथा चली गयी दूरी s हो–

$$v_2 = v_1 + at_2$$

$$s = \frac{(v_1+v_2)t}{2}$$

$$s = v_1.t + \frac{at^2}{2}$$

$$s = v_2 t - \frac{at^2}{2}$$

$$v_2^2 = v_1{}^2 + 2as$$

- **Equation of tangent** ***(स्पर्श रेखा का समीकरण)***

Equation of tangent to the curve $y = f(x)$ at A (x_1, y_1) is (y वक्र पर)

$$y-y_1=\left(\frac{dy}{dx}\right)_{(x_1,y_1)}(x-x_1)$$

(i) The tangent at (x_1,y_1) is parallel to x-axis.

$$\Rightarrow \qquad \left(\frac{dy}{dx}\right)_{x_1,y_1}=0\ (x \text{ के समान्तर})$$

(ii) The tangent at (x_1, y_1) is parallel to y–axis

$$\Rightarrow \qquad \left(\frac{dy}{dx}\right)_{(x_1,y_1)}=\infty\ (y \text{ के समान्तर })$$

(iii) The tangent line makes equal angles with the axes.

$$\Rightarrow \qquad \left(\frac{dy}{dx}\right)_{(x_1, y_1)} = \pm 1$$

- **Equation of Normal** ***(लम्बवत का समीकरण)***

  The equation of normal at (x_1, y_1) to the curve $y = f(x)$ is

$$(y - y_1) = -\frac{1}{\left(\frac{dy}{dx}\right)_{(x_1, y_1)}}(x - x_1)$$

Equiangular polygon ***(समान कोणीय बहुभुज)*** A polygon all of whose interior angles are equal. बहुभुज जिसका प्रत्येक आन्तरिक कोण आपस में बराबर हो।

Equidistant ***(समान दूरी)*** At the same distance. समान दूरी पर।

Equilateral ***(समबाहु)*** A figure that has the same measurement for each side. वह चित्र जिसकी प्रत्येक भुजा बराबर हो।

AB = BC = CA

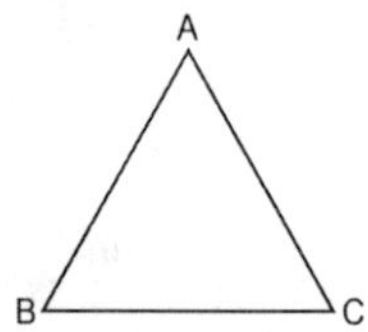

Fig. Equilateral

Equilateral polygon ***(समबाहु बहुभुज)*** A polygon whose all sides are equal. वह बहुभुज जिसकी सभी भुजाएं बराबर हों।

Equilateral triangle ***(समबाहु त्रिभुज)*** A triangle that has three equal sides. वह त्रिभुज जिसकी तीनों भुजाएं बराबर हो तथा तीनों कोण बराबर हों तथा प्रत्येक कोण 60° का हो।

AB = BC = CA

$\angle A = \angle B = \angle C$

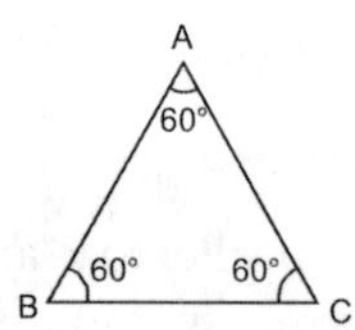

Fig. Equilateral triangle

Equivalent equations ***(तुल्यता समीकरण)*** Two equations whose solutions are the same. दो समीकरण जिनका हल एक ही हो या दोनों सभी के चर राशि का मान एक ही आये।

$$x + 3y = 10 \text{ , and } 2x = 6y = 20.$$

Equiralent rational number ***(तुल्य परिमेप संख्या)*** Two rational number are equiralent if they have the same standard from दो परिमेय संख्या यदि दोनों का मानक रूप एक ही हो तो ऐसी संख्या तुल्य परिमेय संख्या कहलाती है।

Equivalent Relation *(तुल्यता सम्बन्ध)* A relation on a set A which is reflexive symmetric and transitive is called a equivalence relation i.e $a\,\mathrm{R}\,a, a\,\mathrm{R}b \Rightarrow b\mathrm{R}\,a$ and $a\mathrm{R}b, b\mathrm{R}c \Rightarrow a\mathrm{R}c$. समुच्चय A में कोई सम्बन्ध तुल्यता सम्बन्ध कहलाता है। यदि सम्बन्ध R स्वतुल्य सममित तथा संक्रमण हो अर्थात् $x \in \mathrm{A}$ के लिए $x\mathrm{R}x$(स्वतुल्य) $x, y \varepsilon \mathrm{A}$ के लिए $x_1 y \in \mathrm{Aa}$ के लिए $x\mathrm{R}y \in \mathrm{Ra}$ (सममित) तथा $x, y, z \in \mathrm{A}$ के लिए $x\mathrm{R}z \Rightarrow x\mathrm{R}z$ समतुल्य है।

Escribed circles of a triangle and their radius *(त्रिभुज पर बने वृत्त और उसकी त्रिज्या)*

(i) $r_1 = \dfrac{\Delta}{s-a}, r_2 = \dfrac{\Delta}{s-b}, r_3 = \dfrac{\Delta}{s-c}$

(ii) $r_1 = s \tan \dfrac{\mathrm{A}}{2}, r_2 = s \tan \dfrac{\mathrm{B}}{2}, r_3 = s \tan \dfrac{\mathrm{C}}{2}$

(iii) $r_1 = \dfrac{a \cos \frac{\mathrm{B}}{2} \cos \frac{\mathrm{C}}{2}}{\cos \frac{\mathrm{A}}{2}}, r_2 = \dfrac{a \cos \frac{\mathrm{C}}{2} \cos \frac{\mathrm{A}}{2}}{\cos \frac{\mathrm{B}}{2}}$

$$r_3 = \dfrac{a \cos \frac{\mathrm{A}}{2} \cos \frac{\mathrm{B}}{2}}{\cos \frac{\mathrm{C}}{2}}$$

(iv) $r_1 = 4\mathrm{R} \sin \dfrac{\mathrm{A}}{2} \cos \dfrac{\mathrm{B}}{2} \cos \dfrac{\mathrm{C}}{2},$

$r_2 = 4\mathrm{R} \cos \dfrac{\mathrm{A}}{2} \sin \dfrac{\mathrm{B}}{2} \cos \dfrac{\mathrm{C}}{2},$

$r_3 = 4\mathrm{R} \cos \dfrac{\mathrm{A}}{2} \cos \dfrac{\mathrm{B}}{2} \sin \dfrac{\mathrm{C}}{2}$

Euclid *(इक्यूलिड)* Greek geomet or number theorist. ग्रीक निवासी, रेखा गणित के जनक।

- **Euclid 's first theorem** *(इक्यूलिड का प्रथम प्रमेय)* ABC is a right angled triangle with right angle at A. AD, height of the triangle dropped from A on hypotenuse BC,

Hypotenuse side $\vec{AB} = C$

Hypotenuse BC = a, and projection of

AB on BC is BD = n then

$$C^2 = a + n$$

ABC एक समकोण त्रिभुज है। तथा A समकोण है। AD त्रिभुज की ऊँचाई है। BC विकर्ण है।

विकर्ण भुजा $\vec{AB} = C$

विकर्ण BC = a, BD = n तब

$$C^2 = a + n$$

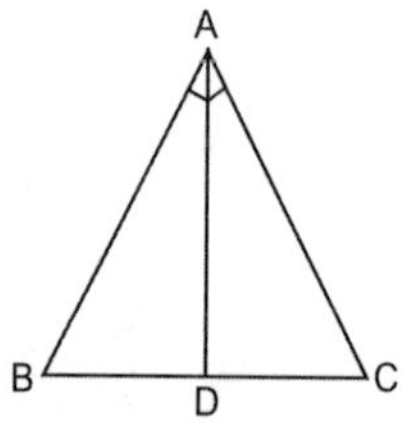

Fig. Euclid 's first theorEm

- **Euclid 's second theorem** ***(इक्यूलिड का द्वितीय प्रमेय)*** ABC is a right triangle with right angle at C.
  CH (altitude relative to the hypotenuse) = h

  $\vec{AH}$ (projection of AC on the hypotenuse) = n

  $\vec{BH}$ (projection of BC on the hypotenuse) = m

  Then $\boxed{b^2 = m + n}$

  त्रिभुज ABC का कोण C समकोण है।

  $\vec{AH} = n$

  $\vec{BH} = m$

  तब $\boxed{b^2 = (m + n)}$

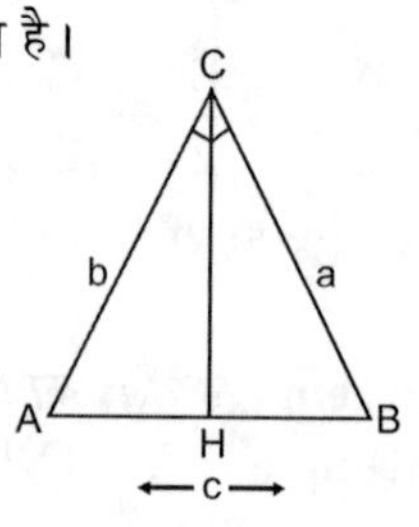

Fig. Euclid's second theorem

Euler-Line ***(यूलर रेखा)*** The Euler line of a triangle is the line connecting the centroid and the circumcentre. वह रेखा जो त्रिभुज के केन्द्र व परिकेन्द्र को मिलाती है।

Euler's theorem ***(यूलर्स प्रमेय)*** According to this theorem. इस प्रमेय के अनुसार

$$c^{i\theta} = \cos\theta + i\sin\theta$$

$$c^{-i\theta} = \cos\theta - \sin\theta$$

$$\sin\theta = \frac{c^{\theta} - e^{\theta}}{2i}$$

$$\cos\theta = \frac{e^{\theta} + e^{-\theta}}{2i}$$

Even function ***(समफलन)*** Any function $f(x)$ of a variable x is said to be even it $f(-x) = f(x)$, if we plot a graph of such a function it is found to be symmetrical about y axis e.g., $y = x^2$. कोई फलन $f(x)$ x का परिवर्तनीय है, तो इसे सम कहेंगे। यदि $f(-x) = f(x)$ को यदि हम ग्राफ पर प्रदर्शित करें तो फलन y-अक्ष पर सममित होगा $y = x^2$.

Even number ***(सम संख्या)*** Those numbers which are divisible by 2, e.g 2, 4, 6, 8, 10 etc. 2 से विभाजित होने वाली संख्याऐं या ऐसी संख्याऐं जिनके अन्त में 0, 2, 4, 6, 8 तो सम संख्यायें कहलाती हैं।

Evaluate The evaluate of a given curve is the locus of the centres of curvature of points on the given curv.

Ex-centre ***(बाह्य केन्द्र)*** It is centre of the ascribed circle.

Exponent ***(घातांक)*** It is the numerical symbol used to indicate the raising of a base number to some indicated power i.g. in x^n the exponent is n. यह एक आंशिक चिन्ह है। किसी संख्या पर लगी घात को घातांक कहते हैं। x^n में x आधार तथा n घातांक है।

Exponential Series ***(घांताकीय श्रेणी)***

$$(i)\quad e^x + 1 + \frac{x}{1!} + \frac{x^2}{2!} + \frac{x^3}{3!} + \ldots\ldots\ldots \frac{x^n}{n!} + \ldots\ldots\ldots \infty$$

$$(ii)\quad e^{-x} = 1 - \frac{x}{1!} + \frac{x^2}{2!} + \frac{x^3}{3!} + \ldots\ldots\ldots \frac{(-1)^n}{n!} x^n + \ldots\ldots\ldots \infty$$

(Replace x by $-x$)

$$(iii)\quad e = 1 - \frac{1}{1!} + \frac{1}{2!} + \frac{1}{3!} + \ldots\ldots\ldots \infty \ \{Putting\ x = 1\ in\ (i)\}$$

(iv) $e^{-1} = 1 - \frac{1}{1!} + \frac{1}{2!} + \frac{1}{3!} + ...\infty$ {*Putting* $x = 1$ *in* (*ii*)}

(v) $\frac{e^x + e^{-x}}{2} = 1 + \frac{x^2}{2!} + \frac{x^4}{4!} + \frac{x^6}{6!} + ...\infty$

(vi) $\frac{e^{x-} e^{-x}}{2} = x + \frac{x^3}{3!} + \frac{x^5}{5!} + ...\infty$

(vii) $a^x = 1 + x(\log_e a) + \frac{x^2}{2!}(\log_e a)^2 + \frac{x^3}{3!}(\log_e a)^3 + ...(a > 0)$

Exponential function ***(चरघातांकीय फलन)*** The function '*f*' defined by $f(x) = a^x$, where '*a*' is any positive real number and *x* is real number is know as general exponential function with base '*a*'.

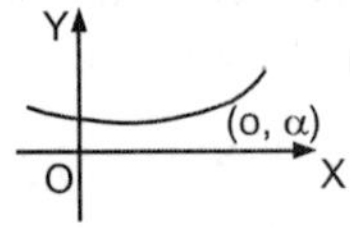

Fig. Exponential function

If base is '*e*' then the function $f(x) = e^x$ for all $x \varepsilon$ R is known as natural exponential function. Its domain is R and its range is $[0, \alpha]$. फलन '*f*' को प्रदर्शित करते हैं। $f(x) = a^x$ जहाँ '*a*' धनात्मक वास्तविक संख्या '*x*' वास्तविक संख्या है। इसे आधार '*a*' पर सामान्य चरघातांकीय फलन से जानते हैं। यदि आधार '*e*' तब फलन $f(x) = e^x$ सभी $x \varepsilon$ R इसे प्राकृतिक चरघातांकीय फलन कहते हैं। डोमेने R हो तब सीमा $[0, \alpha]$ होगी।

Exponential series ***(चरघातांकीय श्रेणी)*** The exponential series is (चरघातांकीय श्रेणी)

$$e^x = 1 + \frac{x}{\angle 1} + \frac{x}{\angle 2} + \frac{x}{\angle 3}....\alpha$$

where base '*e*' is the Eulear number which is approximately equal to 2.732 and *x* is real or complex number. जहाँ आधार '*e*' मूल संख्या है। इसका मान 2.732 होता है। और *x* वास्तविक तथा मिश्रित संख्या है।

Taking $x = 1$, we get

$$e = 1 + \frac{1}{\angle 1} + \frac{1}{\angle 2} + \frac{1}{\angle 3}$$

$$= \sum_{n=0}^{\alpha} \frac{1}{\angle 3}$$

F

Face angle *(पृष्ठीय कोण)* The plane formed by adjacent of a polygonal angle in space. किसी बहुभुज में संलग्न भुजाओं से बना समतल कोण।

Factor *(गुणक)* When two or more natural numbers are multiplied, each of the numbers is a factor of the product. A factor is then a number by which another number is exactly divided (a divisor). दो या दो से अधिक प्राकृतिक संख्याए यदि गुणक हैं तो प्रत्येक किसी के गुणनफल के गुणक है। या किसी एक संख्या को दूसरी संख्या से विभाजित किया जाए तो भी यह प्राप्त होता है। जैसे 10 के गुणक–2, 5 (क्योंकि $10 = 2 \times 5$)

Factor theorem *(गुणनखंड प्रमेय)* Let $p(x)$ be a polynomial of degree greater than or equal to 1 and a be areal number such that $p(a) = 0$, then $(x-a)$ is a factor of $p(x)$. Conversely, if $(x-a)$ is a factor of p, then $p(a) = 0$

यदि $p(x)$ घात $n \geq 1$ वाला बहुपद हो और a कोई वास्तविक संख्या हो तो

(i) $p(a) = 0$ होने पर $(x-a)$, $p(x)$ का गुणनखंड होगा।

(ii) $(x-a)$ में $p(x)$ का गुणनखंड होने पर $P(a) = 0$ होगा।

Factorisation *(गुणनखंड)* Writing a number as the product of its factor which one prime number. किसी अभाज्य संख्या को गुणक के रूप में लिखना।

Factorizing formulae *(गुणन खण्ड सूत्र)*

(i) $(x+y)^2 = x^2 + 2xy + y^2$

(ii) $(x-y)^2 = x^2 - 2xy + y^2$

(iii) $(x+y+z)^2 = x^2 + y^2 + z^2 + 2xy + 2yz + 2zx$

(iv) $(x+y)^3 = x^3 + 3xy(x+y) + y^3$

(v) $(x-y)^3\ x^3 - 3xy(x-y) - y^3$

(vi) $x^2 + y^2 = (x-y)(x+y)$

(vii) $x^3 + y^3 = (x+y)(x^2 - xy + y^2)$

(viii) $x^3 - y^3 = (x-y)(x^2 + xy + y^2)$

(ix) $x^3 + y^3 + z^3 - 3xyz = (x+y+z)(x^2 + y^2 + z^2 - xy - yz - zx)$

(x) $x^4 - y^4 = (x^2 - y^2)(x^2 + y^2) = (x - y)(x + y)(x^2 + y^2)$

(xi) $x^8 - y^8 = (x^4 - y^4)(x^4 + y^4) = (x - y)(x + y)(x^2 + y^2)(x^4 + y^4)$

Family *(समूह)* It is set of related curves figures. For example a family of parallel straight lines is represented by the equation $y = 2x + k$. वह समुच्चय जो ग्राफों और चित्रों से सम्बन्धित हो। जैसे—समूह के समान्तर रेखाओं का समीकरण $y = 2x + k$

- **Family of circles** *(वृत्तों का समूह)* Any circle passing through the intersection of two circles दो वृत्तों के प्रतिच्छेद बिन्दुओं से जाने वाला वृत।

$$s_1 = x^2 + y^2 + 2g_1x + 2f_1y + c_1 = 0$$

$$s_2 = x^2 + y^2 + 2g_2x + 2f_2y + c_2 = 0$$

will be given by the equation दिया हुआ समीकरण

$$s_1 + ks_2 = 0$$

where k is an arbitrary constant. जहाँ k स्वेच्छ अचर है।

- **Any circle concentric with the circle** *(वृत्त और उसका सयुग्मी वृत्त)* $x^2 + y^2 = a^2$, will be given by the equation $x^2 + y^2 = r^2$.

- **Family of Curves** *(वक्रों का समूह)* A set of curves which have geometrical pattern. For example, the equation $x^2 + y^2 = c^2$, represents a family of concentric circles. Different values of c give different curves of the family. वक्रों का समुच्चय जिसमें ज्यामितीय अवस्था समान हो। जैसे—वृत्त का समीकरण $x^2 + y^2 = c^2$ संकेन्द्रीय वृत्तों के समूह को दर्शाता है।

- **Family of lines** *(रेखाओं का समूह)* (*i*) Any line passing through the intersection of two given lines $a_1x + b_1y + c_1 = 0$ a and $a_2x + b_2y + c_2 = 0$ is given *b* the equation.

$$(a_1x + b_1y + c_1) + \lambda(a_2x + b_2y + c_2) = 0$$

(*i*) दो रेखाओं के प्रतिच्छेदन बिन्दुओं से जाने वाली रेखा $a_1x_1 + b_1y + c_1 = 0$ और $a_2x_2 + b_2y + c_2 = 0$ दिये हुए समीकरण है।

$$(a_1x + b_1y + c_1) + \lambda(a_2x + b_2y + c_2) = 0$$

(*ii*) Any line parallel to a given line $ax + by + c = 0$ can be repre-

sented by $ax+by+k=0$
दी हुई रेखा के समान्तर रेखा $ax+by+c=0$ इसे दिखा सकते है। $ax+by+k=0$

Family of planes ***(समतलों का समूह)*** Equation of a plane parallel to a given plane $ax+by+cz+k=0$ is given by दिये हुए समतल का समीकरण

$$ax+by+cz+k=0$$

- **Equation of plane through line of intersection of two planes** ***(दो समतलों के प्रतिच्छेदन बिन्दुओं से जाने वाला समीकरण)***

$\vec{r}\,.\,\hat{n}_1 = d_1$and $\vec{r}\,.\,\hat{n}_2 = d_2$ given by

$\vec{r}\,(\hat{n}_1 - \hat{n}_1 - k.\,\hat{n}_2) = d_1 - kd_2$

In cartesian form If the equation of two planes are कार्तीय अवस्था में दो समतलों के समीकरण

$$a_1x+b_1y+c_1z+d_1=0$$

and $$a_2x+b_2y+c_2z+d_2=0$$

Then the equation of plane passing through the intersection of two planes will दो समतलों के प्रतिच्छेदन बिन्दुओं से होकर जाने वाले समतल का समीकरण $(a_1x+b_1x+c_1z+d_1)+k(a_2x+b_2y+c_2z+d_2)=0$

Note: The two planes intersect on a line whose equation is given by the two simultaneous equations. दो समतलों के प्रतिच्छेन बिन्दुओं से होकर जाने वाली रेखा का समीकरण जिनके दिये हुए दो समीकरण–

$$a_1x+b_1y+c_1z+d_1=0$$

$$a_2x+b_2y+c_2z+d_2=0$$

and it is known as the unsymmertrical form of the equation of a line conditions of parallelism between planes the two represented by और इन्हें असममित अवस्था में जानते हैं। दो समतलों के समान्तर रेखा का समीकरण

$$A_1X+B_1Y+C_1Z+D_1=0$$

$$A_2X + B_2Y + C_2Z + D_2 = 0$$

are parallel if $\theta = 0$ i.e. $\cos\theta = 1$ therefore जब समान्तर हो तब $\theta = 0$ cos $\theta = 1$ इसलिए

$$\frac{A_1}{A_2} = \frac{B_1}{B_2} = \frac{C_1}{C_2}$$

or $$A_1 : B_1 : C_1 = A_2 : B_2 : C_2$$

Condition of orthogonality between planes two plans represented. दो समतलों के लम्बवत् रेखा का समीकरण

$$A_1X + B_1Y + C_1Z + D_1 = 0$$
$$A_2X + B_2Y + C_2Z + D_2 = 0$$

are orthogonal if $\theta = 90$ *i.e.* $\cos\theta = 0$ then लम्बवत् है। यदि $0 - 90 \cos\theta = 0$ तब

$$A_1A_2 + B_1B_2 + C_1C_2 = 0$$

Field *(क्षेत्र)* A set of elements associated with two binary operations subject. ऐसे समुच्चय के अवयव जो द्विआधारी संक्रियायों से जुडे हों।

Figure *(आकृति)* A symbol used to express an integer. यह पूर्णांक में उपयोग की जाती है।

Finite group *(परिमिति समूह)* A group having finite number of elements. यदि किसी समूह के विभिन्न अवयवों की संख्या सीमित हो तो उसे परिमित समूह कहते है।

Finite Set *(परिमित समुच्चय)* A set having a fixed number of elements. यदि किसी समुच्चय के विभिन्न अवयवों की संख्या निश्चित अथवा सीमित हो तो उसे परिमित समुच्चय कहते हैं।

Flotation law *(उत्प्लावन नियम)* According to it, an object floating in a fluid displaces its own weight of fluid. This follows from Archimedes principal for the spacial case of floating objects. जब कोई वस्तु किसी द्रव्य में आंशिक या पूर्ण रूप से डुबोई जाती है तो उसके भार में कमी हटाए गये द्रव के भार के बराबर होती है।

Flow Chart It is chart that indicates the procedure to be followed in solving a problem. Different operations are represented by different symbols.विभिन्न चिन्हों द्वारा बहाव की समस्याओं को हल करते हुए बनाये गये ग्राफ को बहाव का ग्राफ कहते हैं।

Focal Chord ***(नाभिय जीवा)*** The chord of a conic that passes through a focus. शांकव की जीवा जो नाभि से होकर जाती है।

Focal radius ***(नाभिय त्रिज्या)*** A line segment from the focus of an ellipse to a point on the perimeter of the ellipse. रेखाखण्ड जो दीर्घवृत्त के नाभि से खीची गयी हो।

Focus ***(नाभि)*** An imaginary point used in determining the shapes of conic sections like parabolas, hyperbolas and ellipses. स्थिर बिन्दु को शांकव की नाभि कहते हैं। यह परवलय, अतिपरवलय, दीर्घवृत्त में भी होती है।

Force ***(बल)*** It is the agent that changes or tends to change the state of rest or of uniform motion of a body. बल वह धकेल या खिचाव है जो किसी पिण्ड को सिथिज अवस्था से गतिज अवस्था में करता है।

- **Component of Force** ***(बल के अवयव)***

  Component of Force F in two direction is

$$p = \frac{F\sin\alpha}{\sin(\alpha+\beta)}, \text{and } Q = \frac{F\sin\beta}{\sin(\alpha+\beta)}$$

Where α is the angle between P and F and β is the angle between Q and F.

Forced Oscillation ***(बल कम्पन)*** **(Forced vibration)**. Refers to the oscillation of a system or object at a frequency other than its natural frequency. Forced oscillation must be induced by an external periodic force. जिस वस्तु का कम्पन उसके प्राकृतिक कम्पन से भिन्न होता है। यह किसी बाह्य बल के प्रभाव के कारण होता है।

Format ***(फोरमेट)*** It is the information arranged on a sheet of paper. कागज की शीट पर दी जाने वाली सूचना को फोरमेट कहते हैं।

Formula ***(सूत्र)*** Any general rate stated in algebraic equation form e.g. The formula for area of a circle is

$$A = \pi R^2$$

एक सामान्य दर बीजगणतीय समीकरण को सूत्र कहते हैं। जैसे—वृत्त के क्षेत्रफल का सूत्र

$$A = \pi R^2$$

angle $\frac{A}{2}$ in terms of cos A. त्रिकोणमितीय कोणों का अनुपात $\frac{A}{2}$, cos A का पद है।

$$\sin\frac{A}{2}=\sqrt{\frac{1-\cos A}{2}}$$

$$\cos\frac{A}{2}=\sqrt{\frac{1+\cos A}{2}}$$

$$\tan\frac{A}{2}=\sqrt{\frac{1-\cos A}{1+\cos A}}$$

- **Formula for multiple and sub- multiple angles** ***(गुणक और उपगुणक कोणों के सूत्र)***

(*i*) $\sin 2\theta = 2\sin\theta\cos\theta = \frac{2\tan\theta}{1+\tan^2\theta}$

(*ii*) $\cos 2\theta = 2\cos^2\theta - \sin^2\theta = 1-2\sin^2\theta$

$$= 2\cos^2\theta - 1 = \frac{1-\tan^2\theta}{1+\tan^2\theta}$$

(*iii*) $\tan 2\theta = \frac{2\tan\theta}{1-\tan^2\theta}$

(*iv*) $\sin 3\theta = 3\sin\theta - 4\sin^3\theta$

(*v*) $\cos 3\theta = 3\sin\theta - 4\sin^3\theta$

(*vi*) $\tan 3\theta = \frac{3\tan\theta - \tan^3\theta}{1-3\cot^2\theta}$

(*vii*) $\cot 3\theta = \frac{3\cot\theta - \cot^3\theta}{1-3\cot^2\theta}$

Fortran ***(फोरट्रेन)*** It is a language used in digital computers. डिजीटल कम्प्यूटर में प्रयोग की जाने वाली भाषा को फोरट्रेन कहते है।

Frequency polygon ***(बारंबारता बहुभुज)*** It is a method of representing

G

g *(जी)* It means acceleration due to gravity. It also stands for gram. इसे गुरुत्वीय त्वरण कहते हैं। इससे ग्राम भी दर्शाते हैं।

Gallon *(गैलन)* It is a measure of volume.

$$1 \text{ gallon} = 8 \text{ pints.}$$
$$= 4.547 \text{ litres.}$$

It is the space occupies by 10 pounds of water at N.T.P.

धारिता मापने की इकाई है।

1 गैलन = 8 पॉन्ट

= 4.547 लीटर

Gamma function *(गामा फलन)* Gamma of a functions is defined as

$$\overline{|n} = \int_0^\alpha x^{n-1} e^{-x} dx$$

where n is a positive integer

$$\overline{|n} = (n-1)!$$

Some results: $\overline{|1} = \overline{|2} = 1$

$$\overline{|n-1} = n\overline{|n}$$

$$\overline{\left|\frac{1}{2}\right.} = \overline{n}$$

गामा फलन को इस प्रकार से प्रदर्शित करते हैं।

$$\overline{|n} = \int_0^\alpha x^{n-1} e^{-x} dx$$

जहाँ n धनात्मक पूर्णांक है।

$$\overline{|n} = (n-1)!$$

कुछ परिणाम: $\overline{|1} = \overline{|2} = 1$

$$\overline{|n-1} = n\overline{|n}$$

$$\overline{\left|\frac{1}{2}\right.} = \overline{n}$$

Gauss *(गैस)* It is the C.G.S. unit of magnetic flux density. Its symbol is G. चुम्बकीय फ्लक्स घनत्व की इकाई है। इसे G से प्रदर्शित करते हैं।

Generic conic *(द्विघातीय शांकव)* The general equation for this family of curves is

$$ax^2 + 2hxy + by^2 + 2gx + 2fy + c = 0.$$

वक्रों की व्यापक समीकरण

$$ax^2 + 2hxy + by^2 + 2gx + 2fy + c = 0$$

General equation of a circle ***(वृत्त की व्यापक समीकरण)*** If r is radius of the circle and c (a, b) is centre, the equation of circle is यदि किसी वृत्त की त्रिज्या त तथा केन्द्र बिन्दु C (a, b) हो तब

$$(x-a)^2 + (y-b)^2 = r^2$$

or $$x^2 + y^2 + \alpha x + \beta y + \gamma = 0$$

In this $\alpha = -2a$

$\beta = -2b$

$\gamma = a^2 + b^2 - r^2$

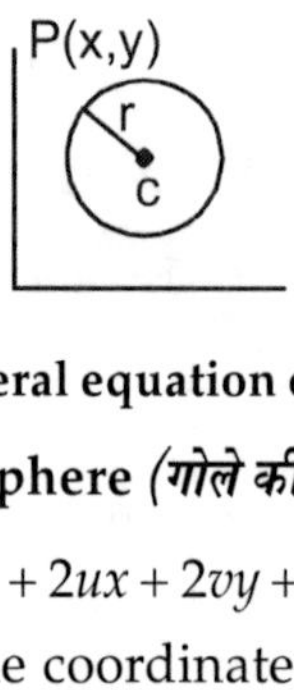

Fig. General equation of a circle

- **General equation of a sphere** ***(गोले की व्यापक समीकरण)*** The equation

$$x^2 + y^2 + z^2 + 2ux + 2vy + 2wz + d = 0$$

represents a sphere. The coordinates of centre will $(-u, -v, -w)$ and its radius will be किसी गोले के केन्द्र के निर्देशांक बिन्दु $(-u, -v, -w)$ हो तब त्रिज्या

$$\sqrt{u^2 + v^2 + w^2 - d}$$

Geometrical representation of complex numbers ***(सम्मिश्र संख्या का ज्यामितीय निरूपण)*** Point P (x, y) represents the complex number $z = x + iy$ in the complex plane.

The length OP known as the modulus of complex number z. Thus $|z| = \sqrt{x^2 + y^2}$ θ, the angle between OP and x-axis is known as **argument or amplitude** of the complex number Z. **The set of**

r $(-1 < r < 1$ *i.e.*, $|r| < 1)$ is $S_\infty = \dfrac{a}{1-r}$

Geometry ***(ज्यामिति)*** It is that branch of mathematics which deals with the study of properties of points, lines, planes, curves, and solids etc. Analytical geometry is a combination of algebra and geometry. गणित की वह शाखा जिसमें बिन्दुओं, रेखाओं समतलों, वक्रकों, आकृतियों और ठोसों का अध्ययन किया जाता है, ज्यामिति कहलाती है। बीजगणित और ज्यामिति की सहभागता को एनालियटिकल ज्यामिति कहते हैं।

Gergonne point ***(गेरगोनी बिन्दु)*** In a triangle, the lines from the vertices to the points of contact of the opposite sides with the inscribed circle meet in a point called the Gergonne point. वह त्रिभुज जिसकी रेखाएं शीर्ष बिन्दुओं पर मिलती है, तथा इसके विपरीत भुजाऐं किसी वृत्त में आकर मिलती है। यह बिन्दु गेरगोनी बिन्दु कहलाता है।

Goldbach conjective ***(गोल्डवेच)*** Every even number greater than 4 is the sum of two odd primes (32 = 13 + 19). Every odd number greater than 7 can be expressed as the sum of three odd prime numbers (11 = 3 + 3 + 5). प्रत्येक सम संख्या 4 से बड़ी हो दो विषम संख्याओं का जोड़ हो। प्रत्येक विषम संख्या 7 से बड़ी हो तथा तीन विषम संख्याओं का जोड़ हो।

Golden ratio ***(गोल्डन अनुपात)*** $\left(\dfrac{1+\sqrt{5}}{2}\right)$.

Golden rectangle ***(गोल्डन आयत)*** A rectangle whose sides are in the golden ratio. वह आयत जिसकी भुजाऐं गोल्डन अनुपात में हों।

Gram (g) ***(ग्राम)*** A units of mass. द्रव्यमान की इकाई है।

Graph ***(आलेखन)*** A graph is a set of points and a set of lines joining these vertices. बिन्दुओं और रेखाओं के मिलाने से आलेखन प्राप्त होती है।

Graphs of hyperbolic functions and inverse hyperbolic functions ***(अतिपरवलीय फलनों के वक्र और अतिपरवलीय फलनों के व्यत्क्रम)***

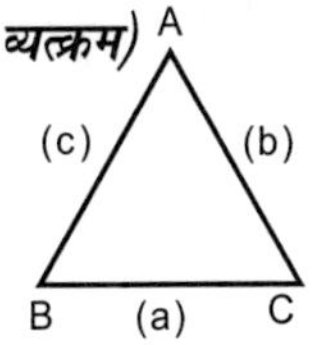

H

Half angle formula *(अर्द्धकोणीय सूत्र)*

(*i*) $$\sin\frac{A}{2}=\sqrt{\frac{(s-b)(s-c)}{bc}}$$

$$\sin\frac{B}{2}=\sqrt{\frac{(s-a)(s-c)}{ac}}$$

$$\sin\frac{C}{2}=\sqrt{\frac{(s-a)(s-b)}{ab}}$$

(*ii*) $$\cos\frac{A}{2}=\sqrt{\frac{s(s-a)}{bc}}$$

$$\cos\frac{B}{2}=\sqrt{\frac{s(s-b)}{ac}}$$

$$\cos\frac{C}{2}=\sqrt{\frac{s(s-c)}{ab}}$$

(*iii*) $$\tan\frac{A}{2}=\sqrt{\frac{(s-b)(s-c)}{s(s-a)}}$$

$$\tan\frac{B}{2}=\sqrt{\frac{(s-c)(s-a)}{s(s-b)}}$$

$$\tan\frac{C}{2}=\sqrt{\frac{(s-a)(s-b)}{s(s-c)}}$$

(*iv*) If r is the radius of incircle of triangle Δ the area of traingle and s its perimeter.
यदि r किसी त्रिभुज के अन्दर के वृत्त की त्रिज्या हो, Δ त्रिभुज का क्षेत्रफल और s परिमाप हो तब

(*a*) $$r=\frac{\Delta}{s}$$

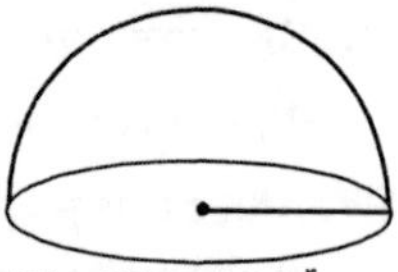

Fig. Hemisphere

(*b*) $$r = \frac{a\sin\frac{B}{2}\sin\frac{C}{2}}{\cos\frac{A}{2}}$$

(*c*) $$\tan\frac{A}{2} = \frac{r}{s-a}$$

$$\tan\frac{B}{2} = \frac{r}{s-b}$$

$$\tan\frac{C}{2} = \frac{r}{s-c}$$

(*v*) If R is the radius of circum circle of the triangle. यदि R किसी त्रिभुज के परिवृत्त की त्रिज्या हो तब

$$R = \frac{a}{2\sin A} = \frac{b}{2\sin B} = \frac{c}{2\sin C}$$

(*vi*) $$r = 4R\sin\frac{A}{2}\sin\frac{B}{2}\sin\frac{C}{2}$$

Half Plane ***(अर्द्ध समतल)*** The part of plan on one side of straight line. समतल का वह भाग जिसकी एक भुजा साथी रेखा हो।

Harmonic Mean (H) ***(हरात्मक माध्य)*** The harmonic mean of two numbers a and b is given by दो संख्याऐं a और b हो तब हरात्मक माध्य

$$H = \frac{2ab}{a+b}$$

Harmonic Motion ***(हरात्मक गति)*** Any regularly repeated sequence that can be expressed as the sum of a set of sine waves. Each component sine wave represents a possible simple harmonic motion. ऐसा निकाय जिसमें तरंगों की ज्याओं के समुच्च का योग हो। तब प्रत्येक तरंग की ज्या सरल आवर्ती गति प्रदर्शित करेगी।

Harmonic Progression ***(हरात्मक श्रेणी)*** It is a sequence of terms in which each term is the reciprocal of the corresponding term of a series in arithmetic progression (A.P)

$$\text{e.g. } 1, \frac{1}{3}, \frac{1}{5}, \frac{1}{7} \text{ .... is a H.P.}$$

ऐसी श्रेणी जिसके पदों के व्युत्क्रम समान्तर श्रेणी में हो, हरात्मक श्रेणी कहते हैं।

H.C.F (Highest Common Factor) ***(म.स.प.) महत्तम समापवर्त्य*** H.C.F of two or more number is the greatest number which is a divisor or factor of all numbers in volved. दो या दो से अधिक संख्याओं में महत्तम समापवर्त्य सबसे अधिक उभनिष्ठ गुणनखंड हो, जिससे दी हुई संख्याऐं विभाजित हो जायें।

When the given numbers have been resolved into prime factors, the H.C.F is the product of all the common factors. Each common factor is considered ones only with the minimum exponent which appears in it e.g. HCF of 480, 360, 600 is 120. It can be found as under

$$480 = 2^5 \times 3 \times 5$$
$$360 = 2^3 \times 3^2 \times 5$$
$$600 = 2^3 \times 3 \times 5^2$$

Thus H. C. F. = $2^3 \times 3 \times 5 = 8 \times 3 \times 5 = 120$

Hectare ***(हेक्टेयर)*** 1 Hectare = 10,000 square metres. 1 हेक्टेयर = 10,000 वर्ग मी.

Hecto ***(हेक्टो)*** A prefix denoting 10^2.

Height ***(ऊँचाई)*** It is the vertical distance of a point above the base line or plane. आधारीय रेखा समतल के लम्बवत् खीचीं गई दूरी को ऊँचाई कहते हैं।

Helix ***(हिलिक्स)*** It is a curve that on the surface of a cylinder or cone and makes a constant angle with the axis. वह वक्र जो बेलन और शंकु के वक्रपृष्ठ को प्रदर्शित करे तथा अक्ष के साथ एक नियत कोण बनाएँ।

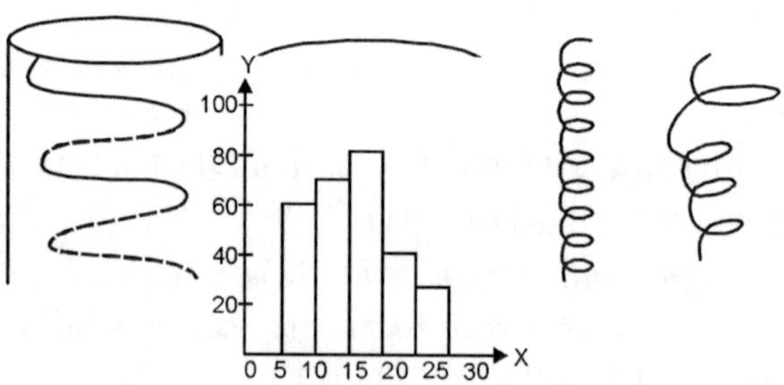

Hemisphere ***(अर्द्ध गोला)*** It is half of a sphere. It is obtained by cutting a sphere through its centre. यह आधा गोला होता है। गोले को केन्द्र से काटने पर प्राप्त होता है।

Henry ***(हेनरी)*** It is the unit of inductance. It is equal to the inductance of a closed circuit that has a magnetic flux of one weber per ampere of current in the circuit. $1H = 1\ Wb\ A^{-1}$. यह बन्द परिपथ में 1 वेबर/एम्पियर के बराबर होती है।

1 हेनरी = 1 वेबर/एम्पियर

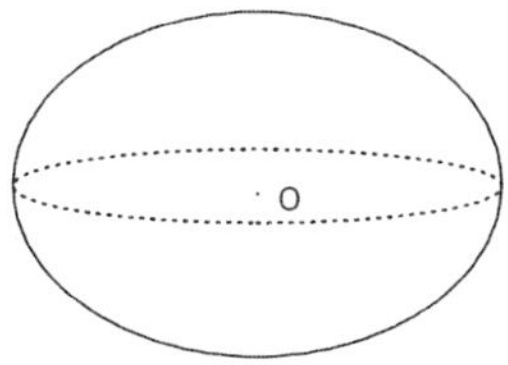

Fig. Helix

Heptagon ***(सप्तभुज)*** It refers to a polygon with seven sides. The sum of internal angles of a heptagon is 900°. ऐसा बहुभुज जिसमें सात भुजाएँ हों। सप्तभुज में अन्दर के कोणों का योग 900° होता है।

Hero's formula ***(हीरो का सूत्र)*** The area (A), of a triangle is given by

$$A = \sqrt{s(s-a)(s-b)(s-c)}$$

in it s in the semi-perimeter = $\frac{p}{2} = \frac{a+b+c}{2}$ = s

$$\text{Also } A = r.p = \frac{a.b.c.}{4R}$$

where r = radius of the circle inscribed in the angle.

R = radius of circumcircle on the triangle.

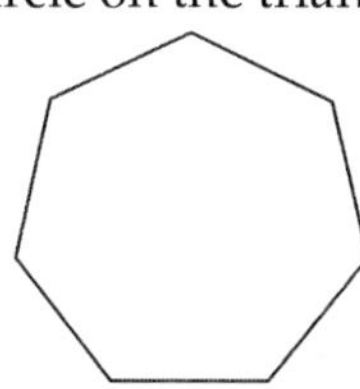

Fig. Hero's formula

त्रिभुज का क्षेत्रफल A हो तब त्रिभुज का क्षेत्रफल

$$A = \sqrt{s(s-a)(s-b)(s-c)}$$

जहाँ s अर्द्ध परिमाप है।

r त्रिभुज के अन्तःवृत्त की त्रिज्या है।

R त्रिभुज के बाह्य की त्रिज्या है।

Heron's (Hero's) Formula ***(हीरोन का सूत्र)*** It is a formula for connecting the area of a triangle with its sides. If a, b, c are the length of the sides of a triangle, its area Δ is given by

$$\Delta = \sqrt{s(s-a)(s-b)(s-c)}$$

इस सूत्र को त्रिभुज के क्षेत्रफल के सूत्र से जोड़ा जाऐं भुजाओं द्वारा, यदि a, b, c लम्बाईयाँ त्रिभुज की भुजाऐं हैं। Δ त्रिभुज का क्षेत्रफल

$$\Delta = \sqrt{s(s-a)(s-b)(s-c)}$$

Hexagon ***(षटभुज)*** A polygon with six sides. ऐसा बहुभुज जिसमें 6 भुजाएं हों।

Hexagonal number ***(षटभुज संख्या)*** A number of the form $n(2n-1)$ ऐसी संख्या जिसकी अवस्था $n(2n-1)$ हो।

Hexagonal prism ***(षटभुज प्रिज्म)*** A prism with a hexagonal base. ऐसा प्रिज्म जिसका आधार षटभुज हो। ऐसा बहुभुज जिसमें एक समान तल हो।

Hexahedron ***(षष्टफलकीय)*** A polyhedron with six faces. A regular hexahedron is cube. ऐसा फलनक जिसमें 6 मुख हो षष्टफलकीय कहलाता है। घन एक षष्टफलकीय को प्रदर्शित करता है।

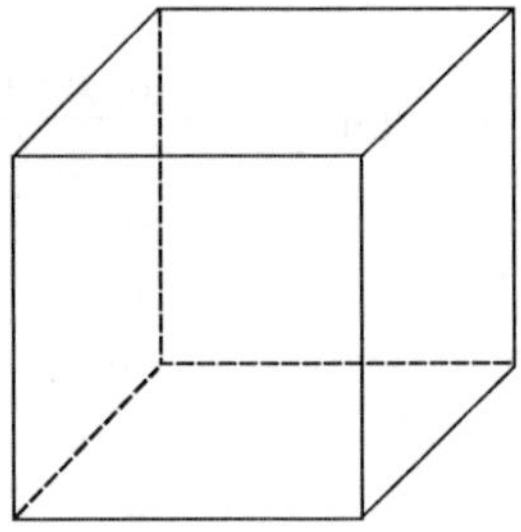

Fig. Hexahedron

Histogram ***(आयत चित्र)*** A histogram or frequency histogram is a graphical representation of a frequency distribution. एक आयत चित्र बारंबारता बंटन का आलेखी निरुपण है।

I

I *(आइ)* It means $\sqrt{-1}$ इसका मान $\sqrt{-1}$ होता है।

Icosahedron *(विंशतिफलकीय)* A polyhedron having 20 faces. वह बहुभुज जिसमें बीस फलक होते हैं।

Identity *(सर्वसमिका)* It is an equation that is true for every value of variable or variables involved. वह समीकरण जो परिवर्तनीय मूल्य के लिये सत्य होता है।

Identity element *(तत्समक अवयव)* An element of a set which combined with another element, under some binary operation, leaves it unchanged. द्विआधारीय संक्रिया में किसी समुच्च का अवयव दूसरे अवयव से जोड़ा जाता है। कोई बदलाव नहीं होता है।

$$i * x = x * i = x \text{ for } x \in s$$

In case of addition 0 is the identity तत्समक में 0 जोडने पर

$$0 + 6 = 6 + 0, 0 + (-3) + 0 \text{ etc.}$$

For multiplication identity is 1. इसका गुणात्मक तत्समक 1 है।

Identity function *(तत्समक फलन)* A function that associates to each real number x, the same number x is known as identity function such as $f(x)$ for x in R. ऐसा फलन जिसके लिए $f(x) = x \forall\ x \in R$ अर्थात R का प्रत्येक अवयव स्वयं का ही प्रतिबिम्ब हो तो ऐसे फलन को तत्समक फलन कहते हैं।

The domain of identity function is R and its range is also R.

When represented graphically it yields a straight line

Image *(प्रतिबिम्ब)* The result of applying a function to a particular number of domain is called the image of the element. In case of $x \to 3x + 4.$ at $x = 4$ we get 16. The number 16 is known as the image of number 4 which is known as object. किसी निश्चित संख्या को किसी फलन के साथ सरल करने से उस अवयव का प्रतिबिम्ब प्राप्त होता है। जैसे $x \to 3x + 4.$ में $x = 4$ रखने पर 16 प्राप्त होता है जो 4 का प्रतिबिम्ब कहलाता है और 4 को वस्तु कहते हैं।

In mapping if a set x is mapped *a* set Y and $x \in X$ is mapped to

$y \in Y$ then y is the image of x.

In geometry; it refers to the result of some transformation

Imaginary Part ***(काल्पनिक भाग)*** The imaginary part of a complex number $a + ib$ is b. सम्मिश्र संख्या $(a + ib)$ में b काल्पनिक भाग है।

Imaginary axis ***(काल्पनिक अक्ष)*** In a grand diagram it is the axis of y. आरंगा चित्र में y-अक्ष को काल्पनिक अक्ष कहते हैं।

Imaginary Number ***(काल्पनिक संख्या)*** It is of the type $a + ib$, where $i = \sqrt{-1}$. इसे $(a + ib)$ के रूप में लिखते हैं। जहाँ $i = \sqrt{-1}$ है।

Imaginary Number ***(काल्पनिक राशि)*** A multiple of $i = (\sqrt{-1})$ solution of an equation in the form $x^2 + 2 = 0$ will need imaginary numbers. प्रत्येक काल्पनिक राशि को एक वास्तविक संख्या और $\sqrt{-1}$ के गुणनफल के रूप में व्यक्त किया जाता है।

Imaginary root ***(काल्पनिक मूल)*** A root of an equation which is an imaginary number. ऐसे मूल की समीकरण जिसमें काल्पनिक संख्या हो।

Implicit relation ***(उपलक्षित सम्बन्ध)*** It is relation between two variables and indirectly with a third variable e.g.

$$x = at^2, y = 4at$$

दो परिवर्तनीय तथा अप्रत्यक्ष रूप से तीसरे परिवर्तनीय के बीच का सम्बन्ध जैसे–

$$x = at^2, y = 4at$$

Important formulae of Algebraic expression

(बीजीय व्यंजकों के सूत्र)

- $(a + b)^2 = a^2 + 2ab + b^2$
- $(a - b)^2 = a^2 - 2ab + b^2$
- $(a + b)(a - b) = a^2 - b^2$
- $(x + a)(x + b) = x^2 + (a + b)x + ab$.
- $(a + b)^3 = a^3 + 3a^2b + 3ab^2 + b^3 = a^3 + b^3 + 3ab(a + b)$.
- $(a - b)^3 = a^3 - 3a^2b + 3ab^2 - b^3 = a^3 - b^3 - 3ab(a - b)$.
- $(a + b + c)^2 = a^2 + b^2 + c^2 + 2ab + 2bc + 2ca$.

- $(a + b)^4 = a^4 + 4a^3b + 6\,a^2b^2 + 4\,ab^3 + b^4$
- $(a - b)^4 = a^4 - 4a^3b + 6a^2b^2 - 4\,ab^3 + b^4.$
- $(a \pm b)^5 = a^5 \pm 5a^4b + 10\,a^3b^2 \pm 10a^2b^3 + 5\,ab^4 \pm b^5.$

Improper fraction ***(विषम भिन्न)*** Refers to a fraction in which the numerator is greater than its denominator e.g. 15/4. वह भिन्न अंक जिसमें भाजक या हर से भाज्य या अंश होता है। जैसे 15/4

Incentre ***(अन्तः केन्द्र)*** It is the point of intersection of bisectors of the altitudes of a triangle. In the ΔABC, K is the incentre. वह बिन्दु जहाँ त्रिभुज के सभी विकर्ण आकर मिलते है, अन्तः केन्द्र कहते हैं। ΔABC में K एक अन्तः केन्द्र है।

Inch ***(इंच)*** It is an imperial unit of length.

$$1 \text{ inch} = \frac{1}{12} \text{ foot}$$

यह लम्बाई मापने की इकाई है।

$$1 \text{ इंच} = \frac{1}{12} \text{ फुट}$$

Incircle ***(अन्तः वृत्त)*** If a circle is drawn, with incentre of the triangle as the centre of the circle, and touching each of the three sides of the triangle then such a circle is called or inscribed circle of the triangle. त्रिभुज के अन्तः केन्द्र को केन्द्र मानकर खींचा गया वृत्त जो त्रिभुज जो त्रिभुज की तीनों भुजाओं से होकर जाता हो।

Incircle of a triangle and its radius ***(त्रिभुज का अंतः वृत्त व उसकी त्रिज्या)***

(i) $r = \dfrac{\Delta}{s}$

(ii) $r = (s - a)\tan\left(\dfrac{A}{2}\right), r = (s - b)\tan\left(\dfrac{B}{2}\right)$ and

$$r = (s - c)\tan\left(\frac{C}{2}\right)$$

(iii) $r = \dfrac{a\sin\left(\frac{B}{2}\right)\sin\left(\frac{C}{2}\right)}{\cos\left(\frac{A}{2}\right)}, r = \dfrac{b\sin\left(\frac{A}{2}\right)\sin\left(\frac{C}{2}\right)}{\cos\left(\frac{B}{2}\right)},$

$$r = \frac{c \sin\left(\frac{B}{2}\right) \sin\left(\frac{A}{2}\right)}{\cos\left(\frac{C}{2}\right)}$$

$$(iv)\ r = 4R \sin\left(\frac{A}{2}\right) . \sin\left(\frac{B}{2}\right) . \sin\left(\frac{C}{2}\right)$$

The length of the intercept made by line $y = mx + c$ with the circle $x^2 + y^2 = a^2$ is (रेखा $y = mx + c$ द्वारा वृत्त $x^2 + y^2 = a^2$ से बनाया खण्ड का माप)

$$= \sqrt{\frac{a^2(1-m^2)-c^2}{1+m^2}}$$

Inclination of line in a plane ***(समतल में रेखा का झुकाव)*** Angle of inclination is the angle made by the line with some fixed line in the plane, measured anti clock wise from the fixed line. The fixed line is generally the x - axis. रेखा द्वारा समतल पर बनाये गये कोण को रेखा का झुकाव कहते हैं।

Inclination of two lines ***(रेखा का झुकाव)*** The angle between two lines in a plane. किसी तल में दो रेखाओं के बीच का कोण।

Inclined plane ***(ढलुआँ तल)*** Any plane that is not horizontal. वह तल जो क्षैतिज नहीं होता है।

Incommensurable quantities ***(अतुल्य राशि)*** Two quantities are said to be incommensurable if their ratio cannot be expressed as the ratio of two integers, e.g. $\frac{\pi}{3}$ are incommensurable quantities. दो राशियाँ अतुल्य कही जाती हैं यदि इन्हें दो पूर्णांक के अनुपात में न व्यक्त किया जा सके जैसे $\pi/\sqrt{3}$ ।

Increment ***(वृद्धि)*** An increase (positive or negative) in the value of variable. किसी परिवर्तनीय मूल्य में धनात्मक अथवा ऋणात्मक वृद्धि।

Infinte ***(अनन्त)*** Not bound. जिसकी कोई सीमा न हो।

Index number ***(सूचकांक)*** Index numbers are specialized averages designed to measure the changes in one variable or a group of related variables over a period of time. There are three types of index numbers which are commonly used (*i*) the price index number (*ii*) the Quantity index numbers (*iii*) the cost of living index numbers. सूचकांक द्वारा एक दी हुई अवधि में एक परिवर्तनीय राशि में सापेक्ष परिवर्तन मापते हैं। तीन सूचकांक सर्वसामान्य के लिए उपयोगी हैं– (*i*) मूल्य सूचकांक (*ii*) मात्रा सूचकांक (*iii*) निर्वाह सूचकांक

$$\text{निर्वाह सूचकांक} = \frac{\text{वर्तमान वर्ष में कुल खर्च}}{\text{आधार वर्ष में कुल खर्च}} \times 100$$

- **INDICES** ***(घातंक)***

  If a be any real number and n is the natural number, then

  $a^n = a \times a \times a \times ..... \times a$

  n factors

  and n is index of a (n, a की घात है) and plural of index in indices.

Infinite function ***(अनन्त फलन)*** Any function of the form Lim $f(x) = \infty$ or $-\infty$ $x \to a$. फलन की अवस्था Lim $f(x) = \infty$ or $-\infty$ $x \to a$.

Infinite series ***(अनन्त श्रेणी)*** A series that contains and infinite number of terms. ऐसी श्रेणी जिसमें लगातार और पदों की संख्या अनन्त हो।

Infinite set ***(अपरिमित समुच्चय)*** Any set having infinite number of elements. ऐसा समुच्चय जिसमें विभिन्न अवयवों की संख्या असीमित हो।

Infinite ***(अनन्त)*** An imaginary number which is greater than any number which could be thought of. ऐसी काल्पनिक संख्या जो सभी संख्याओं से बड़ी हो। जिसके बारे में कुछ सोचा भी ना जा सके।

Inner product ***(अन्तः गुणन)*** In sets, the intersection of two sets is called as the inner product of the two sets. समुच्चय के अन्दर दो समुच्चय प्रतिच्छेद करें तो हम दो समुच्चयों का अन्तः गुणन कहेंगे।

Input ***(सूचना संग्रह)*** Any information fed into the computer in the form of data or instructions. कम्प्यूटर अथवा दूसरे यंत्र में सूचना को श्रेणीबद्ध करना।

In-radius ***(अन्तः त्रिज्या)*** The distance of incentre from any side of a triangle is known as its in radius. अन्तः केन्द्र तथा त्रिभुज की किसी भुजा के बीच की दूरी अन्तः त्रिज्या कहलाती है।

Inscribed circle ***(अन्तः वृत्त)*** Any circle is considered as inscribed in a polygon if each side of the polygon is tangent to circle. The inscribed circle in a triangle has its centre at the point of intersection of the angle bisectors. किसी वृत्त को बहुभुज के अन्दर इस प्रकार रखा जाऐ कि बहुभुज की प्रत्येक भुजा वृत्त पर स्पर्शी हो। अन्तः वृत्त का केन्द्र किसी त्रिभुज के कोण को दो भागों में विभाजित करें।

Integers *(पूर्णांक)* Natural numbers (including zero) and their negatives are known as integers.

$$I = \ldots -4, -3, -2, -1, 0, 1, 2, 3, 4, 5, 6, \ldots$$

शून्य सहित प्राकृतिक संख्याऐं और ऋणात्मक संख्याओं को पूर्णांक कहते हैं।

Integer variable *(भिन्नात्मक पूर्णांक)* Refers to a variable that can have only integral value. जिसमें केवल पूर्णांक मान हो, उसे भिन्नात्मक पूर्णांक कहते हैं।

Integral calculus *(समाकलन कैलकुलस)* It is a branch of mathematics that deals with the integrals of functions. यह गणित की एक शाखा है। जिसमें फलनों का समाकलन किया जाता है।

Integral curves *(समाकल वक्र)* Those curves whose equations are the solutions of a given differential equation. वे वक्र जिनकी समीकरणों का हल अवकलन समीकरणों द्वारा किया गया हो।

Integral Domain *(समाकल डोमने)* Refers to a commutative ring having identity element in it with respect to multiplication and with the property that when $xy = 0$ (0 being identity element with respect to addition) then $x = 0$ or $y = 0$ both $x = y = 0$. क्रमविनिमय वलय सिजमें समान अवयव हो तथा गुणन में प्रयुक्त हैं। जैसे $x = 0, y = 0\ x = y = 0$.

Integral Function *(समाकलन फलन)* *(Entire Function)* Any function that when expanded by Maclaurin's series is valid for any assignable value of the variable. ऐसा फलन जिसका विस्तार मेक्लेरिन श्रेणी में हो, दिये गये मान के लिए मान्य हो।

Integral Index *(समाकल घातांक)* An index (exponent) that is an integer and not a variable. वह घातांक जो पूर्णांक हो और भिन्नात्मक न हो, समाकल घातांक कहलाता है।

Integration *(समाकलन)* It is the process of finding a definite or an indefinite integral. It is inverse of differentiation.

In the expression $\int_a^b f(x)\,dx$; a, b are known as limits of integration, $f(x)$ is known as integrand and x is known as variable of integration. अवकलन की प्रतिलोम संक्रिया को समाकलन कहते हैं। इसमें निश्चित अनिश्चित समाकलनों को प्राप्त किया जाता है। इस सूत्र $\int_a^b f(x)$ में a, b समाकलन की

सीमाएँ हैं। तथा $f(x)$ को समाकल्य कहते हैं।

Some Standard forms *(कुछ महत्त्वपूर्ण तथ्य)*

These are used as formula while integrating the given function.
ये सब जब प्रयोग किये जाते हैं जब दिये हुए फलनों का समाकलन करते हैं।

1. $\int x^n dx = \frac{x^{n-1}}{n+1} + C.n \neq -1$
2. $\int K\, dx = Kx + C$
3. $\int \frac{1}{x} dx = \log x + C$
4. $\int \sin x\, dx = -\cos x + C$
5. $\int \cos x\, dx = \sin x + C$
6. $\int \tan x\, dx = -\log(\cos x) + C$ or $\log \sec x + C$
7. $\int \sec x\, dx = \log(\sec x + \tan x) + C$
8. $\int \operatorname{cosec} dx = \log(\operatorname{cosec} x - \cot x) + C$
9. $\int \cot x\, dx = \log \sin x + C$
10. $\int e^x dx = e^x + C$
11. $\int a^x dx = \frac{a^x}{\log a} + C$
12. $\int \sec^2 x\, dx = \tan x + C$
13. $\int \operatorname{cosec}^2 x\, dx = -\cot x + C$
14. $\int (ax+b)^n x\, dx = \frac{(ax+b)^{n+1}}{a(n-1)} + C,\ n \neq -1$
15. $\int \sin(ax+b) dx = -\frac{1}{a}\cos(ax+b) + C$
16. $\int \cos(ax+b)\, dx = \frac{1}{a}\sin(ax+b) + C$

17. $\int \sec x \tan x \, dx = \sec x + C$

18. $\int \operatorname{cosec} x \, . \cot x \, dx = -\operatorname{cosec} x + C$

19. $\int \frac{1}{ax+b} dx = \frac{1}{a} \log(ax+b) + C$

20. $\int e^{ax+b} dx = \frac{1}{a} e^{ax+b} + C$

21. $\int \frac{1}{\sqrt{1-x^2}} dx = \sin^{-1} x + C = -\cos^{-1} x + C$

२२ए $\int \frac{1}{1+x^2} dx = \tan^{-1} x + C = -\cot^{-1} x + C$

23. $\int \frac{1}{x\sqrt{x^2-1}} dx = \sec^{-1} x + C = -\operatorname{cosec}^{-1} x + C$

Some more standard forms *(कुछ मानक रूप)*

1. $\int \frac{dx}{x^2 - a^2} = \frac{1}{2a} \log \left| \frac{x-a}{x+a} \right| + C$

2. $\int \frac{dx}{a^2 - x^2} = \frac{1}{2a} \log \left| \frac{a+x}{a-x} \right| + C$

3. $\int \frac{dx}{x^2 + a^2} = \frac{1}{a} \tan^{-1} \frac{x}{a} + C$

4. $\int \frac{dx}{\sqrt{x^2 - a^2}} = \log \left| x + \sqrt{x^2 - a^2} \right| + C$

5. $\int \frac{dx}{\sqrt{a^2 - x^2}} = \sin^{-1} \frac{x}{a} + C$

6. $\int \frac{dx}{\sqrt{a^2 + x^2}} = \log \left| x + \sqrt{x^2 + a^2} \right| + C$

Intersecting lines *(प्रतिच्छेदी रेखाएँ)* Two lines intersection is non-empty are said to be intersecting lines. The common point is called the point of intersection. वह दो रेखाएँ जो किसी बिन्दू पर एक दूसरे को काटती हैं प्रतिच्छेदी रेखाएँ कहलाती हैं। इन दोनों रेखाओं के उभयनिष्ठ बिन्दु को प्रतिच्छेदन बिन्दु कहते हैं।

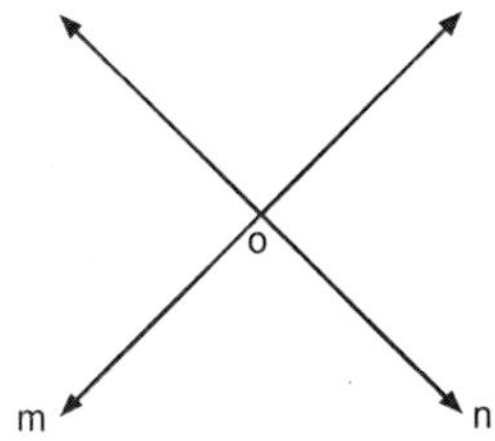

Fig. Intersecting lines

Intersection of sets ***(समुच्चयों का प्रतिच्छेद)*** The intersection of sets consist of all the points that belong to each of the sets. The intersection of sets U and V usually is denoted by $U \cap V$, but sometimes by UV or $U.V$. and is also called the product or meet of U and V. यदि U और V दो समुच्चय हैं तो U और V के उभयनिष्ठ अवयवों का समुच्चय U और V का प्रतिच्छेद समुच्चय (intersection sets) कहलाता है। जिसे $U \cap V$ से प्रदर्शित किया जाता है और इसे U प्रतिच्छेद V पढ़ते हैं।

Interest ***(ब्याज)*** The money borrowed from a lender is called the principal. The additional money which is paid back after a specified period in addition to principal is called interest.

$$\text{Simple interest} = \frac{\text{Principal} \times \text{rate} \times \text{time}}{100}$$

$$\text{I} = \frac{\text{P} \times r \times t}{100}$$

मूलधन के ऊपर दिया गया अतिरिक्त धन (एक निश्चित अवधि के लिए) ब्याज कहलाता है।

$$\text{साधारण ब्याज} = \frac{\text{मूलधन} \times \text{दर} \times \text{समय}}{100}$$

Interior angle ***(अन्तः कोण)*** It is the angle formed at the vertex of a polygon on the inside of the figure by two adjacent sides e.g. $\angle 1$ $\angle 2$ $\angle 3$. बहुभुज के अन्दर शीर्ष बिन्दुओं पर बने कोणों को अन्तः कोण कहते है।

Inverse element ***(प्रतिलोग अवयव)*** In a set, the inverse of an element a_1

under the binary operation, is the element a^{-1} such that $a^*a^{-1} = a^{-1}*a = e$, where e is the identity element of the set. किसी समुच्चय में प्रतिलोग अवयव a_1 द्विआधारी संक्रियाओं में अवयव a^{-1} तब $a * a^{-1} = a^{-1} * a = e$ जहाँ e समुच्चय का तत्समक अवयव है।

Inverse function ***(प्रतिलोम फलन)*** If a function of maps a set A into a set B, then there may exist a reverse mapping denoted by f^{-1} form set B into set A. यदि प्रतिचित्रण $f = A \to B$ एकैकी आच्छादक है। तो प्रतिलोम फलन $f^{-1} : B \to$ अद्वितीय होगा।

Inverse of matrix ***(व्यत्क्रम आव्यूह)*** If A and B are two square matrices such that AB = BA = 1, then B is called the inverse of A and vice-versa.

$$\frac{A(adj\ .\ A)}{|A|} = I, \frac{A(adj.\ A)}{|A|}$$ behaves as the inverse of

A, Hence $A^{-1} = \dfrac{(adj.\ A)}{|A|}$

यदि A और B दो वर्ग आव्यूह हैं, AB = BA = 1 तब B, A का प्रतिलोग होगा।

Inverse number ***(व्युत्क्रम संख्या)*** The inverse of a number n is $\frac{1}{n}(n \neq 0)$. n का व्युत्क्रम $\frac{1}{n}$ होगा।

Inverse ratio ***(व्युत्क्रम अनुपात)*** Inverse ratio of $\frac{x}{y}$ is $\frac{y}{x}$. $\frac{x}{y}$ का व्युत्क्रम अनुपात $\frac{y}{x}$ होगा।

Inverse relation ***(व्युत्क्रम सम्बन्ध)*** If there is a relation R between two sets A and B so that xRy for $x \in A$, $y \in B$, then exists a relation R^{-1} so that $yR^{-1}x$. मान लीजिए R, A से B में एक सम्बन्ध वह समुच्चय है। जहाँ $(x \in A,\ y \in B)$ तो R के प्रत्येक क्रमित युग्म के अवयवों को परस्पर बदल देने से प्राप्त होता है। इसे R^{-1} से निरूपित किया जाता है।

Inverse square law ***(व्युत्क्रम वर्ग का नियम)*** According to it intensity of energy of a force varies as the square of the distance from the source e.g. force of attraction between any two objects $\alpha \frac{a}{d^2}$. दो पिण्डों के बीच की दूरी के वर्ग का व्युत्क्रम बल F के समानुपाती होता है।

Inverse trigonometric functions ***(व्युत्क्रम त्रिकोणमितीय फलन)*** The real function $\sin^{-1}x$, $\cos^{-1}x$ etc. are known as inverse trigonometric functions. The domain and range of these functions are as given in table below: वास्तविक फलन $\sin^{-1}x$, $\cos^{-1}x$ आदि व्युत्क्रम त्रिकोणमितीय फलन कहलाते हैं। डोमेने और रेंज नीचे सारणी में दिये हुए हैं।

CHART *(तालिका)*

Function	Domain	Range	Defination
$\sin^{-1}x$	$[-1, 1]$	$\left[-\frac{\pi}{2}, \frac{\pi}{2}\right]$	$y - \sin^{-1} x \Rightarrow x - \sin y$
$\cos^{-1}x$	$[-1, 1]$	$[0, \pi]$	$y - \cos^{-1} x \Rightarrow x - \cos y$
$\tan^{-1}x$	$]-\infty, \infty[$	$\left[-\frac{\pi}{2}, \frac{\pi}{2}\right]$	$y - \tan^{-1} x \Rightarrow x - \tan y$
$\cot^{-1}x$	$]-\infty, \infty[$	$]0, \pi[$	$y - \cot^{-1} x \Rightarrow x - \cot y$
$\sec^{-1}x$	$]1, \infty[$	$]0, \frac{\pi}{2}]$	$y - \sec^{-1} x \Rightarrow x - \sec y$
	$]\infty, -1[$	$]\frac{\pi}{2}, \pi[$	
$\text{cosec}^{-1}x$	$[1, \infty[$	$]0, \frac{\pi}{2}]$	$y - \text{cosec}^{-1}x \Rightarrow x - \text{cosec}\, y$
	$]-\infty, -1[$	$]-\frac{\pi}{2}, \pi[$	

Inverse Trigonometric functions formulac. *(व्युतक्रमानुपाती त्रिकोणमितीय सूत्र)*

(*i*) $\tan^{-1}x + \tan^{-1}y = \tan^{-1} \frac{x+y}{1-xy}$ if $x > 0, y > 0$ and $xy < 1$

(*ii*) $\tan^{-1}x - \tan^{-1}y = \tan^{-1}\left(\frac{x-y}{1+xy}\right)$

(*iii*) $\tan^{-1}x + \tan^{-1}y\, \Pi + \tan^{-1}\left(\frac{x-y}{1-xy}\right)$ if $x > 0, y > 0$ and $xy < 1$

(*iv*) $\tan^{-1}x + \tan^{-1}y + \tan^{-1}z = \tan^{-1}\left[\dfrac{x+y+2-xy3}{1-xy-y3-3x}\right]$

(*v*) $\sin^{-1}x \pm \sin^{-1}y = \sin^{-1}[x\sqrt{1-y^2} \pm y\sqrt{1-x^2}]$,
if $x, y \geq 0$ and $x^2 + y^2 \leq 1$

(*vi*) $\sin^{-1}x \pm \sin^{-1}y = \sin^{-1}[x\sqrt{1-y^2} \pm y\sqrt{1-x^2}]$,
if $x, y \geq 0$ and $x^2 + y^2 \geq 1$

(*vii*) $\cos^{-1}x \pm \cos^{-1}y = \cos^{-1}[xy \mp \sqrt{1-x^2}\sqrt{1-y^2}]$,
if $x, y > 0$ and $x^2 + y^2 \leq 1$

(*viii*) $\cos^{-1}x \pm \cos^{-1}y = \pi - \cos^{-1}[xy \mp \sqrt{1-x^2}\sqrt{1-y^2}]$,
if $x, y > 0$ and $x^2 + y^2 /> 1$

(*ix*) $\cot^{-1}x \pm \cot^{-1}y = \cot^{-1}\left[\dfrac{xy \mp 1}{y \pm x}\right]$

- **Inverse trigonometric ratios of multiple angles** *(व्युत्क्रमानुपाती त्रिकोणमितीय अनुपात)*

(*i*) $2\sin^{-1}x = \sin^{-1}(2x\sqrt{1-x^2})$, if $-1 \leq x \leq 1$

(*ii*) $2\cos^{-1}x = \cos^{-1}(2x^2-1)$, if $-1 \leq x \leq 1$

(*iii*) $2\tan^{-1}x = \tan^{-1}\left(\dfrac{2x}{1-x^2}\right) = \sin^{-1}\left(\dfrac{2x}{1+x^2}\right) = \cos^{-1}\left(\dfrac{1-x^2}{1+x^2}\right)$

(*iv*) $3\sin^{-1}x = \sin^{-1}(3x - 4x^3)$

(*v*) $3\cos^{-1}x = \cos^{-1}(4x^3 - 3x)$

(*vi*) $3\tan^{-1}x = \tan^{-1}\left(\dfrac{3x-x^3}{1+3x^2}\right)$

Inverse Variation *(व्युत्क्रमानुपाती विचरण)*

- Two quantities x and y vary inversely if the product xy remains constant in other words, x and y are said to vary indirectly, if $xy = k$, Where k is a positive constant.
- दो राशियों और k और y को एक दूसरे के साथ व्युत्क्रमानुपाती विचरण में कहते हैं, यदि

J

J *(जे)* $\hat{j}$ is used for denoting a unit vector in the positive direction of *y*-axis. इससे *y*–अक्ष के धनात्मक दिशा में ईकाई वेक्टर को दर्शाते हैं।

Job *(कार्य)* A job is something that has to be done or in computers it covers all the activities involved in completing any project on a computer from beginning to finish. किसी के द्वारा किया गया कुछ काम अथवा कम्प्यूटर में किसी युक्ति के आरम्भ तथा अन्त के बीच समस्त क्रिया-कलाप।

Joint *(संधि)* A line segment that joins two given point. वह रेखाखण्ड जो दो बिन्दुओं को जोड़ता है।

Jordon Curve *(जार्डन वक्र)* Any continuous, closed curve which does not intersect itself. Such a curve may or may not be of definite length. कोई सतत्, बन्द वक्र जो स्वतः प्रतिच्छेदित नहीं होता है इसकी लम्बाई परिमित अथवा अपरिमित हो सकती है।

Jordan curve theorem *(जार्डन वक्र प्रमेय)* According to this a plane into two regions having the curve divides the common boundary. इसके अनुसार जार्डन वक्र किसी तल को दो भागों में विभाजित करता है जिनकी सीमा रेखा सम होती है।

Joule (J) *(जूल)* It is S.I unit of work. S.I पद्धति में कार्य का मात्रक है।

K

Key punch ***(पंच मशीन)*** It is a machine that is sued to punch the cards. The information is fed on punch card through key punch in coded form. कागजों को ढाँकने की मशीन होती है। टंकित कागज पर सूचनायें संग्रहित होती है।

Kilo ***(किलो)*** A prefix denoting 10^3

$$1 \text{ Kilogram} = 10^3 \text{ gram}$$

$$1 \text{ Kilowatt} = 10^3 \text{ watt}$$

$$1 \text{ Kilometre} = 10^3 \text{ meter}$$

इसे 10^3 से प्रदर्शित करते हैं।

1 किलोग्राम = 10^3 ग्राम

1 किलोवाट = 10^3 वाट

1 किलोमीटर = 10^3 मीटर

Kilo watt hour (K.W.H) ***(गतिकी)*** A practical unit of energy.

$$1 \text{ Kilowatt hour} = 1000 \text{ watt per hour.}$$

विद्युत शक्ति मापने की इकाई है।

1 किलोवाट घण्टा = 1000 वाट/घण्टा

Kinematics ***(गतिकी)*** It is the branch of mathematics that with the study of various modes of motion of objects. गणित की वह शाखा जो वस्तु की विभिन्न गतियों का अध्ययन कराती है।

Kinetic energy (K.E) ***(गतिज ऊर्जा)*** It is the energy associated with an object due to its motion. वस्तु की गति के कारण ऊर्जा

$$\text{K.E.} = \frac{1}{2}mv^2$$

where m = mass of object वस्तु का भार

v = velocity of an object. वस्तु की गति

L

Lami's theorem ***(लामी का प्रमेय)*** According to it when three forces act upon a body and the body is in equilibrium then the forces must be coplanar and each force is proportional to the sine of the angle between the lines of action of the other two forces. यदि किसी पिण्ड पर लगे तीन बल साम्यावस्था में हों, तो उनमें से प्रत्येक बल शेष दो बलों के बीच के कोण की ज्या (sine) का समानुपाती होता है।

$$\text{thus } \frac{\vec{P}}{\sin\alpha} = \frac{\vec{Q}}{\sin\beta} = \frac{\vec{R}}{\sin\gamma}$$

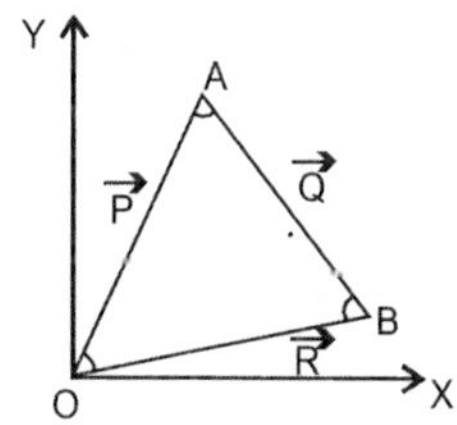

Fig. Lami's theorem

Langrange's mean value theorem ***(लेगरेन्ज का औसत मान प्रमेय)*** It states that if a function $f(x)$ defined [a, b] is such that $f(x)$ is continuous in $x = c \in$ [a ,b] for which

$$f'(c) = \frac{f(b) - f(a)}{b - a}$$

यदि फलन $f(x)$, $[a, b]$ को इस तरह परिभाषित करता है कि $f(x)$, $[a, b]$ में सतत है तो वह एक बिन्दु पर अवश्य स्थित है।

Language ***(भाषा)*** Short form of a Programming Language of a Computer e.g BASIC and PASCAL etc. कम्प्यूटर की प्रोग्राम में छोटी भाषा है। जैसे बेसिक और पासियल।

Laplace equation ***(लाप्लाश समीकरण)*** The equation

$$\frac{\partial^2(u)}{\partial x^2} + \frac{\partial^2 u}{\partial y^2} + \frac{\partial^2 u}{\partial z^2} = 0$$

Such equation are encountered in the study of problems on gravitational field and electromagnetic fields.

समीकरण

$$\frac{\partial^2(u)}{\partial x^2}+\frac{\partial^2 u}{\partial y^2}+\frac{\partial^2 u}{\partial z^2}=0$$

इस समीकरण में गुरुत्व क्षेत्र और वैद्युत चुम्बकीय क्षेत्र की समस्याओं का अध्ययन किया जाता है।

Lateral ***(पार्श्वीय)*** A side of a geometric figure, other than the base e.g. The lateral face of a pyramid is any face pyramid other than its base. किसी ज्यामितीय चित्र में आधार को छोड़कर शेष भाग को पार्श्वीय कहते हैं।

Lateral Surface and Area ***(पार्श्वीय सतह और क्षेत्रफल)*** The lateral surface of a surface with bases, such as a cone of cylinder, is the surface with the bases removed. The lateral area is the area of the lateral surface. आधार से लगा हुआ सतह, जैसे सिलन्डर का शंकु आधार को छोड़कर का सतह है तथा पार्श्वीय सतह का क्षेत्रफल पार्श्वीय क्षेत्रफल कहलाता है।

Latin Square ***(लटिन वर्ग)*** It is a square array of numbers or letters in which each number or letter appears ones is every row of column. e.g. $\begin{vmatrix}1 & 2 & 3 & 4\\ 4 & 3 & 2 & 1\\ 3 & 1 & 4 & 2\\ 2 & 4 & 1 & 3\end{vmatrix}$. अंकों या संख्याओं की एक वर्ग व्यूह रचना जिसमें अंक व संख्या स्तम्भ में केवल एक बार आते हैं।

Latitude ***(अक्षांश)*** The angular distance of a point on the earth from the equator, measured along the maridian though that point. कोणीय दूरी किसी बिन्दु की भूमध्य रेखा से पृथ्वी पर उस बिन्दु तक की दूरी।

Latus rectum ***(नाभिलम्ब)*** Double ordinate through the focus of a conic section. The length of latus rectum of the parabola, $y^2 = 4ax$, is $4a$

The latus rectum of ellipse, $\frac{x^2}{a^2}+\frac{y^2}{b^2}=1$ is $\frac{2b^2}{a}$

वह जीवा जो नाभि से होकर जाती है तथा अक्ष पर लम्ब होती है, नाभिलम्ब कहलाती है। परवलय $y^2 = 4ax$ नाभिलम्ब $4a$ है। दीर्घवृत्त $\frac{x^2}{a^2}+\frac{y^2}{b^2}=1$ का नाभिलम्ब $\frac{2b^2}{a}$ है।

Law of exponents ***(घातांकों के नियम)***

(*i*) If x be any non–zero rational number, and m, n be positive integers then (यदि x एक परिमेय संख्या है तथा m एवं n दो घनात्मक पूर्णांक हैं। तो

$x^m \times x^n = x^{m+n}$

$x^m \times x^n \times x^p \times x^q = x^{m+n+p+q}$

(*ii*) If x is a non–zero rational number, and m, n are positive inteqers such that $m > n$, यदि x एक शून्येतर परिमेय संख्या है तथा m एवं n दो घनात्मक पूर्णांक इस प्रकार है कि $m > n$ तब

$x^m \div x^n = x^{m-n}$

(*iii*) If x is a non–zero rational number and m are positive integers such that $n > m$, यदि x एक शून्येतर परिमेय संख्या है तथा m एवं n धनात्मकघनात्मक पूर्णांक इस प्रकार है कि $m > n$ तब

$$x^m \div x^n = \frac{1}{x^{n-m}}$$

(*iii*) If x is a non–zero rational number and m,n are two positive integers, यदि x एक शून्येतर परिमेय संख्या है तथा m एवं n धनात्मक पूर्णांक है तो

$$(x^m)^n = x^{mn}$$
$$(x \times y)^{-m} = x^{-m} \times y^{-m}$$
$$(x \times y)^m = x^m \times y^m$$
$$x^{-m} = \frac{1}{x^m}$$
$$x^0 = 1$$

- **Laws of impact in elasticity** ***(तन्यता का समघात नियम)*** It two balls moving in the same direction with velocities u_1 and u_2 respectively, collide and after impact their velocities become v_1 and v_2 respectively,

  Then

  $$v_1 - v_2 = e\,(u_1 - u_2) \text{ [provided } u_1 > u_2 \text{and } v_1 > v_2\text{]}$$

  e is called the corefficient of restitution and it depends upon the elasticity of the material of the balls.

  यदि दो गेंदे एक ही दिशा में क्रमश u_1 और u_2 से जा रही हैं और टक्कर के पश्चात उनका वेग क्रमशः v_1 और v_2 हो जाता है। तब $v_1 - v_2 = e(u_1 - u_2)$

  e एक गुणक है जो गेंदो की तन्यता पर निर्भर करता है।

- **Laws of impact in rebound** ***(उत्पतन टक्कर नियम)*** When a ball falls a height, h, on the horizontal plane and rebounds to a height, h_1, then

$$h_1 = e^2 . h$$

where e is coefficient of restitution.

जब किसी समतल पर h ऊँचाई से गेंद गिरायी जाती है तो वह दुबारा h_1 ऊँचाई तक जाती है तब–

$$h_1 = e^2 . h$$

जहाँ e प्रत्यास्थता गुणक है।

- **Laws of surds** ***(करणी का नियम)*** Since $\sqrt[n]{x}$ can be written as $x^{1/n}$ so the laws of surds are

(*i*) For any positive integer n and a positive rational x, the radical $x^{1/n}$ is the positive nth root of x.यदि $\sqrt[n]{x}$ और $\sqrt[n]{y}$ दो करणी समान हो। तब–

$$\left(n\sqrt{x}\right)^n = x$$

or $$\left(4\sqrt{6}\right)^4 = 6$$

(*ii*) If $\sqrt[n]{x}$ and $\sqrt[n]{y}$ are two radicals of the same order, then यदि $\sqrt[n]{x}$ और $\sqrt[n]{y}$ दो करणी समान हो। तब–

$$\left(\sqrt[n]{s}.\sqrt[n]{y}\right)^n = \left(n\sqrt{x}\right)^n . \left(n\sqrt{y}\right)^n = ny$$

$$n\sqrt{x}.\, n\sqrt{y} = n\sqrt{xy}$$

(*iii*) If $\sqrt[n]{x}$ and $\sqrt[n]{y}$ are radicals of the same order, then यदि $\sqrt[n]{x}$ और $\sqrt[n]{y}$ दो करणी समान हो। तब–

$$\left(\frac{\sqrt[n]{x}}{\sqrt[n]{y}}\right)^n = \frac{\left(\sqrt[n]{x}\right)^n}{\left(\sqrt[n]{y}\right)^n} = \frac{x}{y}$$

$$\frac{\sqrt[n]{x}}{\sqrt[n]{y}}=\sqrt{\frac{x}{y}}$$

(*iv*) If m, n are positive integers, then for a positive rational number, a यदि m, n धनात्मक पूर्णांक हो तब कोई वास्तविक संख्या a हो

$$\sqrt[m]{\sqrt[n]{a}}\,\sqrt[mn]{a}=\sqrt[n]{\sqrt[m]{a}}$$

(*v*) If m, n are positive integers, then for a positive number a यदि m,n धनात्मक पूर्णांक हो, तब धनात्मक वास्तविक संख्या

$$\sqrt[m]{a^n}=\sqrt[n]{a^m}$$

- **Law of tangents** ***(स्पर्शिया का नियम)*** (in ΔABC) त्रिभुज ABC में

$$\frac{a-b}{a+b}=\frac{\tan\frac{a-b}{2}}{\tan\frac{a+b}{2}}$$

$$\tan\frac{b-c}{2}=\frac{b-c}{b+c}\cos\frac{a}{2}$$

or

$$\frac{b-c}{b+c}=\frac{\tan\frac{b-c}{2}}{\tan\frac{b+c}{2}}$$

$$\frac{c-a}{c+a}=\frac{\tan\frac{c-a}{2}}{\tan\frac{c+a}{2}}$$

- **Law of triangle** ***(त्रिभुज का नियम)*** It is used for addition of vectors. If the two sides of a triangle can represent two vectors in magnitude as well as in direction then resultant is represented by the third sides taken in opposite order.

  The resultant of $\overrightarrow{BC}$ and $\overrightarrow{CA}$ is $\overrightarrow{BA}$

M

Magic square ***(तर्क वर्ग)*** A square array of N numbers such that sum of the numbers in any row, column, or main diagonal is a constant (known as the magic sum). ऐसा वर्ग जिसमें पंक्ति कॉलम और मुख्य विकर्ण के N संख्याओं का योग नियत रहता है।

23	6	19	2	15
10	18	1	14	22
17	5	13	21	9
4	12	25	8	16
11	24	7	20	3

Magnitude ***(परिमाण)*** The magnitude of a vector is its length. सदिश की लम्बाई को परिमाण कहते हैं।

Main diagonal ***(मुख्य विकर्ण)*** In the matrix [aij], the elements all, a22 ...ann. [aij] आव्यूह में अवयव all, a22 ...ann को मुख्य विकर्ण कहते हैं।

Major arc ***(दीर्घवृत्त)*** An arc of measure greater than 180 degrees. ऐसा चाप जो 180° से बड़ा हो।

Major axis ***(दीर्घ अक्ष)*** The major axis of an ellipse is it's longest chord. दीर्घ वृत्त की दीर्घ अक्ष सबसे बड़ी जीवा होती है।

Malfatti circles ***(मलफती वृत्तियाँ)*** Three equal circles that are mutually tangent and each tangent to two sides of a given triangle. तीन बराबर वृत्त जो एक दूसरे को स्पर्ष करती हों और प्रत्येक किसी दिये गये त्रिभुज के दो भुजाओं को स्पर्श करती हों।

Mapping ***(प्रतिचित्रण)*** A mapping is a function. If members of a set each are halved a new set is formed. Thus halving transforms members of one set into members of another. यदि किसी समुच्चय के प्रत्येक अवयव को किसी सम्बन्ध द्वारा समुच्चय B के किसी विशिष्ट अवयव से सम्बन्धित किया जाये तो इसे प्रतिचित्रण कहते हैं।

Mass ***(द्रव्यमान)*** It is the quantity of matter contained in a body. Mass of a body remains unchanged even if the value of 'g' changes. It is expressed in grams (C. G. S. system), pounds (F. P. S. system).

किसी पदार्थ में द्रव्य की मात्रा, यह g के मान पर निर्भर नहीं करता तथा सी.जी.एस. पद्धति में इसका मात्रक ग्राम तथा एफ.पी.एस. में पाउण्ड है।

Mass-energy equation *(द्रव्य-ऊर्जा समीकरण)* According to it

$$E = mc^2$$

where E = energy ऊर्जा

m = mass द्रव्यमान

c = velocity of light प्रकाश का वेग (3×10^{10} cm/sec)

Mathematics *(गणित)* It is a logical study of shape, arrangement quantity, and many other related concepts. Mathematics generally is divided into three fields **algebra, analysis and geometry.** यह आकार, व्यवस्था, मात्रा तथा कई अन्य मूलभूत नियमों का तुलनात्मक तथा तार्किक अध्ययन है। इसे प्रायः तीन भागों में बांटा गया है–

1. बीजगणित
2. विश्लेषण
3. ज्यामिती।

Matrix *(आव्यूह)* Arrangement of pixels A matrix is made up of numbers arranged in a rectangular shape of rows and columns. संख्याओं के एक निकाय को पंक्तियों तथा स्तम्भों में आयताकार सारणी के रूप में व्यवस्थित करने को आव्यूह कहते हैं।

$$\begin{bmatrix} 0 & -1 & 1 \\ 1 & 2 & -1 \\ 3 & -2 & 0 \end{bmatrix}$$

Matrices *(आव्यूह)* Matrices are represented by the capital letters A, B, C etc. Order of a matrix A matrix m rows n columns has an order $m \times n$. आव्यूह को A, B, C द्वारा प्रदर्शित करते हैं। आव्यूह की कोटी आव्यूह में m पंक्तियों और n स्तम्भें हो तब कोटी $m \times n$ होगी।

An $m \times n$ matrix can be written as

$m \times n$ आव्यूह को इस प्रकार लिख सकते है।

$$A = \begin{pmatrix} a_{11} & a_{12} & a_{1n} \\ a_{21} & a_{23} & a_{2n} \\ a_{m1} & a_{m^3} & a_{mn} \end{pmatrix}$$

or $A = (a_{ij})\ m \times n$ where $|\leq i \leq m / i \leq n$

The m, n numbers are known as Elements of the matrix. m और n संख्याएें आव्यूह की अवयव होते हैं।

Some special cases ***(कुछ महत्त्वपूर्ण तथ्य)***

If $m = n$, the matrix is side to be square matrix and is of the nth degree.

यदि $m = n$, ऐसे आव्यूह को वर्ग आव्यूह या n क्रम का आव्यूह कहते हैं।

If all the elements of a matrix are zeros then is called a *null* matrix. A zero matrix of m x n is denoted by $0_{m \times n}$.

यदि आव्यूह के सभी अवयच शून्य हो तो वह शून्य आव्यूह कहलाता है। शून्य आव्यूह m x n को $0_{m \times n}$ से प्रदर्शित करते हैं।

If matrix of order $1 \times n$ is known as a row matrix (since it has one row) e.g.

यदि आव्यूह $1 \times n$ कोटि का है तो उसे पंक्ति आव्यू कहेंगे।

$$A = (a, b, c, d)$$

A matrix of order $m \times 1$ is known as a column matrix (since it has only one column) e.g. $A = \begin{pmatrix} 1 \\ 2 \\ 3 \end{pmatrix}$. यदि आव्यूह $m \times 1$ कोटि का है तो उसे स्तम्भ आव्यू कहेंगे।

- **A square matrix** ***(विकर्ण आव्यूह)*** $[a_{ij}]$ is known as diagonal matrix if its elements except the main diagonal elements are zeros. यदि किसी वर्ग आव्यूह में मुख्य विकर्ण के तत्त्वों को छोड़कर सभी तत्व शून्य हों तो उसे विकर्ण आव्यूह कहते हैं। e.g.

$$\begin{vmatrix} a & 0 & 0 \\ 0 & b & 0 \\ 0 & 0 & c \end{vmatrix}$$

If the main diagonal elements of a diagonal matrix are equal, then it is know as a scalar matrix. जिस वर्ग आव्यूह के मुख्य विकर्ण के सभी तत्त्व बराबर, शेष तत्त्व शून्य हों, उसे अदिश आव्यूह कहते हैं।

e.g. $$A = \begin{vmatrix} a & 0 & 0 \\ 0 & a & 0 \\ 0 & 0 & a \end{vmatrix}$$

If in a scalar matrix all the diagonal elements are equal to unity then it is know as a unit matrix $x(1)$. जिस वर्ग आव्यूह के मुख्य विकर्ण के सभी तत्व इकाई हों तथा शेष सभी तत्व शून्य हों, तो उसे इकाई आव्यूह कहते हैं। e.g. $$l_2 = \begin{vmatrix} 1 & 0 \\ 0 & 1 \end{vmatrix}$$

$$l_3 = \begin{vmatrix} 1 & 0 & 0 \\ 0 & 1 & 0 \\ 0 & 0 & 1 \end{vmatrix}$$

In represent matrix of order $m \times n$ if in a matrix, elements for which i > j are zeros . Then it is known as upper triangular matrix. आव्यूह की कोटि को $m \times n$ से प्रदर्शित करते हैं। वह वर्ग आव्यूह जिसके मुख्य विकर्ण के नीचे के सभी तत्व शून्य हों उसे उपरित्रिभुजीय आव्यूह कहते हैं।

$$A = \begin{vmatrix} a & b & c & d \\ 0 & e & f & g \\ 0 & 0 & h & i \end{vmatrix}$$

If in a matrix, elements for which i > j are zeros it is known as lower triangular matrix. वह वर्ग आव्यूह जिसके मुख्य विकर्ण के ऊपर के सभी तत्व शून्य हों उसे निम्न त्रिभुजीय आव्यूह कहते हैं।

$$A = \begin{Bmatrix} a & 0 & 0 \\ b & c & 0 \\ d & e & f \end{Bmatrix}$$

A matrix obtained by deleting some rows or columns or both of a given matrix A is known as sub- matrix of A (the given matrix). किसी दिये गये आव्यूह की कुछ पंक्तियों तथा स्तम्भों को निकाल या छोड़ देने पर शेष बचे आव्यूह को दिये गये आव्यूह का उप-आव्यूह कहते हैं।

$$\begin{bmatrix} 1 & 2 \\ 3 & 4 \end{bmatrix} \text{matrix, } A = \begin{bmatrix} 5 & 3 & 2 \\ 1 & 1 & 2 \\ 7 & 3 & 4 \end{bmatrix}$$

Maxima *(उच्चिष्ठ)* The points on a curve where the value is greater than that of the surrounding points. जिस बिन्दू पर वक्र का मान सबसे अधिक हो।

Maximum *(उच्चतम)* The largest of a set of values. सर्वश्रेष्ठ मान वाला।

Mean *(माध्य)* It is the average of a set of numbers calculated by deciding the sum by the number of values

$$\text{mean} = \frac{\text{sum of observations}}{\text{no of obsrvations}}$$

पदों की संख्या का योग, पदों की संख्या से विभाजित कर देने पर माध्य प्राप्त होता है।

$$\text{माध्य} = \frac{\text{पदों की संख्या का योग}}{\text{पदों की संख्या}}$$

Measure of Central Tendency *(केन्द्रीय. प्रवृत्ति के माप)* Qualitative variables which can be measured quantitatively the information contained in the row data, or in the associated frequencey table can also be presented by means of few numerical values. Methods providing such values are called measures of central tendency. ऐसी संख्याएँ जो कि आँकड़ों के कुछ लक्षणों को निरूपित करें, ऐसे आँकड़ों को अंकगणितीय माप या केन्द्रीय प्रवृत्ति के माप कहते हैं।

Mixed surd *(मिश्रित करणी)* A surd which has a rational factor other than unity, the other factor being irrational is called a mixed surd. ऐसी करणी जिसका एक गुणनखंड एक के अतिरिक्त दूसरा कोई अन्य परिमेय संख्या है और दूसरा गुणनखंड कोई अपरिमेय संख्या है मिश्रित करणी कहलाती है उदाहरण– $2\sqrt{3}$, $5\sqrt[3]{12}$, $2\sqrt[4]{5}$.

Median *(माध्यिका)* It is the straight line drawn from one of the angles of a triangle to the middle of the opposite side. In fig AD is median or it is the line segment that joins a vertex to the mid point of the opposite side. त्रिभुज के एक शीर्ष से उसके सम्मुख भुजा के मध्य बिन्दु को मिलाने वाली रेखा माध्यिका कहलाती है।

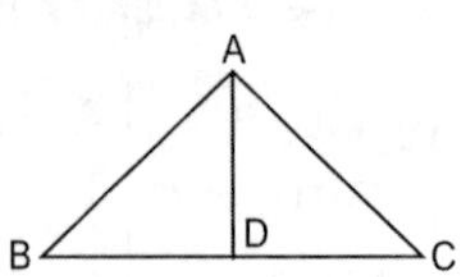

Fig. Median

- **Median** *(माध्यक)* If the values in the row data are arranged in order of increasing or decreasing magnitude, then the middle most value in the arrangement is called the median. To compute the median of n observations–

(*a*) If n is odd, then. यदि n विषम है, तब

$$\text{Median (माध्यक)} = \text{Value of} \left(\frac{n+1}{2}\right)^{th} \text{observation.}$$

(*b*) If n is even, then. यदि n सम है, तब

Median (माध्यक)

$$= \frac{\text{value of}(n/2)^{th}\text{observation} + \text{value of}(n/2+1)^{th}\text{observation}}{2}$$

यदि अपरिष्कृत आकड़ों के मानों को आरोही या अवरोही क्रम में रखा जाए तो इस विन्यास के ठीक बीच के मान को माध्यक कहा जाता है।

$$\text{Median} \quad (\text{m}) = i + \left|\frac{\left(\frac{\text{N}}{2}\right) - \text{F}}{f}\right| \times h$$

N = total frequency = Σf_i
n = lower limit of median class
f = frequency of the median class
F = cumulative frequency of the class preceding the median class
h = class interval (width) of the median class.

Mid-point *(मध्य बिन्दु)* It is the middle point of a straight line or fixed point of a line which divides it into two equal halves. In Fig. P is the mid-point of line AB. किसी सीधी रेखा का मध्य बिन्दु उसे रेखा के दो बराबर भागों में बाँटता है। चित्र में P रेखाखण्ड का मध्य बिन्दु है।

Mensuration *(मेन्शुरेशन) (क्षेत्रमिति)* It is that branch of Mathematics which deals with the study of measurement of geometrical figures and evaluating their length, area, volume etc. गणित की वह शाखा जिसके अन्दर ज्यामितीय चित्र लम्बाई, क्षेत्रफल, आयतन का अध्ययन किया जाता है।

Mensuration Formulae *(क्षेत्रमितीय सूत्र)*

- Area of square = $(\text{side})^2$
  वर्ग का क्षेत्रफल = भुजा)^2
- Area of rectangle = $l \times b$.
  (आयत का क्षेत्रफल)
- Area of 4 walls = $2(l + b) \times h$.
  (4 दीवारों का क्षेत्रफल)
- Area of circle = πr^2
  (वृत्त का क्षेत्रफल)
- Area of right angle $\Delta = \frac{1}{2}(b \times h)$
  (समकोण त्रिभुज का क्षेत्रफल)
- Area of trapezium = $\frac{1}{2}(b_1 + b_2) \times h$
  (समलम्ब चतुर्भुज का क्षेत्रफल)
- Area of parallelogram = $b \times h$
  (समान्तर चतुर्भुज का क्षेत्रफल)
- Area of Δ (using hero's formulae) = $\sqrt{s(s-a)(s-b)(s-c)}$
  त्रिभुज का क्षेत्रफल हीरो के सूत्र द्वारा where $S = \frac{a+b+c}{2}$
- Area of equilateral $\Delta = \frac{\sqrt{3}}{4}a^2$
  (समबाहु त्रिभुज का क्षेत्रफल)
- Area of isosceles $\Delta = \frac{a}{4}\sqrt{4b^2 - a^2}$
  (समद्विबाहु त्रिभुज का क्षेत्रफल)
- Area of Rhombus = $\frac{1}{2}d_1 \times d_2$.
  (समचतुर्भुज का क्षेत्रफल)
- Area of segment = Area of sector – area of Δ.
  खण्ड का क्षेत्रफल = (खण्ड क्षेत्रफल–त्रिभुज क्षेत्रफल)
- Area of sector = $\frac{\theta \times \pi r^2}{360} = \frac{1}{2} r \times$ length of arc.
  (वृत्त खण्ड का क्षेत्रफल)

- lateral S.A. of tetrahedron $= 3\frac{\sqrt{3}}{4}a^2$
(चतुष्फलक का पार्श्ववीय पृष्ठ क्षेत्रफल)
- Lateral S.A. of Pyramid $= \frac{1}{2}$ perimeter of base $\times\, l$.
(पिरामिड का पार्श्व पृष्ठ क्षेत्रफल) ($\frac{1}{2}$ आधार का परिमाप × तरछी ऊँचाई)
- Lateral S.A. of frustum of cone
शंकु का शंकुछिन्नक का क्षेत्रफल
$$= \pi l (R + r)$$
$$\text{where } l^2 = h^2 + (R - r)^2$$
- Length of arc $= \frac{\theta}{360} \times 2\pi r$
(चाप की लम्बाई)
- Curved S.A. of cylinder $= 2\pi rh$.
(बेलन की वक्र पृष्ठ क्षेत्रफल)
- Curved S.A. of cone $= \pi$rl; where $l = \sqrt{r^2 + h^2}$
(शंकु का वक्र पृष्ठ क्षेत्रफल)
- Curved S.A. of hemisphere $= \frac{2}{3}\pi r^2$
(अर्धगोलक का वक्र पृष्ठ क्षेत्रफल)
- Perimeter of rectangle $= 2\,(l + b)$
(आयत का परिमाप)
- perimeter of square $= 4 \times$ side
(वर्ग का परिमाप)
- Perimeter of $\Delta = a + b + c$
(त्रिभुज का परिमाप)
- Sum of angles of a$\Delta = 180^\circ$
(त्रिभुज के कोणों का योग)
- Sum of angles of a $\square = 360^\circ$
(चतुर्भुज के कोणों के योग)
- Surface area of sphere $= 4\,\pi r^2$
(गोले का पृष्ठ क्षेत्रफल)
- Surface area of cuboid $= 2\,(lb + bh + lh)$.
- Surface area of a cube $= 6l^2$

(घन का पृष्ठ क्षेत्रफल)

- Surface area of hemisphere $= 2\pi r^2$
(अर्धगोले का पूर्ण पृष्ठ क्षेत्रफल)
- Total S.A. of frustum of cone $= \pi l\,(r_1 + r_2) + \pi r_1^2 + \pi r_2^2$
(शंकु के शंकुछिन्नक का पूर्ण पृष्ठ क्षेत्रफल)
- Total S.A. of prism = Lateral surface area
प्रिज्म का पूर्ण पृष्ठ क्षेत्रफल 2 (area of one end).
- Total S.A. of cylinder $= 2\pi r(h + r)$.
(बेलन का पूर्ण पृष्ठ क्षेत्रफल)
- Total S.A. of cone $= \pi r\,(l + r)$
(शंकु का पूर्ण पृष्ठ क्षेत्रफल)
- Volume of Tetrahedron $= \dfrac{\sqrt{12}}{12}a^3\,;\, l = \dfrac{\sqrt{3}}{2}a$ units
(चतुष्फलक का आयतन)
- Volume of pyramid (with base equilateral Δ $= \dfrac{\sqrt{3}}{12}a^2h$.
(पिरामिड का आयतन (जब आधार समबाहु त्रिभुज हो)
- Volume of Pyramid $= \dfrac{1}{3}$ area of base $\times h$.
(पिरामिड का आयतन)
- Volume of prism = area of base $\times h$. where $l = \sqrt{h^2 + \dfrac{a^2}{12}}$
(प्रिज्म का आयतन)
- Volume of frustum of cone
(शंकु के शंकुछिन्नक का आयतन) $= \dfrac{1}{3}\pi h(r_1^2 + r_1r_2 + r_2^2)$
- Volume of hemisphere $= \dfrac{2}{3}\pi r^3$
(अर्धगोले का आयतन)
- Volume of sphere $= \dfrac{4}{3}\pi r^3$
(गोले का आयतन)
- Volume of cone $= \dfrac{1}{3}\pi r^2 h$, $l = \sqrt{h^2 + r^2}$
(शंकु का आयतन)
- Volume of material $= \pi r\,(R^2 - r^2)$

(पदार्थ का आयतन)

- Volume of cylinder = $\pi r^2 h$.
  (बेलन का आयतन)
- Volume of cuboid = $l.b.h$.
  (घनाभ का आयतन)
- Volume of cube = $(\text{side})^3$ or $(l)^3$
  (घन का आयतन)

Methods of resolution of equations ***(समीकरण को सरल करने की विधियां)***

(*i*) Consider the equations

$$A_1X+B_1Y=C_1 \qquad ...(1)$$

$$A_2X+B_2Y=C_2 \qquad ...(2)$$

Equation this value be resolved in respect of y to get

$$y=\frac{C_1-A_1x}{B_1}$$

Substituting this value of y in equation

(*ii*) we get an equation only in x

$$A_2x+B_2\frac{C_1-A_1X}{B_1}=C_2$$

Reducing this equation we find

$$x=\frac{B_1C_2-B_2C_1}{A_2B_1-B_2A_1}$$

Knowing the value of x, y, we can be evaluate.

$$y=\frac{C_1-A_1x}{B_1}$$

$$=\frac{C_1-A.\dfrac{B_1C_2-B_2C_1}{A_2B_2-B_2A_1}}{B_1}$$

- **Comparison method** ***(तुलनात्मक विधि)***

Consider the equations

$$Ax+By=C \qquad ...(i)$$

$$A_1x+B_1y=C_1 \qquad ...(ii)$$

By resolving (*i*) and (*ii*) simultaneously in respect of y, we get

$$y=\frac{C-Ax}{B} \qquad ...(iii)$$

N

Napier's analogy *(नेपियर एनालोजी)*

In ΔABC

$$\tan\frac{a-b}{2} = \frac{a-b}{a+b}\cot\frac{c}{2}$$

or
$$\frac{a-b}{a+b} = \frac{\tan\frac{a-b}{2}}{\tan\frac{a+b}{2}}$$

$$\tan\frac{b-c}{2} = \frac{b-c}{b+c}\cot\frac{a}{2}$$

or
$$\frac{b-c}{b+c} = \frac{\tan\frac{b-c}{2}}{\tan\frac{b+c}{2}}$$

$$\tan\frac{c-a}{2} = \frac{c-a}{c+a}\cot\frac{b}{2}$$

$$\frac{c-a}{c+a} = \frac{\tan\frac{c-a}{2}}{\tan\frac{c+a}{2}}$$

Napiers Formula *(नेपियर सूत्र)* If is a relationship between the sides a, b, c and opposite angles α, β, γ of a spherical triangle. वृत्तीय त्रिभुज की भुजाओं a, b, c तथा विपरित कोणों α, β, γ के मध्य सम्बन्ध दर्शाता है।

$$\frac{\sin\frac{a-b}{2}}{\sin\frac{a+b}{2}} = \frac{\tan\frac{\alpha-\beta}{2}}{\tan\frac{\lambda}{2}}$$

$$\frac{\cos\frac{a-b}{2}}{\cos\frac{a+b}{2}} = \frac{\tan\frac{a+b}{2}}{\tan\frac{c}{2}}$$

$$\frac{\sin\frac{\alpha-\beta}{2}}{\sin\frac{\alpha+\beta}{2}} = \frac{\tan\frac{a-b}{2}}{\tan\frac{c}{2}}$$

$$\frac{\cos\frac{\alpha-\beta}{2}}{\cos\frac{\alpha+\beta}{2}} = \frac{\tan\frac{a+b}{2}}{\tan\frac{c}{2}}$$

Natural Numbers *(प्राकृतिक संख्याएं)* The counting numbers 1, 2, 3, 4 are Know as natural numbers. The set of natural numbers is denoted by N. गणना के प्रयोग में आने वाली संख्याएं प्राकृतिक संख्याए कहलाती है। संख्याओं के समुच्चय को N से निरुपित करते हैं।

$$N = \{1, 2, 3, 4....\}$$

Natural logorithm *(प्राकृतिक लघुगुणक)* Any logorithm with Euler's number(e) as its base. A natural log is written as ln. For example, ln(e) = 1. 1 यूलर संख्या के साथ इस आधार पर कोई लघुगुणक, इसे ln से दर्शाते हैं।

Negative *(ऋणात्मक)* A number of quantity which is less than zero negative number are also used to denote quantities which are below some specified point for example in the centrigrade temperature scale a temperature of –24°C is 24° below the Freezing point of water. वह संख्या राशि जो शून्य से कम होती है। इसका प्रयोग कभी-कभी किसी निश्चित मूल्य से नीचे का मूल्य दर्शाने से भी करते हैं। जैसे –24° जल के जमाव के बिन्दु के नीचे का ताप बताता है।

Negative number *(ऋणात्मक संख्या)* A number whose value is less than zero e.g. – 1, – 10, – 100, – 500. वह संख्या जो शून्य से कम हो ऋणात्मक संख्या कहलाती है। जैसे– 1, – 10, – 100, – 500.

Negative Quantity *(ऋणात्मक राशि)* It is a quantity of time temperature, length etc. measured From Zero in a direction opposite to that chosen as positive. समय, ताप, लम्बाई आदि राशि को शून्य से निश्चित दिशा के विपरीत व्यक्त करना।

Neutral Equilibrium *(उदासीन साम्यावस्था)* Equilibrium such that when the system is disturibed a little is not tendency for it to move further nor return. वह अवस्था जिसमें निकाय में थोड़ा अनियमितता करने पर निकाय में पुनः गति या प्रारम्भिक अवस्था में नहीं आता है।

Newton (N) *(न्यूटन)* A unit of force in S.I. units. S.I. मात्रकों में यह बल का मात्रक है। 1 Newton = 1 Kg × 1 metre/ sec^2

Newtonian Mechanics *(न्यूटन यान्त्रिकी)* Mechanics that is based on Newton's laws of motion. वह यान्त्रिकी जो न्यूटन के नियमों पर आधारित हो।

Newton's Law of Collision *(न्यूटन का भिंडत का नियम)*

Let u_1 and u_2 be the velocities of two bodies before collision and v_1 and v_2 that after the collision, along the line of impact or line of collision.

$$\frac{v_2 - v_1}{u_2 - u_1} = -e; \text{ Where e = coefficient of restitution.}$$

$e = 1$ for elastic collision

$e < 1$ for inelastic collision

$e = 0$ for perfectly inelastic collision.

(*i*) In the direct elastic collision both momentum and kinetic energy remain conserved.

(*ii*) In the direct inelastic collision only momentum is conserved.

(*iii*) Rebounds of a particle on smooth plane.

If a smooth ball falls from a height h upon a fixed horizontal plane and if e is the coefficient of restitution, then whole time before the rebounding ends

$$= \sqrt{\frac{2h}{g}}\frac{1+e}{1-e}$$

and the total distance covered before finishing rebounding

$$= \frac{1+e^2}{1-e^2}h$$

Newton's law of gravitation *(न्यूटन गुरुत्वाकर्षण नियम)* The force of attraction between any two particles of mass m_1 and m_2 at a distance from each other is directly proportional to product of their masses and inversely proportional to the distance between them *i.e.,*

$$F \,\alpha \frac{m_1 . m_2}{d^2}$$

or

$$F = G\,\frac{m_1 . m_2}{d^2}$$

Where G is called Gravitational Constant. *(गुरुत्वाकर्षण नियतांक)* किन्हीं दो कणों के मध्य लगने वाला आकर्षण बल पिण्डों के द्रव्यमान (m_1, m_2) के गुणनफल के समानुपाती तथा उनके बीच की दूरी (d) के वर्ग के व्युत्क्रमानुपाती होता है।

Nine point circle *(नौ बिन्दुओं का वृत्त)* In a triangle, the circle that passes through the midpoints of the sides is called the nine point circle. किसी त्रिभुज में वृत्त की भुजाओं के मध्य बिन्दुओं से होकर जायें। तो ऐसे वृत्त को नौ बिन्दुओं का वृत्त कहते हैं।

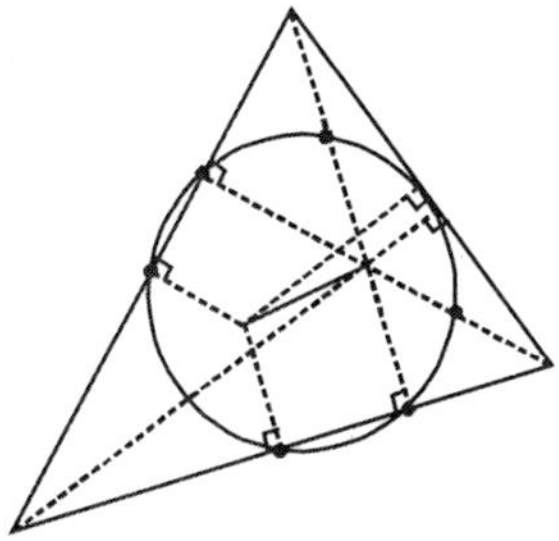

Fig. Nine point circle

Non Collinear *(असरेज)* If the point on a plane does not lie on the same line car straight line), they are said to be non Collinear point. ऐसे बिन्दु जो तल मे एक सीध में न हो।

Non-overlapping *(अवैतिकरण)* If the two solid figures of same type are not overlapping each other or does not overlap one mother, they are said to be non overlapping figures. ऐसी ठोस आकृतियां जो एक दूसरे पर अतिव्यापित नहीं होती है।

Non-parallel lines *(असमान्तर रेखाएँ)* If two lines are not parallel to one another, they are said to be non-parallel lines, AB, CA are non parallel lines. यदि दो रेखाएँ आपस में समान्तर न हो तो एक-दूसरे से असमान्तर कही जाएगी।

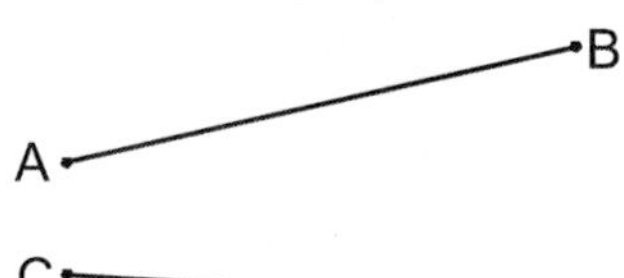

Fig. Non-parallel lines

Non terminating *(अविभाजित)* In division process if the remainder starts repeating after a certain number of steps, then it is Known as non terminating. जो संख्याएँ पूर्ण विभाजित नहीं होती, इसमें अवशेष एक निश्चित संख्या के बाद पुर्नावृत्ति होने लगता है जैसे $\frac{10}{3} = 3.333...$.

Non intersecting ***(अप्रतिच्छेदित)*** In two lines does not intersect (cross) each other, then it is Known as non- intersecting lines. यदि दो रेखाएँ आगे बढ़ायें जाने पर एक दूसरे को कहीं भी प्रतिच्छेदित न करें।

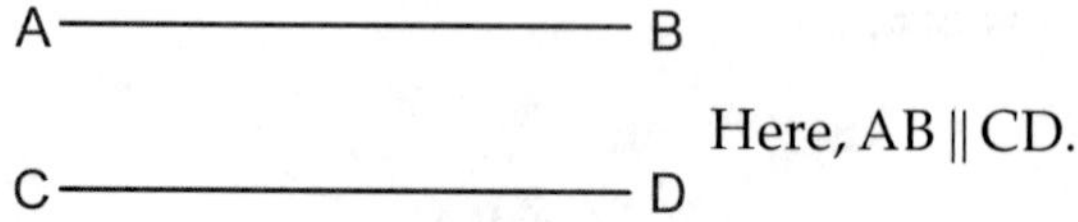

Fig. Non intersecting

Non-recurring ***(अनावृत्ति)*** In division process if the remainder does not start repeating, then it is Known as non - recurring. विभाजित करते समय यदि शेषफल भिन्न-भिन्न आए और संख्या विभाजित न हो तो अनावर्ती संख्या कहलाती है।

Non-rational number ***(अपरिमेय संख्या)*** If the number can not be written in the form of p/q, where $q \neq 0$ are known as non- rational number. वह संख्या जो भिन्न के रुप में (p/q) न लिखा जा सके।

Non-zero ***(अशून्य)*** Except zero, all real numbers are called non zero numbers. शून्य को छोड़कर सभी संख्याएँ अशून्य कहलाती है।

Normal ***(अभिलम्ब)*** The normal a curve at any point is the line perpendicular to the tangent at that point.

A line is said to be normal to a plane if it is perpendicular to all belonging in the plane. For a curve represented by $y = f(x)$, the equation of tangent to the curve at (x_0, y_0) is given by

$$y - y_0 = \frac{dy}{dx}(x - x_0)$$

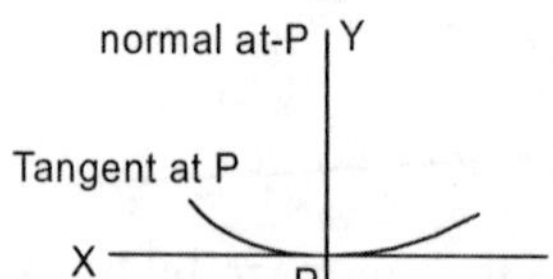

Fig. Normal

As normal to a curve is *a* straight line perpendicular to the tangent and passing through the point of contact, its equation will be

$$y - y_0 = \frac{1}{\frac{dy}{dx}}(x - x_0)$$

वक्र के किसी दिये हुए बिन्दु पर स्पर्शी के लम्बवत् रेखा को अभिलम्ब कहते हैं।

रेखा को समतल का अभिलम्ब जब कहते हैं। यदि वह समतल से जाने वाली सभी रेखाओं पर लम्ब हो।

वक्र $y = f(x)$ से निरुपित करते है।

बिन्दु (x_0, y_0) पर वक्र की स्पर्शी का समीकरण

$$y - y_0 = \frac{dy}{dx}(x - x_0)$$

वक्र के किसी बिन्दु पर अभिलम्ब वह सरल रेखा है जो बिन्दु से होकर जाएें और उसी बिन्दु पर खीचीं गयी स्पर्शी पर लम्ब हो।

$$y - y_0 = \frac{1}{\frac{dy}{dx}}(x - x_0)$$

Point on an ellipse

For an ellipse centred at the origin (दीर्घवृत्त के बिन्दु)

$$\frac{x^2}{a^2} + \frac{y^2}{b^2} = 1$$

At the point P (x, y) of the ellipse the tangent at P to the ellipse is given by the equation

$$\frac{x - x_0}{a^2} + \frac{y - y_0}{b^2} = 1$$

The normal at P to the ellipse is given by

$$y - y_0 = \frac{a^2 y_0}{b^2 x_0}(x - x_0)$$

If the centre of the ellipse is C (h, k) then

$$\frac{(x-h)^2}{a^2}+\frac{(y-k)^2}{b^2}=1 \text{ [equation of ellipse]}$$

At point P (x_o, y_o)
The equation of tangent is

$$\frac{(x-h)(x_0-h)}{a^2}+\frac{(y-k)(y_0-k)}{b^2}=1$$

and the equation of normal of P will be

$$y-y_0=\frac{a^2(y_0-k)}{b^2(x_0-h)}(x-x_0)$$

दीर्घवृत्त के बिन्दुः दीर्घवृत्त का केन्द्र बिन्दु (0, 0) हो।

$$\frac{x^2}{a^2}+\frac{y^2}{b^2}=1$$

दीर्घवृत्त के बिन्दु P (x, y) पर दी हुई स्पर्शी का समीकरण

$$\frac{x-x_0}{a^2}+\frac{y-y_0}{b^2}=1$$

दीर्घवृत्त के बिन्दु P पर अभिलम्ब का समीकरण

$$y-y_0=\frac{a^2y_0}{b^2x_0}(x-x_0)$$

यदि दीर्घवृत्त का केन्द्र C (h, k) हो तब

$$\frac{(x-h)^2}{a^2}+\frac{(y-k)^2}{b^2}=1$$

बिन्दु P(x_0, y_0)
स्पर्शी का समीकरण

$$\frac{(x-h)(x_0-h)}{a^2}+\frac{(y-k)(y_0-k)}{b^2}=1$$

बिन्दु P पर अभिलम्ब का समीकरण

$$y-y_0=\frac{a^2(y_0-k)}{b^2(x_0-h)}(x-x_0)$$

- **Normal equation of the line** *(रेखा का अभिलम्ब समीकरण)* It is $x\cos\theta + y\sin\theta = P$ where P = lenght of the perpendicular from origin upon a line
  Q = angle made by the perpendicular with the positive direction of
  x- axis $x \cos\theta + \sin\theta = P$
  जहाँ P = रेखा के मूलबिन्दु से लम्बवत् लम्बाई है।
  Q = x अक्ष और लम्बवत् रेखा के द्वारा बनाया गया कोण है।
- **Normal of Equation** *(अभिलम्ब का समीकरण)*
  The equation of normal to the circle $x^2 + y^2 + 2gx + 2fy + c = 0$ at any point (x_1, y_1) is
  $$y - y_1 = \frac{y_1 - f}{x_1 + g}(x - x_1)$$
  The equation of normal to the circle $x^2 + y^2 = a^2$ at any point (x_1, y_1) is $xy_1 - x_1y = 0$

Null Matrix *(रिक्त आव्यूह)* It is a matrix with all elements equal to Zero. जिस आव्यूह का प्रत्येक तत्व शून्य हो, उसे रिक्त अथवा शून्य आव्यूह कहते हैं। जिसे O से प्रदर्शित करते है।

Null Sequence *(रिक्त अनुक्रम)* A Sequence whose limit is Zero. ऐसा अनुक्रम जिसकी सीमा शून्य हो।

Null Set *(रिक्त समुच्चय)* It is an empty Set and is devoted by ϕ. Such a set has no members. ऐसा समुच्चय जिसमें कोई अवयव न हो रिक्त समुच्चय कहलाता है। इसे ϕ से निरुपित करते हैं। इस प्रकार के समुच्चय में कोई अवयव नहीं होता है।

Null Vector *(शून्य सदिश)* A Vector whose magnitude is Zero is called a Null vector and devoted by $\vec{O}$ The direction of Null vector is arbitrary . A Null vector is also represented as $\vec{AA}, \vec{BB}$ etc. वह सदिश जिसका मापांक शून्य होता है। शून्य सदिश कहलाता है। जिसे $\vec{O}$ द्वारा निरुपित करते हैं। इसकी दिशा अनिर्धारित रहती है। शून्य सदिश को $\vec{AA}, \vec{BB}$ के द्वारा निरुपित किया जा सकता है।

O

Oblique angle ***(वक्र कोण)*** An angle which is not a right angle, and can be obtuse or acute. कोई भी कोण जो समकोण नहीं होता, यह अधिक कोण या न्यून कोण हो सकता है।

Oblique triangle ***(वक्र त्रिभुज)*** A triangle that is not a right triangle. वह त्रिभुज जो समकोण नहीं होता है।

Obtuse angle ***(अधिक कोण)*** An angle with a degree measure between 90° and 180°. वह कोण जो 90° से अधिक तथा 180° से कम हो अधिक कोण कहलाता है।

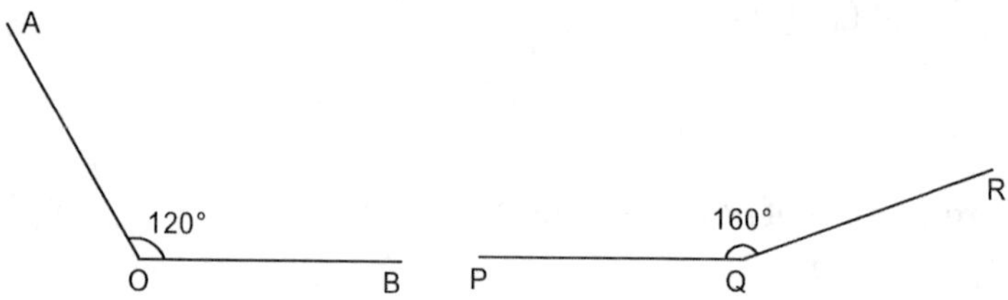

Fig. Obtuse angle

Obtuse triangle ***(अधिक कोण त्रिभुज)*** A triangle with one angle greater than 90 degrees, and other two angle must be acute. वह त्रिभुज जिसका एक कोण 90° से अधिक तथा 180° अंश से कम हो।

Octagon ***(अष्टभुज)*** A polygon with 8 sides. बहुभुज जिसमें 8 भुजा होती है।

Octahedron ***(अष्टफलकीय)*** A polyhedron with 8 faces. बहुफलक जिसमें 8 फलक होते हैं।

Octal number ***(अष्ट्रक संख्या)*** A number in base 8. वह संख्या जिसमें आधार 8 हो।

Odd function ***(विषम फलन)*** A function that satisfies the property.

$$f(-N) = -f(n)$$

यदि $f(-x) = -f(n)$ अर्थात $f(n)$ में n के स्थान पर n रखने पर फलन का चिन्ह बदल जाए तो वह विषम फलन कहलाता है।

Odd number ***(विषम संख्या)*** A natural number that is not divisible by 2 *e.g.* 3, 5, 7, 9... ऐसी संख्याएं जो 2 से विभाजित न हो।

Ohm ***(ओम)*** (Ω) It is a unit of electrical resistance. यह प्रतिरोध को नापने की इकाई है।

One to One ***(एकैकी)*** A function f is said to be one to one if $f(n) = f(y)$ implies that $x = y$. कोई फलन एकैकी कहलाता है जब $f(n) = f(y)$ यदि $n = y$ हो।

Onto ***(आच्छादक)*** A function f is said to map A onto B if for every b in B, there is same a in A such $f(a) = b$. $f: A \to B$ आच्छादक प्रतिचित्रण होगा यदि $f(A) = b$.

Open interval ***(विवर्त अन्तराल)*** An interval that does not include its two end points. एक ऐसा अन्तराल जिसमें उसके अंत बिन्दु सम्मिलित न हों।

Operation ***(संक्रिया)*** It is a way of combining together members of a set. समुच्चय की संख्याओं को एक साथ जोड़ने की विधि।

Operational on rational numbers ***(परिमेय संख्याओं पर संक्रियाएं)***

- If a and b are rational numbers, than (यदि a और b परिमेय संख्या है तब)

(*i*) $a + b$ is a rational number (*ii*) $a + b$ is a rational number

(*iii*) $a \times b$ is a rational number (*iv*) $a - b$ is a rational number

- For any rational numbers a, b and c: (किसी परिमेय संख्या a,b,c के लिए)

(*i*) $a + b = b + a$ (*ii*) $a \div b = b \times a$

(*iii*) $(a + b) + c = a + (b + c)$ (*iv*) $a + 0 = 0 + a = a$

(*v*) $a \times 1 = 1 \times a = a$ (*vi*) $a \times (b + c) = a \times b + a \times c$

(*vii*) $a \times (b \times c) = c \times (a \times b)$ (*viii*) $a \times 0 = 0 \times a = 0$

- If $x = \frac{a}{b}$ is a non zero rational number, than $x^{-1} = \frac{b}{a}$ is a rational number.
- (*i*) $(a^{-1})^{-1} = a$
  (*ii*) $a \times a^{-1} = a^{-1} \times a = 1$
- If a and b are two rational numbers than $\frac{a+b}{2}$ is a rational number lying between a and b. यदि a और b दो परिमेय संख्या है तब $\frac{a+b}{2}$ भी एक परिमेय संख्या है जो a और b के बीच स्थित होता है।
- Between a and b, infinitely many rational numbers can be found. a और b के मध्य अपरिमित रूप से अनेक परिमेय संख्यायें स्थित होती है।

Operations with indices ***(घातांक के साथ संक्रियाएँ)*** **Addition and subtraction :** The sum or the difference of powers can be carries out only if the terms involved have the same base and the same exponents. समान आधार और समान घातों वाले पदों को जोड़ने या घटाने से एक पद प्राप्त करना।

e.g. $$3a^4 + 2a^4 = 5a^4$$

$$6a^5 - 4a^5 = 2a^5$$

- **Multiplication** ***(गुणनफल)***

  (*i*) When the bases are same. जब आधार समान हो।

  $$x^n . x^m = x^{n+m}$$

  (*ii*) When the exponents are same. जब घातें समान हो।

  $$x^m . y^{1_n} = (x . y)^{1_n}$$

- **Division** ***(विभाजन)*** (i) When bases are same. जब आधार समान हों।

  $$x^m \div n^n = x^{m-n}$$

  (*ii*) When exponents are same. जब घातें समान हों।

  $$x^n \div y^n = \left(\frac{x}{y}\right)^n$$

- **Raising to power** ***(घात लगाना)***

  $$(x^m)^n = x^{m.\,n}$$

  $$\left[\left(x^m\right)^n\right]^l = x^{m.\,n.l}$$

Operations using fraction ***(भिन्नों का सरणीकरण)*** **Addition and subtraction:** If the terms have denominator then add the numerators (or subtract the numerators) keeping the common denominator. e.g. $\frac{6}{7}+\frac{3}{7}=\frac{9}{7}$.

If the terms to be added or subtracted have denominators then first concert them into terms having same denominator (multiply the terms by L.C.M. of denominators). Then proceed as in above case.

यदि हर समान हो तब उसके अंश को जोड़ देते हैं। जिन पदों के हर असमान होते है। उन्हें जोड़ने या घटाने के लिए सबसे पहले इनके हर ल.स.म द्वारा बराबर करत हैं।

- **Multiplication** ***(गुणनफल)*** To multiply fractions, multiply the numerators by numerator and denominator by denominator. भिन्नों के गुणा में अंश और अंश तथा हर और हर का गुणा करते हैं।

- **Division** ***(विभाजन)*** It involves the multiplication of dividend by the reciprocal of the divisor.
  Two number are called reciprocal numbers if their product is equal to e.g. $\frac{x}{y}$ is reciprocal of $\frac{y}{x}$ or $\frac{2}{3}$ is reciprocal $\frac{3}{2}$.
  भाजक और भाज्य के व्यत्क्रम का गुणनफल विभाजन कहलाता है। दो संख्याये व्यत्क्रम संख्याऐं जब होगी जब उनका गुणनफल 1 हो। जैसे– $\frac{x}{y}$ का व्यत्क्रम $\frac{y}{x}$ है। और $\frac{3}{2}$ का व्यत्क्रम $\frac{3}{2}$ है।

- **Power** ***(घात)***

$$\left(\frac{3}{7}\right)^2 = \frac{3}{7}\times\frac{3}{7} = \frac{3^2}{7^2}.\left(\frac{5}{9}\right)^1 = \frac{5}{9}.\left(\frac{7}{11}\right)^0 = 1$$

Ordinal numbers ***(क्रमवाच्य संख्या)*** Numbers showing over or position e.g., first. second etc. ऐसे अंक 1st, 2nd, 3rd, 4th जो क्रम व स्थिति दर्शाते हों।

Ordinate ***(कोटि)*** A vertical coordinate on a plane. किसी सतह का लम्बवत निर्देशांक।

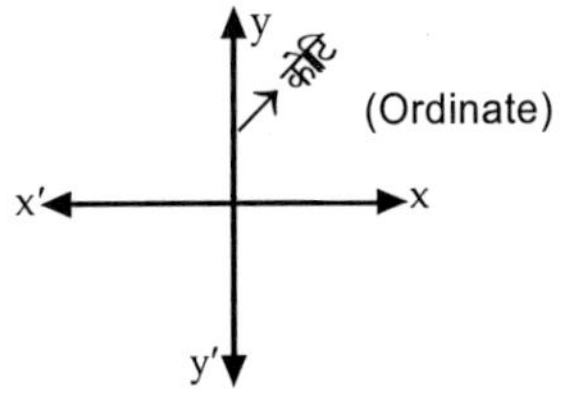

Fig. Ordinate

Origin ***(मूल बिन्दु)*** The point on *a* graph that represents the point where the f are y axes meet ; $(x, y) = (0, 0)$. वह बिन्दु जहाँ x अक्ष y अक्ष एक दूसरे को लम्बवत काटती हो।

Orthic triangle ***(लम्बवतीय त्रिभुज)*** The triangle whose vertices are the feet of the altitudes of = given triangle. Example: Δ ABC. किसी दिये गये त्रिभुज की भुजाओं पर डाले गये लम्बवत के जिस त्रिभुज के शीर्ष हों उसे लम्बवतीय त्रिभुज कहते हैं। जैसे त्रिभुज ABC चित्र में।

P

Pandigital ***(पैनडिजिटल)*** A decimal integer is called pandigital if it contains each of the digits from 0 to 9. कोई दशमलव गुणांक पैनडिजिटल कहलाता है यदि उमें 0-9 तक सभी अंक सम्मिलित हों।

Pair of straight lines through origin :

(*i*) The homogeneous equation of the second degree $ax^2 + 2hxy + by^2 = 0$ always represent a pair of straight lines through the origin if $h^2 \geq ab$.

The equation of the two lines will be दो रेखाओं का समीकरण होगा–

$$ax + (h + \sqrt{h_2 - ab})y = 0$$

and $$ax + (h - \sqrt{h_2 - ab})y = 0$$

(*ii*) The angle θ between the straight lines given by the equation $ax^2 + 2hxy + by^2 = 0$ is equal to

$$\tan^{-1}\left[\frac{\sqrt{h^2 - ab}}{a + b}\right]$$

The two line will be coincident if $h^2 = ab$ and the two lines will be perpendicular if $a + b = 0$.

(*iii*) Equation to the straight lines bisecting to the two angles between the straight lines given by $ax^2 + 2hxy + by^2 = 0$ will be

$$\frac{x^2 - y^2}{a - b} = \frac{xy}{h}$$

(*iv*) The conditions that the general equation of the second degree. $ax^2 + 2hxy + by^2 + 2gx + 2fy + c = 0$ may represent two straight lines is

$$\begin{vmatrix} a & h & g \\ h & b & f \\ g & f & c \end{vmatrix} = 0$$

मूल बिन्दु से गुजरने वाली सरल रेखाओं का युग्म–

(*i*) द्विघातीय समघात समीकरण $ax^2 + 2\,hxy + by^2 = 0$ मूल बिन्दु से गुजरने वाली सरल रेखाओं के युग्म को निरुपित करती है। यदि $h^2 \geq ab$.

(*ii*) दो सरल रेखाओं के बीच का कोण जो समीकरण $ax^2 + 2\,hxy + by^2 = 0$ से निरुपित होती है, होगा–

$$\tan^{-1}\left[\frac{\sqrt{h^2 - ab}}{a+b}\right]$$

यदि $h^2 = ab$ तो दो रेखाएँ संपाती होंगी। यदि $a + b = 0$ तो दो रेखाएँ परस्पर लम्ब होंगी।

(*iii*) समीकरण $ax^2 + 2hxy + by^2 = 0$ से निरुपित सरल रेखाओं के बीच के कोणों के अर्धकों का समीकरण–

$$\frac{x^2 - y^2}{a-b} = \frac{xy}{h}$$

(*iv*) वह प्रतिबन्ध जिससे कि द्विघातीय व्यापक समीकरण $ax^2 + 2hxy + by^2 + 2gx + 2\,fy + c = 0$ दो सरल रेखाएँ निरुपित करें–

$$\begin{vmatrix} a & h & g \\ h & b & f \\ g & f & c \end{vmatrix} = 0$$

Parabola *(परवलय)* A parabola is the locus of a point which moves in a plan such that its distance from a fixed point (called focus) in the plan is always equal to its distance from fixed straight sine (called the directrix) in the same plane. परवलय उस बिन्दु का बिन्दुपथ हैं जिसकी एक स्थिर बिन्दु (नाभि) और एक स्थिर सरल रेखा से दूरियाँ सदैव बराबर रहती है।

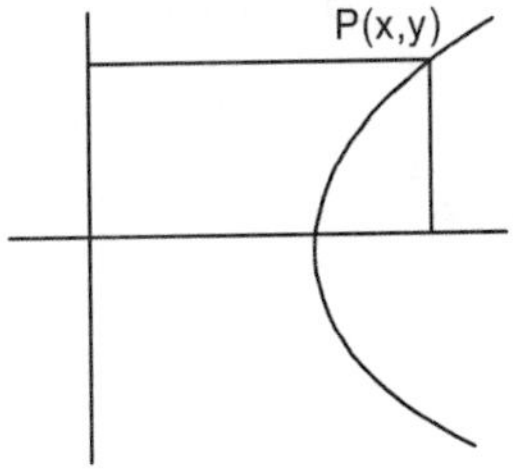

Fig. Parabola

Parabolic segment–It refers to the area bound by a chord of a parabola perpendicular to its axis and the curve cut off by the chord.

The area of such a segment is given by

$$\text{Area} = \frac{2cd}{3}$$

where c = length of the chord

d = its distance from the vertex of the parabola.

परवलीय खण्ड–किसी परवलय का जीवा द्वारा घिरा वक्र क्षेत्रफल जिसका अक्ष जीवा के लम्बवत हो।

जिसका क्षेत्रफल होगा $= \frac{2cd}{3}$

जहाँ C = जीवा की लम्बाई

d = परवलय के शीर्ष से जीवा की दूरी है।

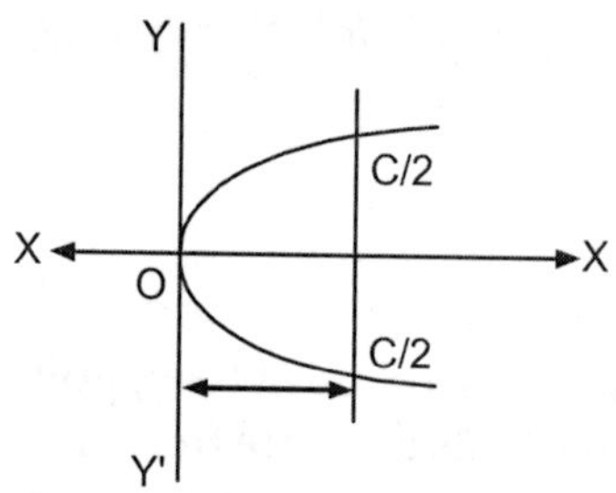

Fig. Parabolic segment

Paraboloid ***(परवलायड़)*** A surface that is formed by rotating a parabola about its axis. किसी परवलय को उसके अक्ष से घुमाने पर निर्मित सतह।

Paraboloid ***(ठोस अनुवृत्त)***

(*i*) Elliptical (अण्डाकारिता)

$$\frac{x^2}{a^2} + \frac{y^2}{b^2} = \frac{z}{c}$$

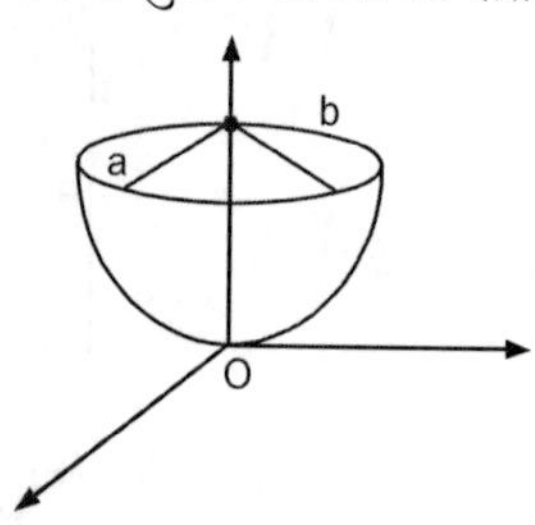

Fig. Paraboloid

(*ii*) Hyperbalic paraboloid (अतिपरवलीय अनुवृत्त)

$$\frac{x^2}{a^2}+\frac{y^2}{b^2}=\frac{z}{c}$$

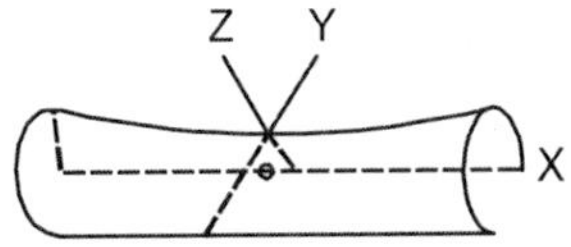

Fig. Hyperbalic paraboloid

Parallel line ***(समान्तर रेखा)*** Two lines which do not intersect in a plane however they are extended are called parallel lines. दो रेखा एक ही तल से बढ़ाई जाय और यदि कहीं भी एक दूसरे को न काटे तो दोनों रेखाएं समान्तर रेखा कहलाएंगी।

Parallel Planes ***(समान्तर समतल)*** Planes lying in space that do not have any common point no matter how far they are extended. For example, equation $2x + 3y - 5z + d = 0$ represents parallel planes for changing values of d. ऐसे समतल जिनमें कोई (उभयनिष्ठ) बिन्दु न हो और उन्हें आगे बढ़ाने पर एक-दूसरे को न काटे। इन्हें $2x + 3y - 5z + d = 0$ से निरुपित करते हैं। इनका मान d के मान पर निर्भर करता है।

Parallelepiped ***(समान्तर चतुष्फलक)*** A solid figure with six faces such that the planes containing two opposite faces are each face in a parallelogram. छः फलकों वाली एक ठोस आकृति जिसमें दो विपरीत फलकों को धारण करने वाले समतल समान्तर है। जिसका प्रत्येक फलक समान्तर चतुर्भुज हों।

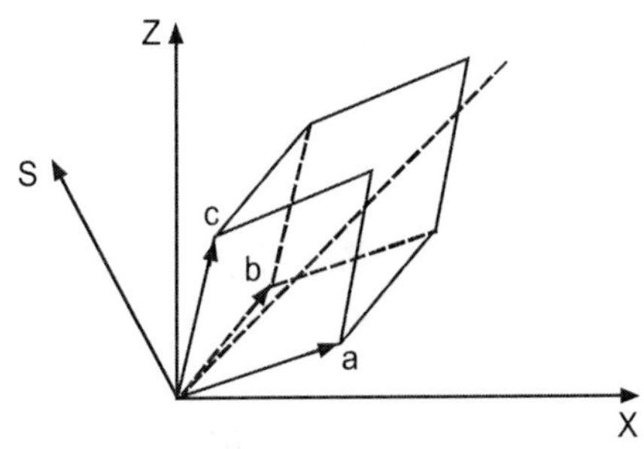

Fig. Parallelepiped

Parallelism ***(समानता)*** The state of being parallel not interesting. समान्तर होने की दिशा।

Parallel vectors ***(समान्तर सदिश)*** If the support lines of vectors are parallel then they are known as parallel vectors. यदि सदिशो की संगत भुजाएँ समान्तर हैं, तो सदिश भी समान्तर होंगे।

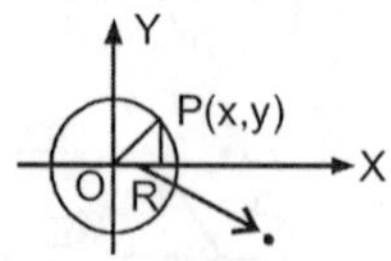

Fig. Parallel vectors

Parallelogram ***(समान्तर चतुर्भुज)*** A quadrilateral with opposite sides parallel. एक चतुर्भुज जिसकी सम्मुख भुजाएं समान्तर हो। चित्र ABCD एक समान्तर चतुर्भुज है।

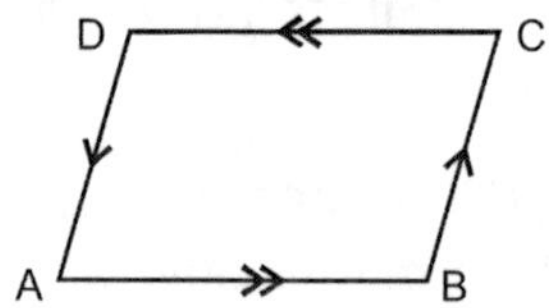

Fig. Parallelogram

Parametric form of the equation of a circle ***(वृत्त की प्राचलिक समीकरण)*** If r is the radius of the circle and P (x, y) is a point on the circle such that OP makes an angle α with the x–axis. then. यदि r वृत्त की त्रिज्या और वृत्त पर इस प्रकार है कि कोई बिन्दु P (x,y) OP रेखा x – अक्ष के साथ α कोण बनाती है, तब

$$\left.\begin{aligned} x &= r\cos\alpha \\ y &= r\sin\alpha \end{aligned}\right] 0 \le \alpha \le 2\pi$$

are the parametric form of the circle,

वृत्त की प्रचलित अवस्था है,

in terms of parameter, α $x^2 + y^2 = r^2$

इन दो पदो की परिमाप, α

$$\frac{\partial^2 u}{\partial x^2} + \frac{\partial^2 u}{\partial y^2} + \frac{\partial^2 u}{\partial z^2} = 0$$

Partial differential equation/PDE ***(आंशिक आवकलन समीकरण)*** Any equation relating a function of several valuables to its partial derivatives in different directions. विभिन्न दिशाओं में कई चरों के फलन को उसके आंशिक व्युत्पन्न से संबंधित कोई समीकरण।

Partial fractions ***(ऑशिक भिन्ने)*** They are the fraction of the form. भिन्नों की अवस्था

$$\frac{A}{(ax+b)^n}, \frac{Ax+B}{(ax^2+bx+c)^n}$$

Where n is a positive integer. जहाँ n एक धन पूर्णांक है।

Pascal's triangle ***(पासकल का त्रिभुज)*** It is a pattern of numbers as shown below. संख्याओं को नीचे व्यक्त किया गया एक तरीका–

1

1 1

1 2 1

1 3 3 1

1 4 6 4 1

1 5 10 10 5 1

Pedal triangle ***(पैडल त्रिभुज)*** If AD, BE and CF are the perpendiculars from A, B and C on opposite sides, respectively, meeting at P then P is known as the orthoceullic of the Δ ....यदि AD, BE और CF क्रमशः A, B और C से विपरीत भुजाओं पर लम्ब है तथा ये सब P बिन्दु पर मिलती है तब P का त्रिभुज को औरथोसेलिक कहेंगे–

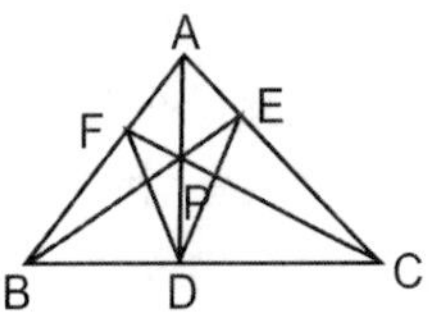

Fig. Pedal triangle

ABC and ΔDEF is known as Pedal triangle.

Sides and angle of the pedal triangle. पैडल त्रिभुज की भुजाएँ और कोण

$$\text{side EF} = a \cos A$$
$$\text{side DF} = b \cos B$$
$$\text{side DE} = c \cos C$$
$$\angle DEF = 180 - 2B$$
$$\angle DFE = 180 - 2C$$
$$\angle EDF = 180 - 2A$$

Pentagon ***(पंचभुज)*** A five sided polygon. एक बहुभुज जिसमें 5 भुजाएं हों।

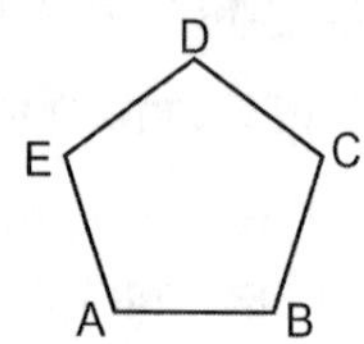

Fig. Pentagon

Pentagonal number ***(पंचकोणिक संख्या)*** A number of the form $n(3n - 1)/2$. कोई संख्या जो $n(3n - 1)/2$ के रूप में हो।

Percent ***(प्रतिशत)*** A fraction with etc. denominator as 100 is called a percent or, the amount out of 100. 4/5 is equal to 80/100, and is then 80% Also, a ration with its second term as 100 is called percents. किसी दी गई संख्या के प्रति सैकड़ा भाग को प्रतिशत कहते हैं। जैसे 80% (प्रतिशत) का अर्थ 80/100 होगा। प्रतिशत का चिन्ह % से प्रदर्शित करते हैं।

Perfect cube ***(पूर्ण घन)*** If x is an integer then x^3 is *a* feat perfect cube= As $(-2)^3 = -8$, $(-3)^3 = -27$, $(2)^3 = 8$, $(3)^3 = 27$.

Ans. 8, 27, 8, 27, are perfect cubes.

जिन अंकों को गुणनखण्ड के तीन-तीन का जोड़ा बनाया जा सके। जैसे $27 = 3 \times 3 \times 3$ अथवा $(3)^3$।

Perfect number ***(पूर्ण संख्या)*** A number that is the sum of all its factors except itself for example 6. वह संख्या जो अपने को छोड़कर बाकी सभी गुणनखण्डों का योग होता है। जैसे–$6 = 1 \times 2 \times 3 = 1 + 2 + 3 = 6$

Perfect power ***(पूर्ण घात)*** An integer is a perfect power if it is of the form mn where mn where m and n are integers and $n > 1$. कोई गुणांक पूर्ण घात होता है यदि वह mn के रूप में हो, तथा जिसमें m और n गुणांक।

Perpendicular ***(लम्बवत)*** At right angle to a line or plane. किसी रेखा या तल पर 90 अंश का कोण बनाती हुई रेखा।

Pi (π) ***(पाई)*** The ratio of the circumference of a circle to its diameter. The value of pi is 3.145926, correct to seven decimal places. यदि किसी वृत्त की परिधि से उसके व्यास का अनुपात होता है। इसका मान 3.14 होता है।

Perpendicular bisector ***(लम्ब समद्विभाज)*** The perpendicular bisector of a side of a triangle is the line that is perpendicular to the side and which also bisects it. वह रेखाखण्ड जो कि भुजा पर लम्ब हो (90 अंश) तथा उस भुजा को 2 बराबर भागों में बाट दें। जैसे चित्र में रेखा 'l', AB का लम्ब समद्विभाजक है।

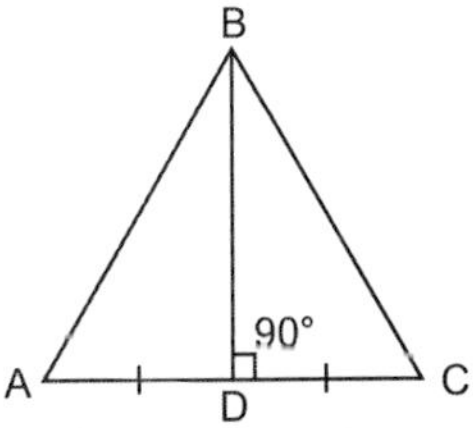

Fig. Perpendicular bisector

Phase difference ***(अवस्था परिवर्तन)*** The equation of a simple wave is $y = a \sin \dfrac{b^2}{\alpha(1+e\cos\theta)} 2\pi$ सरल तरंग का समीकरण $y = a \sin\left(\dfrac{ft-x}{\lambda}\right)2\pi$

The phase of this wave will be $\left[\dfrac{2\pi(ft-x)}{\lambda}\right]$

phase difference between two points $x = x_1, x = x_2$ is $\dfrac{2\pi(x_1 - x_2)}{\lambda}$

दो बिन्दुओं के बीच अवस्था परिवर्तन $x = x_1, x = x_2$ $\dfrac{2\pi(x_1 - x_2)}{\lambda}$

Pint ***(पिन्ट)*** It is a measure of volume. यह आयतन नापने की इकाई है।

1 gallon = 8 pints (1 गैलोन = 8 पिन्टस)

1 litre = 1.76 pints. (1 लीटर = 1.76 पिन्टस)

Polar coordinates ***(ध्रुवीय निर्देशांक)*** A system of polar coordinates is identified by. ध्रुवीय निर्देशांक प्रणाली को निम्न द्वारा पहचानते है।

(*a*) a Pole O

(*a*) ध्रुव O

(*b*) a Polar axis OX.

(b) ध्रुवीय अक्ष) OX

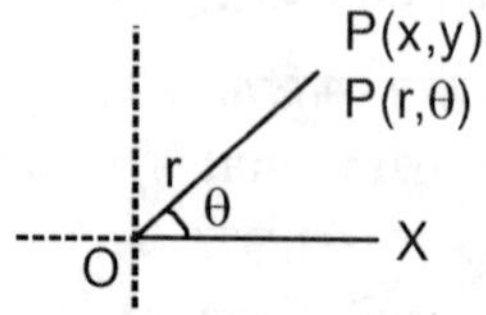

Fig. Polar coordinates

A point in the plane is characterised by radius vector (r) OP and by the angle θ formed by the radius with the semi-axis OX. किसी समतल पर वह बिन्दु जो त्रिज्य सदिश (r) OP तथा अर्द्ध अक्ष OX द्वारा बने कोण Q से प्राप्त होता है।

For the point P (x, y) the respective polar coordinates are

बिन्दु P (x, y) के ध्रुवीय निर्देशांक

$r = + \sqrt{x^2 + y^2}$

$\theta = \tan^{-1} \dfrac{x}{y}$

The cartesian coordinates of a point P (r, θ) are given by $x = r\cos\theta$, $y = r\sin\theta$.

कार्तीय P (r, θ) निर्देशांक हो तब $x = r\cos\theta$, $y = r\sin\theta$

- **Polar equation of a straight line** ***(सरल रेखा का ध्रुवीय समीकरण)***

$$r = \frac{K}{\cos(\alpha - \theta)}$$

where K = distance of straight line from the orign.

जहाँ K = मूल बिन्दु से सरल रेखा की दूरी है।

α = angle which K forms with the X-axis

α = x अक्ष और K के बीच का कोण है।

r,θ = Polar variables.

r, θ = ध्रुवीय चर

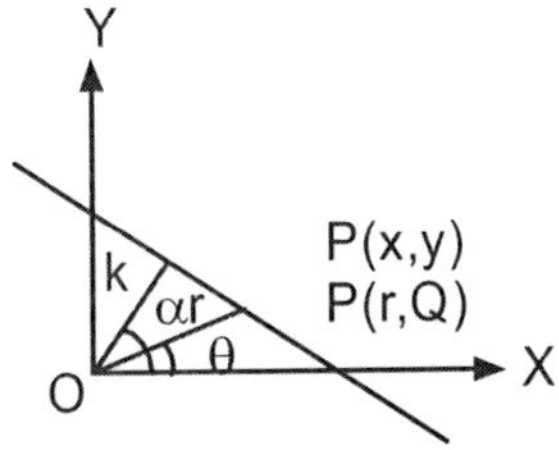

Fig. Polar equation of a straight line

Polar equation of the ellipse ***(दीर्घवृत्त की ध्रुवीय समीकरण)*** If we assume that pole is the centre of the ellipse and greater axis which is oriented to the right is the polar axis, then the equation of the ellipse is यदि हम मान लें कि दीर्घवृत्त का केन्द्र ध्रुव है तथा वही अक्ष ध्रुवीय की ओर झुकी हुई है तब दीर्घ वृत्त का समीकरण–

$$r^2 = \frac{b^2}{1-c^2\cos\theta}$$

If we assume the pole to be the focus to the right (F_1) and take the polar axis as the greater axis oriented to the right, the polar equation of the ellipse is

$$r^2 = \frac{b^2}{\alpha(1+e\cos\theta)}$$

यदि हम ध्रुव को केन्द्र (F_1) तथा ध्रुवीय अक्ष और बड़ी अक्ष के बीच झुकाव है, तव दीर्घवृत्त का समीकरण–

$$r = \frac{b^2}{\alpha(1+e\cos\theta)}$$

Position vector ***(स्थिति सदिश)*** For any point P (x, y, z) the vector y is given by $\vec{y} = x.\hat{i} + y.\hat{i} + z.\hat{k}$

कोई बिन्दु सदिश तब by $\vec{y} = x.\hat{i} + y\hat{i} + z.\hat{k}$

is called the position vector.इसे स्थिति सदिश कहते हैं।

Pound ***(पाउण्ड)*** It is a unit of British Currency

1 Pound = 100 pence.

यह ब्रिटिश मुद्रा की इकाई है।

1 पाउण्ड = 100 पेन्स

It is a unit of mass (E.P.S system)

1 Pound = 16 ounce

1 stone = 14 pounds

यह द्रव्यमान का (E.P.S प्रणाली) में मात्रक है।

1 पाउण्ड = 16 ओन्स

1 स्टोन = 14 पाउण्ड

Pound *(पाण्उड)* It is a unit of force (E.P.S system) यह (E.P.S) प्रणाली में बल का मात्रक है।

1 poundal = 0.138255 Newton.

1 पाउण्डल = 0.138255 न्यूटन

Pound weight *(पाण्उड वजन)* It is the weight of one pound mass. एक पाउण्ड द्रव्यमान के वजन के बराबर होता है।

Power *(घात)* It is the rate of doing work. It also refers to the exponential term *e.g.* 2^4 means the power of base 2 is 4. किए गए काम की दर को घात कहते हैं। इसे घातीय पद के रूप में लिखते हैं। जैसे– 2^4 में 2 आधार तथा 4 घात है।

- **Powers and roots of complex number** *(सम्मिश्र संख्या की घातें तथा वर्गमूल)*

$(\text{Cos}\,\theta + i\,\text{Sin}\theta)^n = \text{Cos}\,n\,\theta + i\,\text{Sin}\,n\,\theta$, for $n = \pm 1, \pm 2, \pm 3.....$

$(\text{Cos}\,\theta + \text{i}\,\text{Sin}\,\theta)^{-1} = \text{Cos}\,(-\theta) + \text{Sin}\,(-\theta)$

then (तब) $a^{1/n} = z =$

$$\sqrt[n]{P}\left\{\cos\left(\frac{\theta}{n} + K\frac{2\pi}{n}\right) + i\sin\left(\frac{\theta}{n} + K\frac{2\pi}{n}\right)\right\}$$

where (जहाँ) k = 0 1, 2 .... (n–1)

Nth Roots of units (इकाइयों का N वाँ वर्गमूज सम्मिश्र संख्या)

For a complex number 1, we have

$I = (\cos\theta + \sin\theta)$

$$(\therefore \sqrt[n]{I} = \cos\frac{2\pi}{n}.k + i\sin\frac{2\pi}{n}.k)$$

Where (जहाँ) $K = 0, 1, 2, 3, \ldots\ldots\ldots\ldots.(n-1)$

- **Powers of trigonometric functions** ***(त्रिकोणमितीय फलनों की घाते)***

(*i*) $\sin^2\alpha = \frac{1}{2}(1-\cos 2\alpha)$

(*ii*) $\cos^2\alpha = \frac{1}{2}(1+\cos 2\alpha)$

(*iii*) $\sin^3\alpha = \frac{1}{4}(3\sin\alpha - \sin 3\alpha)$

(*iv*) $\cos^3\alpha = \frac{1}{4}(3\cos\alpha + \cos 3\alpha)$

(*v*) $\sin^4\alpha = \frac{1}{8}(\cos 4\alpha - 4\cos^2\alpha + 3)$

(*vi*) $\cos^4\alpha = \frac{1}{8}(\cos 4\alpha + 4\cos 2\alpha + 3)$

(*vii*) $\sin^5\alpha = \frac{1}{16}(10\sin\alpha - 5\sin 3\alpha + \sin 5a)$.

(*viii*) $\cos 5\alpha = \frac{1}{16}(10\cos\alpha + 5\cos 3\alpha + \cos 5a)$

Place value ***(स्थानीय मान)*** The value of the position of a digit in a number For example in the number 7863, the 8 is in the hundreds place and etc. value in 800. किसी संख्या में किसी अंक की स्थिति का मान स्थानीय मान कहलाता है। जैसे संख्या 7863 में अंक 8 का स्थानीय मान 800 होगा।

Plane ***(समतल)*** A flat surface that starches off into infinity. कोई समतल सतह जो अनंत तक खींची जा सके।

Plane geometry ***(समतल ज्यामिती)*** The study of two dimensional figures. द्विविमीय आकृतियों का अध्ययन समतल ज्यामिती कहलाता है।

Point ***(बिन्दु)*** A point in geometry is undefined. A geometric point is considered to be a particular location in geometric space. A tiny hole by a pin or a small dot made by a sharp pencil on a sheet of paper, gives us an idea of a point. किसी कागज पर एक नुकीली वस्तु, पैंसिल व कल से बनाया गया एक सूक्ष्म चिन्ह या कोई सूक्ष्म छिद्र हमें बिन्दु की जानकारी देता है।

Prime factorisation *(अभाज्य गुणनखण्ड)* The calculation of every prime factor in a given the prime factor of 12 are 3, 2. अभाज्य संख्याओं से युक्त गुणक।

Prime factors *(अभाज्य)* Prime factors of a number are a list of prime numbers the product of which is the number concerned. ऐसा गुणनखण्ड जिसमें अभाज्य संख्याए हो।

Prime number *(अभाज्य संख्या)* A natural number other than 1, every divisible by 1 and itself, The number 2, 3, 5, 7, 11, 13, 17, 19... ऐसी संख्याएं जो केवल 1 (एक) से या स्वयं से विभाजित हो।

Principal *(मूलधन)* The money borrowed from a lender is called the principal.

$$P = \frac{SI \times 100}{T \times R}$$

उधार लिया हुआ धन मूल धन कहलाता है।

Polygon *(बहुभुज)* A geometric figure that is bounded by many straight lines such as triangle, square, pentagon hexagon, heptagon, octagon etc. रेखाचित्र जो कई सरल रेखाओं से घिरा हो जैसे—वर्ग, पंचभुज, षटभुज, अष्टभुज आदि।

Polynomial *(बहुपद)* In algebra, an expression consisting of two or more terms, such $x^2 - 2xy + y^2$. बीजगणितीय व्यंजक जिसमें 2 या 2 से अधिक पद हों।

Positive number *(धनात्मक संख्याए)* A real number greater than zero. शून्य (0) से बड़ी वास्तविक संख्यायें, धनात्मक संख्यायें कहलाती है।

Power set *(घात समुच्चय)* Let A be set. Then the collection or family of all subsets of A is called the power set of Q and is denoted by P (A). That is $P(A) = \{S/S \subset A\}$

मान लीजिये A एक समुच्चय है। इसके सभी उपसमुच्चयों के समुच्चय को A का समुच्चय कहा जाता है। इसके प्रतीक P(A) से निरूपित किया जाता है; अर्थात-

$$P(A) = \{S/S \subset A\}$$

Properties of determinants *(सारणिक के गुण)* Following properties are associated with determinants of degree 3 or higher. निम्न गुण 3 घात पर उससे ज्यादा वाली घातों में लगते हैं।

(*i*) There is no change in the value of the determinant if rows and columns are interchanged with each other. यदि किसी सारणिक की पंक्तियों का स्तम्भों में तथा स्तम्भों का पंक्तियों में परस्पर विनिमय कर दिया जाए तो सारणिक के मान में कोई परिवर्तन नहीं होता है।

(*ii*) If two adjacent rows or columns of a determinant are interchanged then the sign of the determinant gets changed. यदि किसी सारणिक की किन्हीं दो आसन्न पंक्तियों का परस्पर विनिमय कर दिया जाए, तो सारणिक का चिन्ह बदल जाता है। परन्तु उसका संख्यात्मक मान वही रहता है।

(*iii*) If any two rows or two columns of a determinants are proportional then the value of determinant will be zero. यदि किसी सारणिक में कोई दो पंक्तायों या दो स्तम्भ समानुपातिक हैं तो उस सारणिक का शून्य होता है।

(*iv*) If each element in a row or column of a determinants be multiplied by the same factor, then the determinant is multiplied by that factor. यदि किसी सारणिक की किसी पंक्ति अथवा स्तम्भ के प्रत्येक अवयव को किसी संख्या से गुणा कर दिया जाए तो सारणिक में उस संख्या से गुणा हो जाता है।

(*v*)
$$\begin{vmatrix} a_1+\alpha & b_1 & c_1 \\ a_2+\beta & b_2 & c_2 \\ a_3+\gamma & b_3 & c_3 \end{vmatrix} = \begin{vmatrix} a_1 \\ a_2 \\ a_3 \end{vmatrix} + \begin{vmatrix} \alpha & b_1 & c_1 \\ \beta & b_2 & c_2 \\ \gamma & b_3 & c_3 \end{vmatrix}$$

(*vi*) If each element of a column (or row) of a determinant be added or subtracted the equimultiples of corresponding constituents of one or more column (or rows), there occurs no change in determinant. यदि किसी सारणिक की किसी पंक्ति या स्तम्भ के अवयव में दूसरी पंक्तियों अथवा स्तम्भों के संगत अवयवों के सम अपवर्त्य जोड या घटा दिए जाए तो सारणिक के मान में कोई परिवर्तन नहीं होता है।

(*vii*) If A and B are the square matrices of the same order then det. IAB I = det. A. det. B.

Properties of definite Integrals ***(निश्चित समाकलन के गुण)***

(*i*) $\int_a^b f(x)\,dx = -\int_b^a f(x)\,dx$

(*ii*) $\int_a^b f(x)\,dx = \int_a^c f(x)\,dx + \int_c^b f(x)\,dx, a < c < b.$

(*iii*) $\int_a^a f(x)\,dx = 0$

(*iv*) $\int_a^a f(x)\,dx = \int_0^a f(a-x)\,dx$

(*v*) $\int_{-a}^{a} f(x)\,dx = 2\int_a^{-a} f(x)\,dx$, if $f(x)$ is an even function यदि (x) सम फलन है $= 0$, if $f(x)$ is an odd function. यदि x विषम फलन है।

Properties of logarithms ***(लघुगुणक के गुण)***

$$\log_a xy = \log_a x + \log_a y$$

$$\log_a \left(\frac{x}{y}\right) = \log_a x - \log_a y$$

$$\log_a x^n = n \log_a x$$

$$\log_a x^{\frac{1}{n}} = \frac{1}{n} \log_a$$

Properties of vector addition ***(सदिशों के जोड़ के गुण)***

(*i*) It is commutative property $\vec{a} + \vec{b} = \vec{b} + \vec{a}$ विनिमय का गुण

(*ii*) It is associative property. $\vec{a} + (\vec{b} + \vec{c}) = (\vec{a} + \vec{b}) + \vec{c}$ सहचार्य का गुण

(*iii*) For any closed polygon $A_1 A_2 A_3$ ....A_n. बन्द बहुभुज

$$A_1\vec{A}_2 + A_2\vec{A}_3 + \ldots\ldots A_n\vec{A}_1 = 0$$

Sepecially in case of a triangle ABC . Δ ABC में

$$A\vec{B} + B\vec{C} + C\vec{A} = 0$$

(*iv*) For any vector $\vec{a}$, $\vec{a} + \vec{0} = \vec{a}$ where $\vec{0}$ is a zero vector. कोई सदिश $\vec{a}$, $\vec{a} + \vec{0} = \vec{a}$ जहाँ से शून्य वेक्टर है।

(*v*) For any vector $\vec{a}$, $\vec{a}+(-\vec{a})=(-\vec{a})+\vec{a}=0$, vector $(-\vec{a})$ is known as additive inverse of vector $\vec{a}$. कोई सदिश $\vec{a}$, $\vec{a}+(-\vec{a})$ = $\vec{a}+(-\vec{a})$ + $\vec{a}=0$ सदिस को सदिश का योगात्मक व्यत्क्रम कहते हैं।

Proper subset ***(उचित उपसमुच्चय)*** A proper subset *A* of set *B* is that subset which does not contain all the elements of *B*. It is represented by $A \subset B$. यदि *A*, समुच्चय *B* का उपसमुच्चय हो और *B* में कम से कम एक अवयव ऐसा है जो *A* में न हो, तो *A* को *B* का उचित उपसमुच्चय कहते हैं। इसे $A \subset B$ से निरुपित करते हैं, और इसे *A* उचित उपसमुच्चय *B* पढ़ते हैं।

Profit ***(लाभ)*** If the selling price (SP) of an article is greater than the cost price (CP), the difference between the selling price and cost price is called Profit thus if SP > CP, then.

$$\text{Profit} = \text{SP} - \text{CP}.$$

यदि किसी वस्तु को उसके क्रय मूल्य, से अधिक पर विक्रय किया जाता है तो लाभ कहलाता है।

अतः यदि, विक्रय मूल्य > क्रय मूल्य, तब

लाभ = विक्रय मूल्य − क्रय मूल्य।

Profit% ***(प्रतिशत लाभ)***

$$\frac{\text{profit}}{\text{CP}} \times 100, \quad \frac{\text{लाभ}}{\text{क्रय मूल्य}} \times 100$$

Probability of an event ***(प्रायिकता)*** If there are n elementary events associated with *a* random experiment and *m* of them are favourable to an even A , then the probability of happening or occurrence of A is denoted by P (A) and is

defined as the ratio $\frac{m}{n}$.

Then $P(A) = \frac{m}{n}$.

यदि किसी प्रयोग में प्रतिदर्श समष्टि घटनायें *n* है, तथा जिसमें समसम्भावी *m* है तो घटना A की प्रायिकता P(A) परिभाषित होगी अनुपात $\frac{m}{n}$ अर्थात $P(A) = \frac{m}{n}$.

- **Addition theorem of Probability** *(योगात्मक परिमेय)*

(*i*) When events are mutually exclusive–

If A and B are mutually exclusive events then

$$n(A \cap B) = 0 \Rightarrow P(A \cap B) = 0$$

$$\therefore \quad P(A \cup B) = P(A) + P(B)$$

(*ii*) When events are not mutually exclusive–

If A and B are two events which are not mutually exclusive then.

$$P(A \cup B) = P(A) + P(B) - P(A \cap B)$$

or $$P(A + B) = P(A) + (B) - P(AB)$$

- **Multiplication theorem of Probability** *(गुणात्मक परिमेय)*

(*i*) When events are independent.

$$P(A/B) = P(A) \quad \text{and} \quad P(B/A) = P(B), \text{ then}$$

$$P(A \cap B) = P(A).P(B) \quad \text{or} \quad P(AB) = P(A).P(B)$$

(*ii*) When events are not independent :

$$P(A \cap B) = P(A).P(B/A) \quad \text{or} \quad P(B).P(A/B)$$

$$P(AB) = P(A).P(B/A) \quad \text{or} \quad P(B).P(A/B)$$

- **Some Important results** *(कुछ परिणाम)*

(*a*) Let A and B be two events, then

(*i*) $P(A) + P(\bar{A}) = 1$

(*ii*) $P(A + B) = 1 - P(\overline{AB})$

(*iii*) $P(A/B) = \dfrac{P(AB)}{P(B)}$

(*iv*) $P(A + B) = P(AB) + P(\bar{A}B) + P(A\bar{B})$

(*v*) $A \leq B \Rightarrow P(A) \leq P(B)$

(*vi*) $P(\bar{A}B) = P(B) - P(AB)$

(*vii*) $P(AB) \leq P(A)\, P(B) \leq P(A + B) \leq P(A) + P(B)$

(*viii*) $P(AB) = P(A) + P(B) - P(A + B)$

(*ix*) $P(\text{Exactly one event}) = P(A\bar{B})\;\; P(\bar{A}B)$

(*x*) $P(\bar{A}+\bar{B}) = 1 - P(AB)$

$$= P(A) + P(B) - 2P(AB)$$

$$= P(A + B) - P(AB)$$

(*xi*) $P(\text{neither A nor B}) = P(\bar{A}+\bar{B}) = 1 - P(A + B)$

Prism *(प्रिज्म)* A solid with parallel bases, congment polygons, and sides that are all parallelograms.

Q

Quadrangular prism *(चतुष्कोणीय प्रिज्म)* A prism whose base is a quadrilateral. एक प्रिज्म जिसका आधार चतुर्भुज होता है।

Quadrangular pyramid *(चतुष्कोणीय पिरामिड)* A pyramid whose base is a quadrilateral. ऐसा पिरामिड जिसका आधार चतुर्भुज होता है।

Quadrant *(चतुर्थांस)* Each of the four regions created by the coordinate axis. निर्देशांक अक्ष द्वारा काटा गया एक भाग।

Quadratic equation *(वर्ग समीकरण)* An equation of the from $ax^2 + bx + c = 0$, where a, b, c are real number and $a \neq 0$ is called quadratic equation. समीकरण जो $ax^2 + bx + c = 0$ के रूप में हो जहाँ, a, b, c वास्तविक संख्याए हो तथा $a \neq 0$ शून्य न हो वर्ग सेमी. कहलाता है। या द्विघातीय समीकरण कहलाती है।

Quadrotic equation $\alpha = \dfrac{-b+\sqrt{b^2-4ac}}{2a}$

$$\beta = \frac{-b-\sqrt{b^2-4ac}}{2a}$$

यदि वर्ग समीकरण $ax + bx + c = 0\ (a \neq 0)$ के α और β मूल है तो

If roots of quadratic equation $ax^2 + bx + c = 0\ (a \neq 0)$ are α and b then

(*i*) $(\alpha - \beta) = \sqrt{(\alpha+\beta)^2 - 4\alpha\beta} = \pm \dfrac{\sqrt{b^2-4ac}}{a} = \dfrac{\pm\sqrt{D}}{a}$

(*ii*) $\alpha^2 + \beta^2 = (\alpha+\beta)^2 - 2\alpha\beta = \dfrac{b^2-2ac}{a^2}$

(*iii*) $\alpha^2 - \beta^2 = (\alpha+\beta)\ \sqrt{(\alpha+\beta)^2 - 4\alpha\beta} = -\dfrac{b\sqrt{b^2-4ac}}{a^2} = \dfrac{\pm\sqrt{D}}{a}$

(*iv*) $\alpha^2 + \beta^3 = (\alpha+\beta)^3 - 3\alpha\beta\ (\alpha+\beta) = -\dfrac{b(b^2-3ac)}{a^3}$

(*v*) $\alpha^3 - \beta^3 = (\alpha-\beta)^3 + 3\,\alpha\beta(\alpha-\beta)$

$$= \sqrt{(\alpha+\beta)^2 - 4\alpha\beta}\ \{(\alpha+\beta)2 - \alpha\beta\}$$

$$= \frac{(b^2 - ac)\sqrt{b^2 - 4ac}}{a^3}$$

(*vi*) $\alpha^4 + \beta^4 = \{(\alpha+\beta)^2 - 2\alpha\beta\}^2 - 2\alpha^2\beta \mid = \left(\frac{b^2 - 2ac}{a^2}\right)^2 - 2\frac{c^2}{a^2}$

(*vii*) $\alpha^4 - \beta^4 = (\alpha^2 - \beta^2)(\alpha^2 + \beta^2) = \frac{-b(b^2 - 2ac)\sqrt{b^2 - 4ac}}{a^4}$

(*viii*) $\alpha^2 + \alpha\beta + \beta^2 = (\alpha+\beta)^2 - \alpha\beta$

(*ix*) $\frac{\alpha}{\beta} + \frac{\beta}{\alpha} = \frac{\alpha^2 + \beta^2}{\alpha\beta} = \frac{(\alpha+\beta)^2 - 2\alpha\beta}{\alpha\beta}$

(*x*) $\alpha^2\beta + \beta^2\alpha = \alpha\beta(\alpha+\beta)$

(*xi*) $\left(\frac{\alpha}{\beta}\right)^2 + \left(\frac{\beta}{\alpha}\right)^2 = \frac{\alpha^4 + \beta^4}{\alpha^2\beta^2} = \frac{(\alpha^2 + \beta^2)^2 - 2\alpha^2\beta^2}{\alpha^2\beta^2}$

Quadratic function ***(वर्ग फलन)*** A function that has an equation of the form $y = Ax^2 + Bx + C$ where "A" does not equal to 0. ऐसा फलन जिसमें वर्ग समीकरण $ax^2 + bx + c = 0$ (जहाँ A शून्य) न हो आता है।

Quadratic Surd ***(द्विघात करणी)*** A surd of order 2 is called a quadratic surd. e.g $\sqrt{3}$

करणीघात 2 वाली करणी को द्विघात करणी कहते हैं, उदाहरण– $\sqrt{3}$

Quartic Surd ***(चतुष्क घात करणी)*** A surd of order 4 is called quartic surd, e.g $\sqrt[4]{5}$.

करणीघात 4 वाली करणी को चतुष्क घात करणी कहते हैं, जैसे– $\sqrt[4]{5}$

Quadrilateral ***(चतुर्भुज)*** If polygon having four sides:

Examples of quadrilaterals are squares, rectangles, parallelogram and trapezoids.

चार भुजाओं वाला बहुभुज जैसे–आयत, वर्ग, समान्तर चतुर्भुज, समलम्ब आदि।

R

R–Abbreviation for the real numbers *वास्तविक संख्याओं का संक्षेप।*

Radian *(रेडियन)* A unit of angular measurement such that there are 2π radians in a complete circle.

One radian = $180 / \pi$ degrees

One radian is approximately $57.3°$

कोणीय मापन की इकाई, किसी पूर्ण वृत्त का कोणीय 2π रेडियन होता है।

$$\pi \text{ रेडियन} = 180°$$

$$1 \text{ रेडियन} = 57.3°$$

Radius *(त्रिज्या)* The distance from the centre to a point on a circle or the line segment from the center to a point a circle, 'A O' is called as radians of the circle with centre '0'. वृत्त केन्द्र से परिधि तक की दूरी त्रिज्या कहलाती है। चित्र में OA वृत्त त्रिज्या है।

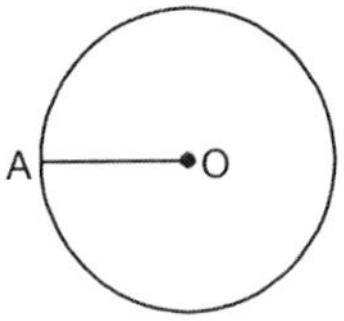

Fig. Radius

Radii of inscribed and circumscribed circumferences *(अन्तः वृत्त और परिवृत्त की त्रिज्याएँ)*

$$r = \frac{\Delta}{s}, \text{For } \Delta ABC, s = \frac{a+b+c}{2}$$

$$r = (s-b)\, tan\, \frac{A}{2} (s-b)\ Tan\, \frac{B}{2} = (s-c)\, Tan\, \frac{C}{2}$$

$$r = \sqrt{\frac{(s-a)(s-b)(s-c)}{s}}$$

Where r = radit of inscribed circle. जहाँ r = अन्तः वृत्त की त्रिज्या है।

$$R = \frac{a}{2\sin A} = \frac{b}{2\sin B} = \frac{c}{2\sin C}$$

$$R = \frac{a.b.c.}{4\Delta}$$

where R = radius of circumscribed circle. जहाँ R = परिवृत्त की त्रिज्या है।

Range *(परास)* The range of a set of numbers is the largest value in the let minus the smallest value in the set. किसी समुच्चय के अधिकतम मान के न्यूनतम मान का अन्तर ही परास है।

Rate *(दर)* A ratio comparing two different units. For example kilometres per hour and went beat per minute are rates. दो भिन्न मात्रक के तुलनात्मक अनुपात जैसे किलोमीटर, प्रतिघण्टा, प्रति मिनट हृदय स्पन्दन।

Ratio *(अनुपात)* A comparison expressed as indicated division For example, there is a ratio of three boys to the girls in our class is ($\frac{3}{2}$ or 3: 2). किसी दो राशि से तुलना करना अनुपात कहलाता है। यहाँ 3 : 2 तीन अनुपात 2 लिया जाता है।

Rationalising factor *(परिमेयकारी गुणक)* If the product of two surds is a rational number, then each one of them is called the rationalising factor of the other, e.g $\sqrt{5}$ is a rationalising factor of $3\sqrt{5}$, because $3\sqrt{5} \times \sqrt{5} = 3 \times 5 = 15$ which is a rational number. यदि दो करणीयों का गुणनफल एक परिमेय संख्या हो तो उनमें से प्रत्येक को दूसरे का परिमेयकारी गुणक कहते हैं।

Relation between Hyperbolic and Circular Function *(अति परवर्तीय व वृत्तीय फलन में सम्बन्ध)*

(*i*) $\sin(ix) = i \sin x$
$\sin h$ (ix $= i \sin x$
$\sin hx = -i \sin(ix)$
$\sin x = i \sin h(ix)$

(*ii*) $\cos(ix) = \cos hx$
$\cos h(ix) = \cos x$
$\cos h x = \cos(ix)$
$\cos x = \cos h(ix)$

(*iii*) $\tan(ix) = i \tan h(x)$
$\tan h(ix) = i \tan x$
$\tanh(x) = -i \tan(ix)$
$\tan(x) = -i \tan(ix)$

(*iv*) $\cot(ix) = -i \cot h x$
$\cot h(ix) = -i \cot x$
$\cot hx = i \cot(ix)$
$\cot x = 1 \cot h(ix)$

(*v*) $\sec(ix) = \sec h x$
$\sec h(ix) = \sec x$

(*vi*) $\text{cosec}(ix) = -i\, \text{cosec}\, h x$
$\text{cosec}(ix) = -i\, \text{cosec}\, x$

$\sec h\, x = \sec$ (ix) $\quad \text{cosec}\, h\, x = i\, \text{cosec}\,(ix)$

$\sec x = \sec h$ (ix) $\quad \text{cosec}\, x = i\, \text{cosec}\, h\,(ix)$

Rational numbers ***(परिमेय संख्या)*** A number that can be expressed as fraction or in the form of p/q or ratio of two numbers where the denominator does not equal to zero (0) i.e. $q \neq 0$ e.g. 5, $\frac{3}{2}$ 0.4, 0.23. etc. ऐसी संख्या जिसे p/q के रूप में लिखा जाय p और q पूर्णांक हो तथा q शून्य न हो। $\frac{4}{5}$ परिमेय संख्या है कि $\frac{4}{0}$ परिमेय नहीं हैं।

Rational Number (Concept) ***(तथ्य)***

1. A number of the form $\frac{p}{q}$, where p and q are integers and $q \neq 0$ is called rational number.
2. A rational number $\frac{p}{q}$ is said to be in standard form (10 west form) if q is positive and HCF of p and q is 1
3. 10 west form of $\frac{p}{q}$ is called standard form if $q > 0$
4. Every integer is a rational number and every fraction is a rational number.
5. If $\frac{p}{q}$ is a rational number and m is a non-zero integer than
$$\frac{p}{q} = \frac{p \times m}{q \times m}$$
6. If $\frac{p}{q}$ is a rational number and m is common divisor of p and q
than $$\frac{p}{q} = \frac{p \div m}{q \div m}$$
7. If $\frac{p}{q}$ and $\frac{r}{s}$ are two rational numbers, $q, s > 0$ then
(*i*) $\frac{p}{q} > \frac{r}{s}$, if $p \times s > q \times r$
8. If x and y are two rational numbers, then either
(*i*) $x > y$ or (*ii*) $x = y$ or (*iii*) $x < y$

9. Every rational number can be represented on a number line.
10. Every rational number has a obsolute value which is greater than zero or equal.

1. संख्या $\frac{p}{q}$, जहाँ p एवं q कोई भी पूर्णांक हैं तथा q शून्येतर है, परिमेय संख्या कहलाती है।
2. परिमेय संख्या $\frac{p}{q}$ सरलतम या लघुतम पदों में कहलाती है, यदि p तथा q का म.स. $=1$ हो।
3. लघुतम पदों में परिमेय संख्या $= \frac{p}{q}$ मानक रूप में कहलाती है, यदि $q > 0$ हो।
4. प्रत्येक पूर्णांक एक परिमेय संख्या है और प्रत्येक भिन्न भी एक परिमेय संख्या है।
5. यदि $\frac{p}{q}$ एक परिमेय संख्या है और एक शून्येतर पूर्णांक है, तो

$$\frac{p}{q} = \frac{p \times m}{q \times m}$$

6. यदि $\frac{p}{q}$ एक परिमेय संख्या है और m, p तथा q का सार्व भाजक है, तो होगा।

$$\frac{p}{q} = \frac{p \div m}{q \div m}$$

7. यदि $\frac{p}{q}$ एवं $\frac{r}{s}$ दो परिमेय संख्याएँ हैं तथा $q, s > 0$, तब $\frac{p}{q} > \frac{r}{s}$ होगा, यदि $p \times s > q \times r$ हो।
8. यदि x एवं y दो परिमेय संख्याएँ हैं, तो या तो (*i*) $x > y$ या (*ii*) $x = y$ या फिर (*iii*) $x < y$ होता है।
9. प्रत्येक परिमेय संख्या, संख्या रेखा पर निरूपित की जा सकती है।
10. प्रत्येक परिमेय संख्या का एक निरपेक्ष मान होता है, जो शून्य या शून्य से बड़ा होता है।

Ray *(रे)* तीर A line has one end point but continues infinitely in the other direction. ऐसी रेखा जिसमें एक अन्त बिन्दु हों।

Real number *(वास्तविक संख्याए)* Any number, positive or negative, that is not imaginary. $\frac{4}{3}$, 2.5, 0 and – 8 are all examples of real numbers or

The union of the set of rational numbers and irrational numbers.

ऐसी संख्याए जो काल्पनिक न हो भले ही धनात्मक या ऋणात्मक हो।

Real variable ***(वास्तविक चर)*** A variable whose value ranges over the real numbers. चर जिसका मूल्य परास वास्तविक संख्या के ऊपर होता है।

Reciprocal ***(विलोम)*** The reciprocal of a number a, is $\frac{1}{a}$ (a, can not be zero). किसी संख्या का विलोम $\frac{1}{a}$ होगा।

Rectangle ***(आयत)*** A quadrilateral that has four 90 degrees angles. Squares are a type of rectangle, or A parallelogram whose opposite sides are equal are each angle in 90°. आयत एक समान्तर चतुर्भुज है, जिसकी आमने सामने की भुजाएँ बराबर होती है। प्रत्येक कोण 90° का होता है।

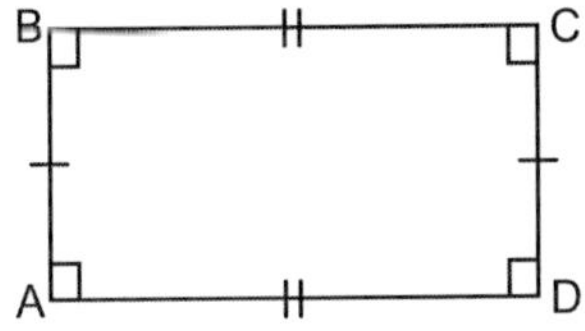

Fig. Rectangle

Rectangle number ***(आयत संख्या)*** Refers to a number that has more than two factors. Such a number can be represented by rectangular configuartion of dots e.g. वह संख्या जिसके दो या दो से अधिक खण्ड हो, इन खण्डों की संख्या को आयत संख्या कहते हैं। जैसे–

$18 = 2 \times 9 \quad \text{or } 3 \times 6$

Rectangular axis ***(आयतीय अक्ष)*** The x and y axis are called rectangular axis as they are $\perp$ to each other. x और y आयतीय अक्ष कहलाती हैं। ये एक दूसरे पर लम्ब होती हैं।

Rectangular coordinates ***(आयतीय निर्देशांक)*** These are the cartesian coordinates with axis of coordinates mutually perpendicular. यह कार्तीय निर्देशांक x अक्ष के साथ लम्बवत निर्देशांक है।

Right angle ***(समकोण)*** An angle formed by two perpendicular lines ; a 90° angle. वह कोण जो 90 अंश का हो पर दो रेखाएं लम्बवत् हो।

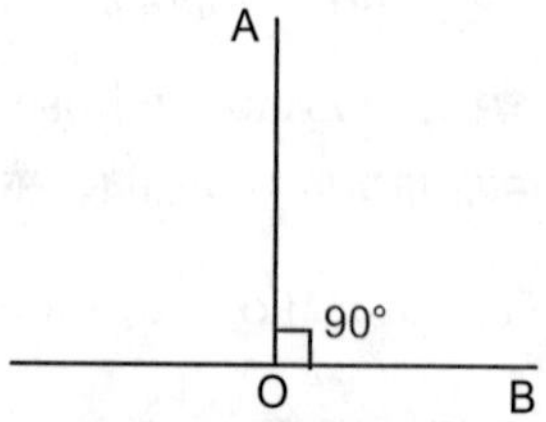

Fig. Right angle

Right angled triangle ***(समकोण त्रिभुज)*** It is a triangle in which one of the angles is 90°. वह त्रिभुज जिसमें एक कोण 90° हो। समकोण त्रिभुज कहलाता है।

$$\angle B = 90°$$

Δ ABC is a right angled triangle. Δ ABC समकोण त्रिभुज है।

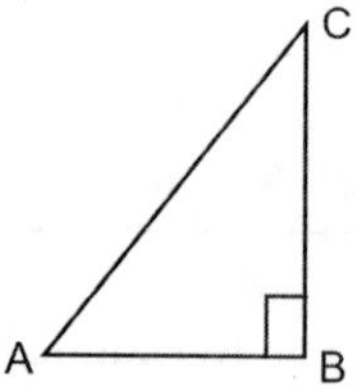

Fig. Right angled triangle

Right circular cone ***(समकोणीय शंकु)*** A right circular cone is a solid generated by the revolution of a right angled triangle about one of the sides Containing the right angle. कोई समकोणीय त्रिभुज, समकोण बनाते हुए, इसकी एक भुजा के परित घूमता है। तब इस प्रकार निर्मित ठोस समकोणीय शंकु कहा जाता है।

Right Prism ***(लम्ब प्रिज्म)***

(*i*) Lateral surface area = Perimeter of base × Height

$$A_l = P_B \times h$$

पार्श्व पृष्ठ का क्षेत्रफल = आधार की परिमाप × ऊँचाई

(*ii*) Total surface area = 2 × area of one end × lateral surface area

$$A_T = A_L \times 2\,A_o$$

सम्पूर्ण पृष्ठ का क्षेत्रफल = 2 × एक किनारे का क्षेत्रफल × पार्श्व पृष्ठ का क्षेत्रफल

(*iii*) Volume = area of base × height

$$V = A_o \times h$$

आयतन = आधार का क्षेत्र. × ऊँचाई

Right Pyramid ***(लम्ब पिरामिड)***

(*i*) Cateral/Curved surface area

$$= \frac{1}{2} \text{ (Perimeter of base)} \times \text{Slant height}$$

वक्र पृष्ठ का क्षे० = $\frac{1}{2}$ आधार का क्षे० × त्रियक ऊँचाई

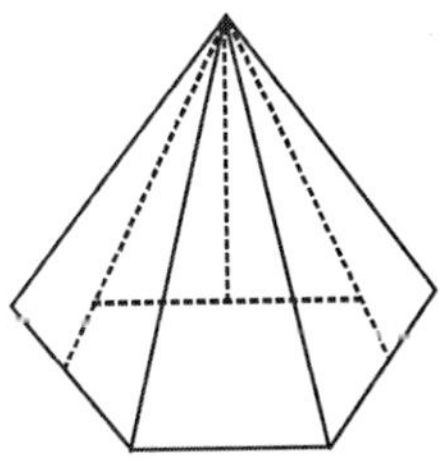

Fig. Right Pyramid

(*ii*) Total surface area = area of base + lateral surface area

$$A_T = A_o + A_L$$

सम्पूर्ण पृष्ठ का क्षे० = आधार का क्षे० × सम्पूर्ण पृष्ठ का क्षे०

(*iii*) volume = $\frac{1}{3}$ (Area of base) × height

$$V = \frac{1}{3} A_o \times h$$

आयतन = $\frac{1}{3}$ आधार का क्षे. × ऊँचाई

Ring ***(छल्ला)*** It is shown as a shaded region

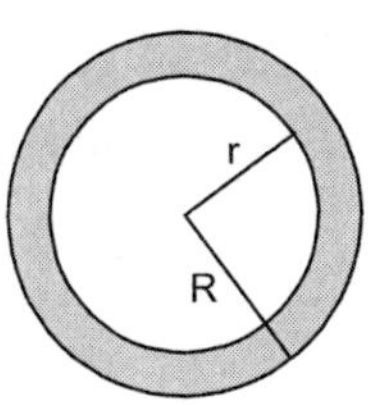

Area of ring (छल्ले का क्षे.) $= \pi (R^2 - r^2)$

$= \pi (R + r)(R - r)$

Perimeter (परिमाप) $= 2\pi (R + r)$

Properties ***(गुण)*** If is cone that has a circular a base and axis is perpendicular to base.

(*i*) Volume = $\frac{1}{3}\pi r^2 . h$

(*ii*) Slant height = $\sqrt{h^2 + r^2}$

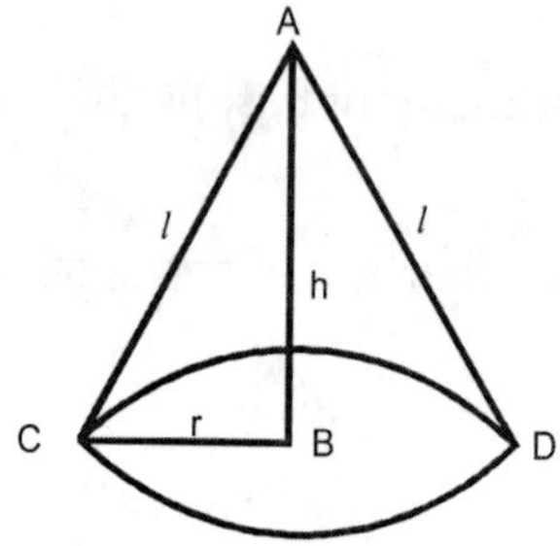

Fig. Properties

(*iii*) Total surface Area = $\pi r\ (l + r)$

(*iv*) Lateral / curved surface area = $\pi . r . l$

वह शंकु जिसका आधार वृत्त हो तथा आधार के लम्बवत अक्ष हो।

(*i*) आयतन = $\frac{1}{3}\pi r^2 . h$

(*ii*) तिरछी ऊँचाई = $\sqrt{h^2 + r^2}$

(*iii*) सम्पूर्ण पृष्ठ = $\pi r\ (l + r)$

(*iv*) वक्रपृष्ठ = $\pi . r . l$

Right circular cylinder ***(समकोणीय बेलन)*** It is a solid described by the revolution of a rectangle about one of its sides which remain fixed.

(*i*) Curved/lateral surface = $2\pi rh$

(*ii*) Total surface area = $2\ \pi r\ (r + h)$

(*iii*) Volume = $\pi r^2 h$

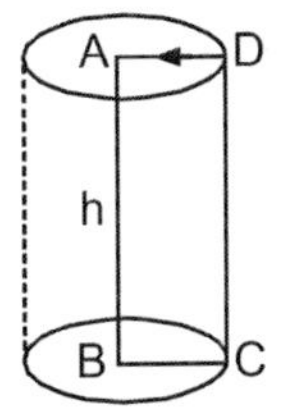

Fig. Right circular cylinder

एक समकोणीय वृत्तकार बेलन एक ठोस होता है। जो किसी आयत के इसकी एक भंजा के परितः घूमने से बनता है।

(*i*) वक्रपृष्ठ = $2\pi rh$

(*ii*) सम्पूर्ण पृष्ठ = $2\,\pi r\,(r + h)$

(*iii*) आयतन = $\pi r^2 h$

Right triangle ***(समकोण त्रिभुज)*** A triangle that contains a light angle then ΔABC is right angle triangle, with right angle at 'B'. वह त्रिभुज जिसका एक कोण 90° हो।

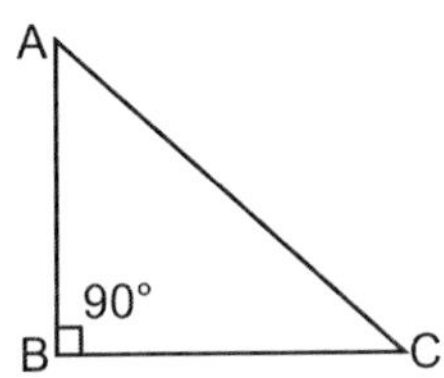

Fig. Right triangle

Root ***(मूल)*** The root of an equation is the same as the solution to the equation. समीकरण का हल ही उसका मूल होता है।

Root of unity ***(इकाई के मूल)*** A solution of the equation $x^n = 1$, where n is *a* positive integer. $x^n - 1$ समीकरण का हल, जहाँ n एक धनात्मक पूर्णांक है।

Root mean square (rms) ***(वर्ग माध्य मूल)*** The rms of a list is the square root of the mean of the squares of the elements in the list. To compute the rms of a list, you square all the enteries, then average the numbers you get, and finally take the square-root of the average. श्रेणी के अवयवों के वर्ग का माध्य निकालकर उनका वर्ग मूल करके किसी श्रेणी का वर्ग माध्य मूल ज्ञात किया जाता है।

Roman numerals ***(रोमन अंक)*** A system of writing integers, used by the Romans, in which I denote 1, V = 5 , X = 10, L = 50, C = 100, D = 500, M = 1000 etc. रोमन अंक जैसे– I = 1, V = 5, C = 100 आदि।

Roman Numerals	Equivalent
I	1
II	2
III	3
IV	4
V	5
VI	6
VII	7
VIII	8
IX	9
X	10
XI	11
XII	12
XIII	13
XIV	14
XV	15
XVI	16
XVII	17
XVIII	18
XIX	19
XX	20
XXX	30
XL	40
L	50
LX	60
LXX	70
LXXX	80
XC	90
C	100
C C	200

C C C	300
C D	400
D	500
D C	600
D C C	700
D C C C	800
C M	900
M	1000
M D	1500

Root of a complex number ***(सम्मिश्र संख्या का वर्गमूल)*** If 'a' is a complex number = p (cos θ + *i* sin θ). ('a' सम्मिश्र संख्या है।)

Then (तब)
$$a^{\frac{1}{n}} = z = \sqrt[n]{p}\left[\cos\left(\frac{\theta}{n}+k.\frac{2\pi}{n}\right) + i\sin\left(\frac{\theta}{n}+k.\frac{2\pi}{n}\right)\right]$$

where (जहाँ) k = 0, 1, 2, ... $(n-1)$ gives the n roots.

Rotational Transformations ***(घर्णीय परिवर्तन)***

If coordinates of any point $P(x, y)$ with refrence to new axis will be (x', y') then

	$x\downarrow$	$y\downarrow$
$x'\rightarrow$	$\cos\theta$	$\sin\theta$
$y'\rightarrow$	$-\sin\theta$	$\cos\theta$

Rules of derivation ***(निगमन के नियम)*** If $f(x)$ and $g(x)$ are two functions that can be derived in x, then we have यदि दो फलन $f(x)$ और $g(x)$ हैं x का निगमन करें तब

$$[f(x) \pm g(x)]' = f(x) \pm g(x)$$
$$[f(x).\, g(x)]^1 = f(x).\, g(x) + f(x).\, g'(x)$$
$$\left|\frac{f(x)}{g(x)}\right| = \frac{f'(x).\, g(x) - f(x)g'(x)}{[g(x)]^2}, g(x) = 0$$

If f is a functions of t and t is a function of x, then

$$\frac{dy}{dx} = \frac{dy}{dt} \times \frac{dt}{dx} \text{ or } \frac{dy}{dx} = \frac{dy}{dt} l \frac{dx}{dt}$$

Derivatives of some important functions
(कुछ फलनों के अवकलन गुणांक)

$\frac{d}{dx}(x^n) = n.x^{n-1}$ $\frac{d}{dx}(a^x) = a^x \log a$

$\frac{d}{dx}(\sin x) = \cos x$ $\frac{d}{dx}(e^x) = e^x$

$\frac{d}{dx}(\cos x) = -\sin x$ $\frac{d}{dx}(\log x) = \frac{1}{x}$

$\frac{d}{dx}(\tan x) = \sec^2 x$ $\frac{d}{dx}(\text{sin-1 x}) = \frac{1}{\sqrt{1-x^2}}$

$\frac{d}{dx}(\text{cot x}) = -\text{cosec2}\ x$ $\frac{d}{dx}(\cos^{-1} x) = \frac{-1}{\sqrt{1-x^2}}$

$\frac{d}{dx}(\sec x) = \sec x \tan x$ $\frac{d}{dx}(\tan^{-f} x) = \frac{1}{1+x^2}$

$\frac{d}{dx}(\operatorname{cosec} x) = -\operatorname{cosec} x \cot x$ $\frac{d}{dx}(\cot^{-1} x) = \frac{1}{x\sqrt{x^2-1}}$

$\frac{d}{dx}\left(\sqrt{x}\right) = \frac{1}{2\sqrt{x}}$ $\frac{d}{dx}(\sec^{-1} x) = \frac{1}{x\sqrt{x^2-1}}$

$\frac{d}{dx}\left(\log_a^x\right) = \frac{1}{x} \log a$ $\frac{d}{dx}(\operatorname{cosec}^{-1} x) = \frac{-1}{x\sqrt{x^2-1}}$

Note : Remember $\frac{d}{dx}(\sin x) = \cos x$, but

$\frac{d}{dx}(\sin y) = \cos y \frac{dy}{dx}$ as by chain rule

$$\frac{d}{dx}(\sin y) = \frac{d}{dy}(\sin y). \frac{dy}{dx}$$

S

Scalar *(अदिश)* A real number. एक वास्तविक संख्या।

Scalar quantity *(अदिश राशि)* A quantity that has magnitude but no direction, such as mass, and density. ऐसी राशियाँ जिसमें से केवल परिमाण का बोध हो। जैसे द्रव्यमान, घनत्व।

Scalar matrix *(अदिश आव्यूह)* A diagonal matrix whose all the diagonal elements are equal is called a scalar matrix e.g.

$$\begin{vmatrix} 3 & 0 & 0 \\ 0 & 3 & 0 \\ 0 & 0 & 3 \end{vmatrix}$$

यदि किसी वर्ग आव्यूह में मुख्य विकर्ण पर स्थित तत्व बराबर हों और शेष सभी शून्य हो तो उसे अदिश आव्यूह कहते हैं।

Scale *(स्केल)* A system of marks in a given order, and at known intervals, used on rulers, thermometers etc. as, an aid in measuring various quantities. संख्या-प्रणाली का क्रम नापने का चिन्ह, जो कि थर्मोमीटर, रूलर आदि में प्रयुक्त होता है।

Scalar triple product *(अदिश तिगुणन)*

If $a = a_1 l + a_2 m + a_3 n$, $b = b_1 l + b_2 m + b_3 n$
and $c = c_1 l + c_2 m + c_3 n$, then

$$[abc] = \begin{vmatrix} a_1 & a_2 & a_3 \\ b_1 & b_2 & b_3 \\ c_1 & c_2 & c_3 \end{vmatrix} = [lmn]$$

- **Properties of scalar product** *(अदिश गुणन के गुण)*

  (*i*) $(a.\,b).\,b$ is not defined

  (*ii*) $(a + b)^2 = a^2 + 2a.b + b^2$

  (*iii*) $(a - b)^2 = a^2 - 2a.b + b^2$

  (*iv*) $(a + b)\,.\,(a - b) = a^2 - b^2 = a^2 - b^2$

(*v*) $|a+b| = |a| + |b| \Rightarrow a \,||\, b$

(*vi*) $|a+b|^2 = |a|^2 + |b|^2 \Rightarrow a \perp b$

(*vii*) $|a+b| = |a-b| = a \perp b$

Scalene-triangle *(विषमबाहु त्रिभुज)* A triangle with three unequal sides. ऐसा त्रिभुज जिसकी तीनों भुजाएं असमान हो।

Secant *(छेदन रेखा)* A straight line of unlimited length cutting a given curve. किसी दिये गये वक्र की असमीमित लम्बाई वाली एक सीधी रेखा काटती हुई।

Second *(सेकण्ड)* The unit of measure of an angle that is $\frac{1}{60}$ of a minute.

कोण माने की इकाई $1^1 = 60''$

1 मिनट = 60 सेकण्ड

Secondary Data *(गौण आँकड़े)* The data which are not originally collected rather obtained from published or unpublished sources are known as secondary data. ऐसे आँकड़े को जो एक व्यक्ति द्वारा संग्रह किए गए हों और अन्य अनुसंधान-कर्ता अपने अध्ययन में प्रयोग कर लें, गौण आँकड़े कहलाते हैं।

Sector *(सेक्टर)* A region bounded by two radii of a circle and an are whose end points lie on those radii. किसी वृत्त की दो त्रिज्याओं द्वारा घिरा हुआ भाग जिसके अंतबिन्दु उन त्रिज्याओं पर पड़ते हों।

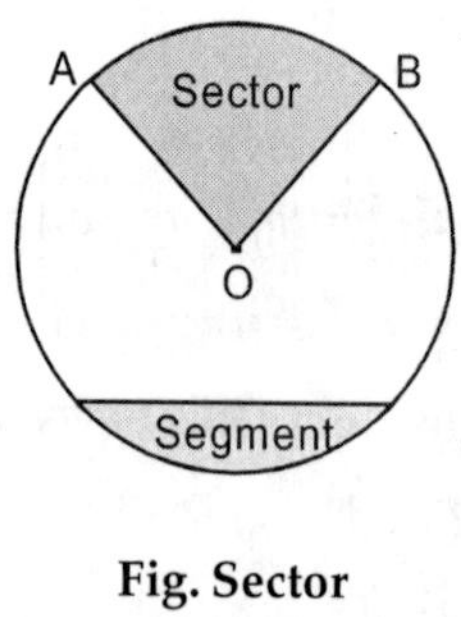

Fig. Sector

Segment *(खण्ड)* A past out off from any figure by a line or plans (or planes). किसी रेखा द्वारा काटा गया किसी आकृति का भाग।

✤ **Segment** (*i*) major segment

= ADB

(*ii*) Minor segment

= ACB

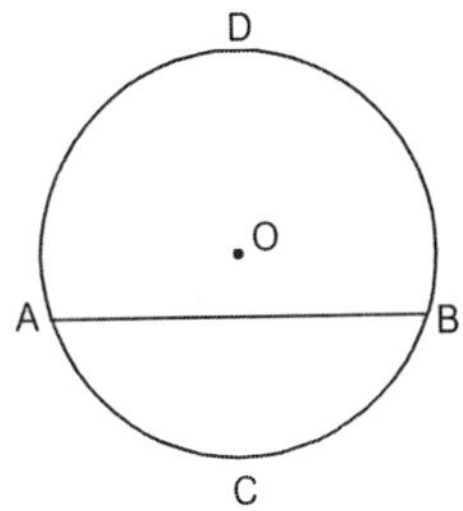

Fig. Segment

Skew lines ***(त्रियक रेखायें)*** Non - intersecting, non parallel lines in space. असमान्तर एवं अप्रतिच्छेदी रेखाओं को त्रियक रेखायें कहते हैं।

Selling Price ***(विक्रय मूल्य)*** The price at which an article is sold is known as its selling price. The selling price is abbreviated as S.P. जिस मूल्य पर कोई वस्तु बेची जाती है, वह उस वस्तु का विक्रय मूल्य कहलाता है। इसे S.P. से प्रदर्शित करते हैं।

Sequence ***(क्रम)*** An ordered set of numbers derived according to a rule, each member being determined either directly or from the preceding terms. किसी नियम के अनुसार प्राप्त क्रमिक समूह की संख्यायें, जिसमें से प्रत्येक पिछले पद से प्राप्त हो अथवा सीधे-सीधे।

Series ***(श्रेणी)*** The sum of a finite or infinite sequence. सीमित अथवा असीमित क्रमों का योग।

Set ***(समुच्चय)*** A set is a collection of thing, with out regard to their order. वस्तुओं के सुपरिभाषित समूह या संग्रह को समुच्चय कहते हैं।

Similar figures ***(समरूप चित्र)*** Two geometric figures are similar if their sides are in proportion and all their angles are the same Here $\Delta ABC \rightarrow (\Delta PQR$, sin $\frac{AB}{BC} = \frac{PQ}{QR}$, and $\angle A = \angle P$, $\angle B = \angle Q$ etc.

दो ज्यामितीय आकृतियां समरूप कहलायेंगी यदि उनकी भुजायें समानुपातिक होंगी और उनके कोण बराबर होंगे।

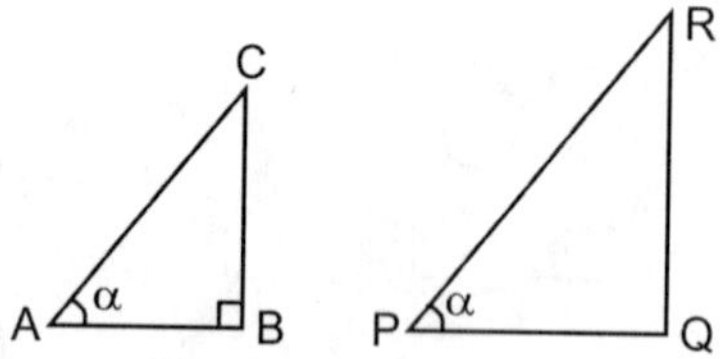

Fig. Similar figures

Similar surds ***(समरूप करणियाँ)*** Surds having same irrational factors are called similar or like surds. वे करणियाँ जिनके अपरिमेय गुणनखंड समान हों समरूप करणियाँ कहलाती हैं, जैसे $\sqrt{3},\ \sqrt[2]{3},\ \frac{1}{5}\sqrt{3}$

Semi circle ***(अर्धवृत्त)*** A semi -circle is one half of a circle (either) of the parts of a circle which are out off by a diameter). किसी वृत्त का एक-आधा भाग अर्धवृत्त कहलाता है।

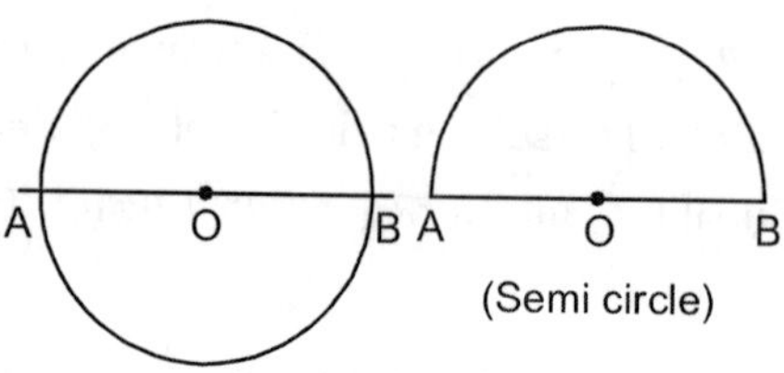

Fig. Semi circle

Separation of Inverse Trigonometric and Inverse Hyperbolic functions ***(व्युत्क्रमानुपाती त्रिकोणमितीय और अति पर दलीय फलन को अलग करना)***

(*i*) $\tan^{-1}(x+iy) = \frac{1}{2}\tan^{-1}$

$$\left(\frac{2x}{1-x^2-y^2}\right) + \frac{1}{2}\tan^{-1}\left(\frac{2y}{1+x^2+y^2}\right)$$

$$= \frac{1}{2}\tan^{-1}\left(\frac{2x}{1-x^2-y^2}\right) + \frac{1}{4}\log\left[\frac{x^2+(1+y)^2}{x^2+(1-y)^2}\right]$$

(*ii*) $\sin^{-1}(\cos\theta + i\sin\theta) = \cos^{-1}\left(\sqrt{\sin\theta}\right) + i\sinh^{-1}\left(\sqrt{\sin\theta}\right)$

OR

$$= \cos^{-1}\left(\sqrt{\sin\theta}\right) + i\log\left(\sqrt{\sin\theta} + \sqrt{1+\sin\theta}\right)$$

(*iii*) $\cos^{-1}(\cos\theta + i\sin\theta) = \sin^{-1}\left(\sqrt{\sin\theta}\right) - i\sinh^{-1}\left(\sqrt{\sin\theta}\right)$

or

$$= \sin^{-1}\left(\sqrt{\sin\theta}\right) - i\log\left(\sqrt{\sin\theta} + \sqrt{1+\sin\theta}\right)$$

(*iv*) $\tan^{-1}(\cos\theta + i\sin\theta) = \frac{\pi}{4} + \frac{1}{4}\log\left(\frac{1+\sin\theta}{1-\sin\theta}\right)$, $(\cos q) > 0$ and

$$\tan^{-1}(\cos\theta + i\sin\theta) = \left(\frac{\pi}{4} + \right)\frac{1}{4}\log\left(\frac{1+\sin\theta}{1-\sin\theta}\right), (\cos\theta) < 0$$

Shortest distance ***(न्यूनतम दूरी)*** Suppose the equation of the lines are (रेखाओं का समीकरण)

$$\frac{x-\alpha}{l} = \frac{y-\beta}{m} = \frac{z-\gamma}{n}$$

and $$\frac{x-\alpha'}{l'} = \frac{y-\beta'}{m'} = \frac{z-\gamma'}{n'}$$

Then $(\alpha-\alpha')(mn'-m'n)+(\beta-\beta')$

$$\text{S.D. न्यूनतम दूरी} = \frac{(nl'-n'l)+(\gamma-\gamma')(lm'-l'm)}{\sqrt{\Sigma(mn'-m'n)^2}}$$

$$= \begin{vmatrix} \alpha-\alpha' & \beta-\beta' & \gamma-\gamma' \\ l & m & n \\ l' & m' & n' \end{vmatrix}$$

$$= \sqrt{\Sigma(mn'-mn)^2}$$

Similarity ***(समरूपता)*** The property of being similar is called similarity. समरूप होने का गुण, समरूपता कहलाता है।

Simplification ***(सरल करना)*** The process of reducing an expression or a statement to a brifer form. किसी पद व कथन को छोटा कर उसे सूक्ष्म रूप में लाना।

Simplest form of a rational number ***(परिमेय संख्या का लघुत्तम रूप)***:

A rational number in the form of $\frac{x}{y}$ is said to be in its simplest form if x and y are integers having no common factor other than 1 and $y \neq 0$ $\frac{x}{y}$ रूप वाली परिमेय संख्या जिसमें x और y का 1 के अतिरिक्त कोई भी समगुणन खण्ड नहीं होता है। जैसे– $\frac{6}{9}$ का लघुतम रूप $-\frac{2}{3}$ है।

- **Standard form of a rational number** ***(परिमेय संख्या का मानक रूप)*** : A rational number in the simplest form or lowest form is said to be in the standard form if the denominator is positive. लघुतम पद वाली परिमेय संख्या का हर धनात्मक है तो इसे संख्या का मानक रूप कहते है जैसे $\frac{-26}{39}$ का मानक रूप $\frac{-2}{3}$ है।

Sign of trigonometrical ratios ***(त्रिकोणमितीय अनुपातिक चिन्ह)***

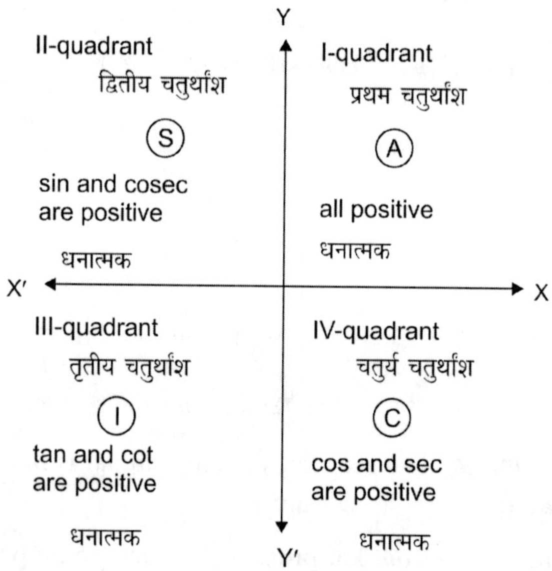

Some useful identities ***(कुछ सर्वसमिकाएँ)***

(*i*) $\tan(A+B+C) = \dfrac{\sum \tan A - \tan A \tan B \tan C}{1 - \sum \tan A . \tan B}$

(*ii*) $\tan\theta = \cot\theta - 2\cot 2\theta$

(*iii*) $\tan 3\theta = \tan\theta . \tan(60-\theta) . \tan(60+\theta)$

(*iv*) $\tan(A+B) - \tan A - \tan B = \tan A . \tan B . \tan(A+B)$

(*v*) $\sin\theta \sin(60-\theta) \sin(60+\theta) = \dfrac{1}{4}\sin 3\theta$

(*vi*) $\cos\theta \cos(60-\theta) \cos(60+\theta) = \dfrac{1}{4}\cos 3\theta$

Some useful series ***(कुछ महत्वपूर्ण सारिणी)***

(*i*) $\sin\alpha + \sin(\alpha+\beta) + \sin(\alpha+2\beta) + ... +$ to n terms

$$= \frac{\sin\left[\alpha + \left(\frac{n-1}{2}\right)\beta\right]\left[\sin\left(\frac{n\beta}{2}\right)\right]}{\sin\left(\frac{\beta}{2}\right)}; \beta \neq 2n\pi$$

(*ii*) $\cos\alpha + \cos(\alpha+\beta) + \cos(\alpha+2\beta) + ... +$ to n terms

$$= \frac{\cos\left[\alpha + \left(\frac{n-1}{2}\right)\beta\right]\left[\sin\left(\frac{n\beta}{2}\right)\right]}{\sin\left(\frac{\beta}{2}\right)}; B \neq 2n\pi$$

(*iii*) $p = \cos\alpha . \cos 2\alpha . \cos 2\alpha ... \cos(2^{n-1}\alpha)$

$$= \begin{cases} \dfrac{\sin 2^n \alpha}{2^n \sin\alpha}, if\, \alpha \neq n\pi \\ 1, if\, \alpha = 2k\pi \\ -1, if\, \alpha = (2k-1)\pi \end{cases}$$

Slope ***(ढाल)*** The slope of a line is the change in the vertical coordinates/ the change in the horizontal coordinates of any two points on the line. लम्बवत निर्देशाकों के परिवर्तन से किसी रेखा में उत्पन्न झुकाव को उस रेखा का ढाल कहा जाता है।

Solid geometry ***(ठोस ज्यामिति)*** The area of geometry that envolves 3d objects. त्रिविमीय ज्यामितीय वस्तुओं का क्षेत्रफल।

Space ***(स्थान)*** A three-dimensional region, Any abstract space. कोई त्रिविमीय क्षेत्र।

Speed ***(गति, चाल)*** Distance passed over per unit time. गतिमान वस्तु द्वारा निश्चित समय से तय की दूरी उस वस्तु की चाल कहलाती है।

i.e., $S = \frac{D}{T}$ when S = speed (चाल)

D = Distance (दूरी)

T = time (समय)

Sphere ***(गोला)*** A three dimensional object in which all points are equal distance from the centre a ball share. एक त्रिविमीय वस्तु के सभी बिन्दु केन्द्र से समान दूरी पर हो।

Square ***(वर्ग)*** A quadrilateral with four equal sides and 4 right angles. चर्तुर्भज जिसकी चारों भुजाएं बराबर हो तथा प्रत्येक कोण 90° अश का हो।

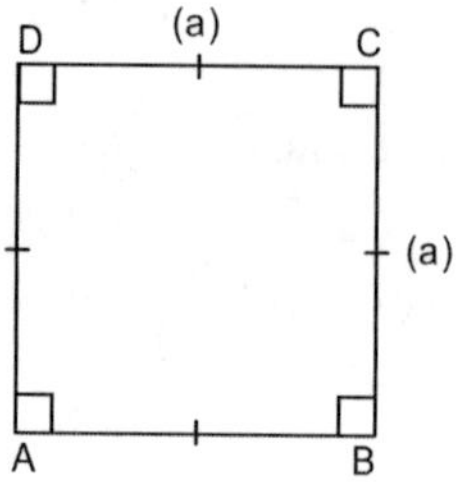

Square root ***(वर्गमूल)*** The square root of a given number is that number which when multiplied with itself produces the given number. वह पूर्णाक जिसे स्वयं से गुणा करने पर दी गई संख्या प्राप्त होती है, तो उसे वर्गमूल कहते है ।

- **Square root of a complex number** ***(मिश्र संख्या का वर्ग मूल)***

The square root of $z = a + ib$ is

$$\sqrt{a+ib} = \pm\left[\sqrt{\frac{|z|+a}{2}} + i\sqrt{\frac{|z|-a}{2}}\right] \text{ for } b > 0 \text{ or}$$

$$\pm\left[\sqrt{\frac{|z|+a}{2}} - i\sqrt{\frac{|z|-a}{2}}\right] \text{ for } b < 0$$

T

Trigenometric function ***(त्रिकोणियमिति फलन)*** A trigonometric function of an angle which is defined as the ratio of the length of the leg opposite to the leg adjacent to an angle in its right triangle Also. किसी कोण का त्रिकोणमिति फलन जो विपरीत भुजाओं की लम्बाई का अनुपात होता है।

Tangent ***(स्पर्श रेखा)*** A tangent is a straight line touching a circle at one and only one point and which is perpendicular to the radians of the circle.

वह रेखा जो वृत्त के परिधि पर एक और केवल एक ही बिन्दू को स्पर्श करती है । वृत्त की त्रिज्या स्पर्श रेखा पर लम्ब होती है ।

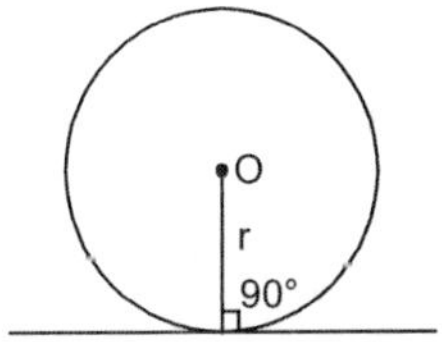

Fig. Tangent

Terminating decimal ***(भाज्य दशमलव)*** A decimal that contains a finite number of digits for example, 0.408 is terminating decimal. ऐसा दशमलव अन्तर हो, किन्तु विभाजित हो जाए।

Tetrahedron ***(चतुषफलकीय)*** A four sided polyhedron. एक बहुभुज जिसमें चार भुजायें होती हैं।

Theorems ***(प्रमेय)*** The conclusion obtained through logical reasoning based on previously proved results & some axioms constitute a statement which is know as a theorem or a proposition. अभिगृहीतों पर आधारित तर्कसंगत विवेचन जिसका निगमन कर सकें, इस प्रक्रिया को गुण धर्मों या परिणामों को सिद्ध करना कहते हैं, और इस प्रकार सिद्ध किए गए परिणामों को प्रमेय कहते हैं।

Theorems of limit ***(सीमाओं पर प्रमेय)*** If $f(x)$ and $\phi(x)$ are two functions and- (यदि $f(x)$ और $\phi(x)$ दो फलन है और) $\lim_{n\to a} f(x) = A$, $\lim_{n\to a} \phi(x) = A \pm B$, then (तब)

(*i*) $\lim\limits_{x\to a} \{f(x) + \phi(x)\} = \lim\limits_{x\to a} f(x) \pm \lim\limits_{x\to a} \phi(x) = A \pm B,$

(ii) $\lim_{x \to a} (kf(x)) = K \lim_{x \to a} f(x) = KA;$

(iii) $\lim_{x \to a} \{f(x).\,\phi(x)\} = \lim_{x \to a} f(x).\, \lim_{x \to a} \phi(x) = A\,B.$

(iv) $\lim_{x \to a} \frac{f(x)}{\phi(x)} = \frac{\lim_{x \to a} f(x)}{\lim_{x \to a} \phi(x)} = \frac{A}{B}$ if (यदि) $B \neq 0$.

(v) $\lim_{x \to a} f(x) = \lim_{h \to 0} f(h + a).$

Thousand ***(हजार)*** Ten hundred (1000). 1 हजार = 10,000 (दस हजार)

Time : ***(अवधि)*** **Time is the measurement of how long something lasts.**

$$\text{Time} = \frac{\text{Distance Travelled}}{\text{Speed}}$$

$$\text{समय} = \frac{\text{तय की गई दूरी}}{\text{चाल}}$$

Transitive property ***(संक्रमक गुण)*** The property that state that if a = b b = c then a = c. ऐसा गुण जो यह दर्शाये कि यदि a = b, b = c है तब a = c होगा।

Transversal line ***(तिर्यक रेखा)*** In geometry, it given two more lines in the plane then a transversal line is line distiance from the original line and in a single point. Here PQ is transversal in at M and N respectively. दो समान्तर रेखाओं के काटने वाली चित्र में PQ तिर्यक रेखा है।

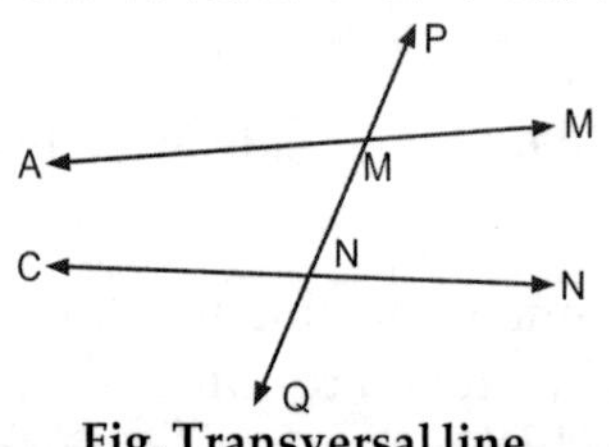

Fig. Transversal line

Trapezium ***(समलम्ब चतुर्भज)*** A quadrilateral in which one pair of opposite sides is parallel. ऐसा चतुर्भुज जिसमें कोई एक जोड़ी सम्मुख भुजाएं समान्तर हो। चित्र में ABCD समलम्ब है। जहाँ AB || DC.

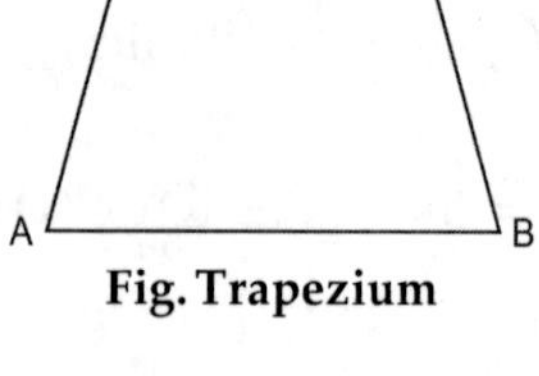

Fig. Trapezium

Triangle ***(त्रिभुज)*** If AB, (are three non- collinear points A fig formed by going three non Collinear points.

Then the figure made up by the three line segments AB, BC, and CA is called triangle with vertices A, B, and C.

तीन भुजाओं से घिरी हुई आकृति त्रिभुज कहलाती है। त्रिभुज में तीन कोण, तीन भुजाएं होती है।

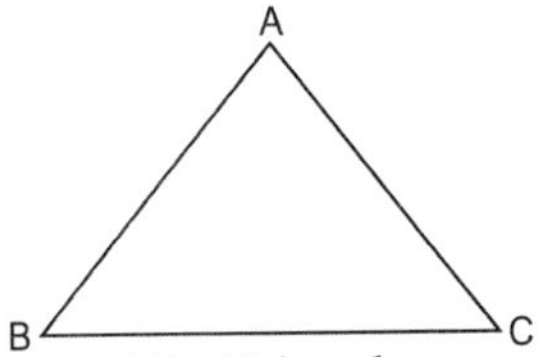

Fig. Triangle

Triangular number *()* A number of the form $n\ (n+1)\ /2$. वह संख्या जो $n(n+2)/2$ के रूप में हो।

Trigonometric rations ***(त्रिकोणमितीय अनुपात)*** The ratios of the lengths of pairs of sides in a right triangle; *i.e.*, sine, cosine and tangent.

$\frac{a}{\sin A} = \frac{b}{\sin B} = \frac{c}{\sin C}$ जहाँ a, b, c त्रिभुज की भुजाएं हो।

Trigonometric Ratios of 0^0 and 90^0 ***(0^0 और 90^0 के त्रिकोणमितीय अनुपात)***

θ T. ratios	0^0	30^0	45^0	60^0	90^0
sin θ	0	$\frac{1}{2}$	$\frac{1}{\sqrt{2}}$	$\frac{\sqrt{3}}{2}$	1
cos θ	1	$\frac{\sqrt{3}}{2}$	$\frac{1}{\sqrt{2}}$	$\frac{1}{2}$	0
tan θ	0	$\frac{1}{\sqrt{3}}$	1	$\sqrt{3}$	Not defined अपरिभाषित
cosec θ	Not defined अपरिभाषित	2	$\sqrt{2}$	$\frac{2}{\sqrt{3}}$	1
sec θ	1	$\frac{2}{\sqrt{3}}$	$\sqrt{2}$	2	Not defined अपरिभाषित
cot θ	Not defined अपरिभाषित	$\sqrt{3}$	1	$\frac{1}{\sqrt{3}}$	0

Trigonometric Ratios of Complementary Angle *(पूरक कोण का त्रिकोणमितीय अनुपात)*–

$$\sin(90-\theta) = \cos\theta.$$
$$\cos(90-\theta) = \sin\theta.$$
$$\tan(90-\theta) = \cot\theta.$$
$$\text{cosec}(90-\theta) = \sec\theta.$$
$$\sec(90-\theta) = \text{cosec}\,\theta.$$
$$\cot(90-\theta) = \tan\theta.$$

Trigonometrical function or circular function *(त्रिकोणमितीय फलन या वृत्तीय फलन)* such as $\sin x$, $\cos x$, $\cos 2x + \tan x$, $\sec x$, $\text{cosec}\, x$, $\tan x$ etc.

Trigonometry *(त्रिकोणमिति)* The branch of mathematics in involving triangles that combines arithmetic, algebra, and geometry It is used in surveying navigation and physics. गणित की वह शाखा जो त्रिभुज के बारे में अंकगणितीय, बीजगणितीय तथा रेखा गणितीय अध्ययन कराये।

Trinomial *तीन-पद-वाला व्यंजक)* An algebric expression consisting of 3 terms. तीन पदों वाला बहुपद $ax + by + c$ or $x + y + z$.

Trinomial surds *(त्रिपदी करणी)* An expression consisting of three terms atleast two of which are monomial surds, is called a trinomial surd. वह करणी जिसमें कम से कम तीन पद हों और जिनमें से कम से कम दो एक पदी करणियाँ हो

जैसे– $\sqrt{2}+\sqrt{3}+\sqrt{5}$

Twin primes *(युगल अभाज्य)* Two prime numbers that differ by 2. For example 11 and 13 are twin primes. दो अभाज्य संख्या जिनमें 2 का अन्तर हो जैसे 11 और 13 में 2 का अन्तर है।

U

Unbiased *(आकारहीन)* Not biased, having zero bias. जिसका आकार नहीं अर्थात शून्य हो।

Undefined function *(अपरिभाषित फलन)* If $y = \frac{x^2-9}{x-3}$ then for $x = 3$, $y = \frac{0}{0}$ which is meaningless and undefined and indefinite too. Therefor for $x = 3$, y has no any definite value. This type of function for x = 3, will be called as undefined function. यदि $y = \frac{x^2-9}{x-3}$ तो $x = 3$ के लिए $y = \frac{0}{0}$ होता है जो अर्थहीन एवं अनिश्चित है। अतः $x = 3$ के लिए y का कोई निश्चित मान नहीं है। ऐसे फलन के $x = 3$ को अपरिभाषित फलन कहा जाता है।

Unlike Surds *(असमरूप करणियाँ)* Surds having no common irrational factors are called unlike surds. वे करणियाँ जिनके अपरिमेय गुणनखंड समान न हों असमरूप करणियाँ कहलाती हैं–

जैसे– $\sqrt{2}$, $3\sqrt{5}$, $5\sqrt{3}$

Unit *(मात्रक)* A standard of measurement such as at inch, a foot a centimeter is pound or a dollar. मापन के लिए उपयुक्त इकाई उसका मात्रक कहा जाता है। जैसे इंच, फुट, सेंमी आदि।

Unit circle *(एकल वृत्त)* A unit - circle is a circle with radius unity. जिसकी त्रिज्या इकाई एक हो।

Unit cube *(एक घन)* A cube with unit edge length. जिस घन की भुजा लम्बाई एक हो।

Unit fraction *(एकल भिन्न)* A fraction whose numerator is 1. जिस भिन्न का अंश 1 एक हो, यूनिट फ्रैक्सन कहा जाता है।

Unit rate *(इकाई दर)* A rate with a denominator of 1. दर जिसकी इकाई हर एक हो।

Unit square *(इकाई वर्ग)* A unit square is square of side length 1. जिस वर्ग की भुजा 1 इकाई हो।

Unity ***(इकाई)*** One unit. एक इकाई।

Universal set ***(समष्टीय समुच्चय)*** A set that contains all set in a given context is called the universal set It is denoted by 'U'. यदि किसी निश्चित संदर्भ में दिए हुए समस्त समुच्चय एकनिश्चित समुच्चय के उपसमुच्चय हो तो इस निश्चित समुच्चय को समष्टीय समुच्चय कहा जाता है। इसे U से प्रदर्शित किया जाता है।

Universal Set ***(समष्टीय समुच्चय)*** The set of all object admissible in a particular problem or discussion. किसी निश्चित संदर्भ में दिए हुए समस्त समुच्चय एक निश्चित समुच्चय के उपसुच्चय हो तो इस निश्चित समुच्चय को समष्टीय समुच्चय कहा जाता है।

Unit vector ***(एकल सदिश)*** A vector of unit magnitude is called the units vector. The unit vector in the direction of a vector $\vec{a}$ is denoted by $\hat{a}$, reads 'a, cap' Thus $|\hat{a}| = 1$. ऐसा सदिश जिसका परिमाण 1 (एक) हो इसे $\hat{a}$ से प्रदर्शित करते है।

V

Valuation ***(मूल्यांकन)*** Act of finding or determining the value of. मान ज्ञात करने की क्रिया।

Variable ***(चर)*** A symbol used to represent an unspecified member of some set or A numerical value of a characterise that can differ from individual to individual. परिवर्तन राशियों को चर राशियां कहते हैं। जिन्हें साधारणतः अक्षरों t, u, v, w, x, y, z से प्रदर्शित किया जाता है।

Vector ***(सदिश)*** A quantity that has magnitude (length) and direction. It may be represented or directed line segment. E.g., force, velocity, displacement etc. ऐसी राशियाँ जिसमें परिमाण व दिशा दोनों का बोध हो जैसे—बल, विस्थापन, वेग आदि।

Vector (or cross) product ***(सदिश गुणनफलन)*** Let $\vec{a}, \vec{b}$ be two non- zero non parallel vector. Then the vector product $\vec{a} \times \vec{b}$ in that order defined as a vector whose magnitude is $|\vec{a}|\,|\vec{b}|$ where θ is the angle between $\vec{a}$ and $\vec{b}$ and whose direction is perpendicular to the plane of $\vec{a}$ and $\vec{b}$ in such a way that $\vec{a}, \vec{b}$ and this direction constitute a right handed system. In other words $\vec{a} \times \vec{b} = |\vec{a}|\,|\vec{b}| \sin\theta\, \vec{n}$. यदि दो $\vec{a}$ और $\vec{b}$ सदिशो और के परिणाम क्रमशः a और b हो तथा उनके बीच का कोण θ हो तो इन दोनो सदिशो का सदिश गुणनफल (vector product) एक ऐसा सदिश है। जिसका परिणाम $|\vec{a}|\,|\vec{b}| \sin\theta$ और जिसकी दिशा एकांक सदिश में जो कि दोनों सदिशों पर $\vec{a}$ और $\vec{b}$ पर लम्ब है की दिशा है। सदिश तथा दक्षिणवर्ती अभिन्यास (Right handed system) मे लिए जाते है।

- **Angle between two vectors** ***(दो सदिशों के बीच का कोण)***

  If θ is the angle between a and b, then

$$\sin\theta = \frac{|a \times b|}{|a||b|}$$

If $\hat{n}$ is the unit vector perpendicular to the plane of a and b then

$$\hat{n} = \frac{a \times b}{|a \times b|}$$

Note : If i, j, k be three mutually perpendicular unit vectors, then

(*i*) $i \times j = j \times j = k \times k = 0$

(*ii*) $i \times j = k, j \times k = i, k \times i = j$

(*iii*) $j \times i = -k, k \times j = -i, i \times k = -j$

(*iv*) If vector a and b are parallel then $|a \times b| = 0$

(*v*) If vector a and b are perpendicular then $|a \times b| = |a|\,|b|$

- **Properties of vector product** ***(सदिश गुणन के गुण)***

If a, b, c are any vectors and m, n any scalars then

(*i*) $a \times b \neq a$ (Non-commutativity)
but $a \times b = -(b \times a)$ and $|a \times b| = |b \times a|$

(*ii*) $(ma) \times b = a \times (mb) = m\,(a \times b)$

(*iii*) $(ma) \times (nb) = (mn)\,(a + b)$

(*iv*) $a \times (b \times c) \neq (a \times b) \times c$

(*v*) $a \times (b + c) = (a \times b) + (a \times c)$ (Distributivity)

(*vi*) $a \times b = a \times c \Rightarrow b = c$

Vector or cross product of two vectors ***(दो सदिशों के सदिश गुणनफल)***

$$\therefore a \times b = |a|\,|b| \sin\theta\, \hat{n} = ab \sin\theta\, \hat{n}$$

Vector product in terms of components (अवयव के रूप में)

If $a = a_1 i + a_2 j + a_3 k$ and $b = b_1 i \mid b_2 j + b_3 k$ then

$$a \times b = (a_2 b_3 - a_3 b_2)\, i + (a_3 b_1 - a_1 b_3)\, j + (a_1 b_2 - a_2 b_1) k$$

$$= \begin{vmatrix} i & j & k \\ a_1 & a_2 & a_3 \\ b_1 & b_2 & b_3 \end{vmatrix}$$

Variance of individual observations ***(विचलन)***

(*i*) If $x_1, x_2, \ldots x_n$ are n values of a variable x, then by definition

$$\text{var}\,(x) = \frac{1}{n}\left[\sum_{i=1}^{n}(x_i - \overline{x})^2\right] = a^2 \quad \ldots(i)$$

or

$$\text{var}\,(x) = \frac{1}{n}\sum_{i=1}^{n} x_i^2 - \overline{x}^2 \quad \ldots(ii)$$

(*ii*) Variance of a discrete frequency distribution

If $x_1, x_2, \ldots x_n$ are n observations with frequencies $f_1, f_2, \ldots f_n$ then

W

Watt *(वाट)* A metric unit of measure of power. शक्ति मापने की इकाई।

Weight *(भार)* The gravitational pull on a body. किसी पिण्ड पर गुरुत्व के कारण लगने वाला बल।

Whole number *(पूर्ण संख्याएं)* All the natural numbers along with 0, thus whole numbers are 0, 1, 2, 3, 4... प्राकृतिक संख्याएं तथा शून्य मिलकर पूर्ण संख्याएं बनाती है।

Work done by the force *(कार्य)*

If a constant force F acting on a particle displaces it from point A to B, then work done by the force W = f.d (where d = $\overline{AB}$)

कार्य–यदि एक नियत बल किसी कण पर लग रहा है और कण A से B स्थान पर पहुँच जाता है तब कार्य = बल × विस्थान।

X

X *(एक्स)* Roman numeral for 10. 10 (दस) के लिये रोमन अंक

X axis *(एक्स-अक्ष)* The horizontal axis in the plane. किसी तल का क्षैतिज अक्ष।

X- intercept *(अन्तः खण्ड)* If a line cuts x- axis at A (in the fig) then distance from origin (0) to A i.e. OA′ is called as x- intercept. चित्र में, मूल बिन्दु से बिन्दु A तक की दूरी X-अन्तःखण्ड कहलाता है।

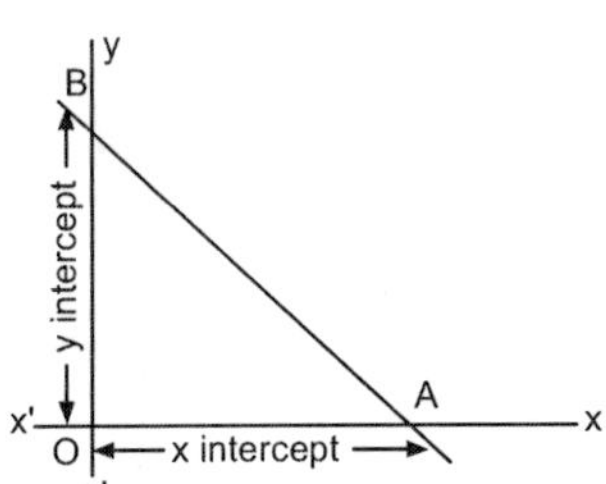

Fig. X- intercept

Y

Yard *(याड)* A measure of length equal to 3 feet. छत्तीस इंच का गज अथवा लम्बाई का मापक जो बराबर होता है 3 फीट के।

Y- axis *(वाई-अक्ष)* The vertical axis in the plane. किसी तल का लम्बवत अक्ष।

Year *(वर्ष)* A measure of lime equal to the period of one revolution of the earth about the axis sum. Approximately equal to 365 days. समय का मापक व परिमाण जो बराबर है पृथ्वी के सूर्य का एक चक्कर लगाने में लगने वाले समय के जो लगभग 365 दिन होता है।

Y- intercept *(वाई अन्तःखण्ड)* If a straight line cuts y- axis at B, then the distance from origin (0) to B is 'OB' is as y- intercept. y-अक्ष का काटने वाला खण्ड y-अन्तःखण्ड कहलाता है। चित्र में OB y-अन्तःखण्ड है।

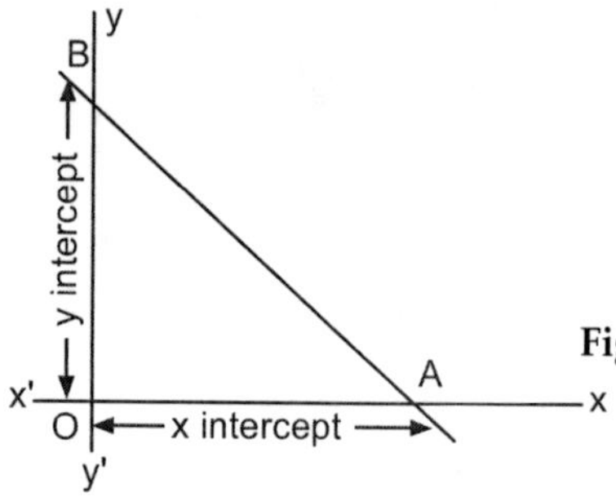

Fig. Y-intercept

Z

Zero *(शून्य)* 0. First whole number. प्रथम पूर्ण संख्या।

Zero vector *(शून्य सदिश)*

A vector whose magnitude is zero is called zero vector. ऐसा सदिश जिसका मान शून्य होता है वह शून्य सदिश कहलाता है।

Zero element *(शून्य अवयव)* The element 0, is a zero element of e group of a + 0 = a, and 0 + a = a for all elements a. अवयव 0 (शून्य), a + 0 = a एवं 0 + a = a के समूह का, a के समस्त अवयवों के लियें, शून्य अवयव कहलायेगा।

Zeros of a function ***(शून्य फलन)*** The values of the domain of a function which are mapped on to zero or, less formally the points at which the value of a function is zero. किसी फलन के डोमेन की वे समस्त अवयव व मूल जिनका प्रतिचित्रण शून्य से हो अथवा वे बिन्दु जिन पर किसी फलन का मूल शून्य (0) हो जाये।

Z- intercept ***(Z-अन्तःखण्ड)*** The distance on the z- axis up to the point at which a line crosses, the z - axis. z-अक्ष पर किसी रेखा द्वारा काटी गई किसी बिन्दु तक की दूरी, z-अन्तःखण्ड कहलाता है।

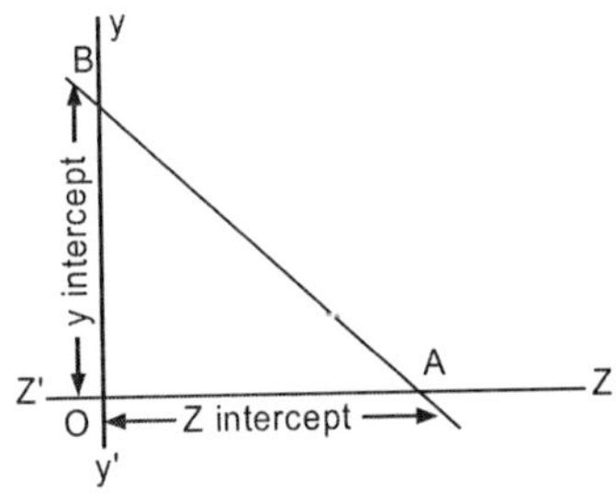

Fig. Z- intercept

Zero-angle ***(शून्य कोण)*** If the initial and find positions of a ray coincide without making any revolution, we say the angle formed is zero angle.

Measure of a zero-angle = 0°.

यदि किसी किरण के प्राथमिक एवं अंत बिन्दु बिना कोई चक्कर लगाये एक ही स्थान व बिन्दु पर मिल जाये, तो उससे निर्मित कोण शून्य कोण कहलायेगा।

शून्य कोण का माप = 0°

MATHEMATICAL TABLES
(गणितीय सारणी)

LOGARITHMS
(लघुगुणक)

	0	1	2	3	4	5	6	7	8	9	Mean Difference		
											1 2 3	4 5 6	7 8 9
10	0000	0043	0086	0128	0170						5 913	172126	303438
						0212	0253	0294	0334	0374	4 812	162024	283236
11	0414	0453	0492	0531	0569						4 812	162023	273135
						0607	0645	0682	0719	0755	4 711	151822	262933
12	0792	0828	0864	0899	0934						3 711	141821	252832
						0969	1004	1038	1072	1106	3 710	141720	242731
13	1139	1173	1206	1239	1271						3 610	131619	232629
						1303	1335	1367	1399	1430	3 710	131619	222529
14	1461	1492	1523	1553	1584						3 6 9	121519	222528
						1614	1644	1673	1703	1732	3 6 9	121417	202326
15	1761	1790	1818	1847	1875						3 6 9	111417	202326
						1903	1931	1959	1987	2014	3 6 8	111417	192225
16	2041	2068	2095	2122	2148						3 6 8	111416	192224
						2175	2201	2227	2253	2279	3 5 8	101316	182123
17	2304	2330	2355	2380	2405						3 5 8	101315	182023
						2430	2455	2480	2504	2529	3 5 8	101215	172022
18	2553	2577	2601	2625	2648						2 5 7	91214	171921
						2672	2695	2718	2742	2765	2 4 7	91114	161821
19	2788	2810	2833	2856	2878						2 4 7	91113	161820
						2900	2923	2945	2967	2989	2 4 6	81113	151719
20	3010	3032	3054	3075	3096	3118	3139	3160	3181	3201	2 4 6	81113	151719
21	3222	3243	3263	3284	3304	3324	3345	3365	3385	3404	2 4 6	81012	141618
22	3424	3444	3464	3483	3502	3522	3541	3560	3579	3598	2 4 6	81012	141517
23	3617	3636	3655	3674	3692	3711	3729	3747	3766	3784	2 4 6	7 911	131517
24	3802	3820	3838	3856	3874	3892	3909	3927	3945	3962	2 4 5	7 911	121416
25	3979	3997	4014	4031	4048	4065	4082	4099	4116	4133	2 3 5	7 910	121415
26	4150	4166	4183	4200	4216	4232	4249	4265	4281	4298	2 3 5	7 810	111315
27	4314	4330	4346	4362	4378	4393	4409	4425	4440	4456	2 3 5	6 8 9	111314
28	4472	4487	4502	4518	4533	4548	4564	4579	4594	4609	2 3 5	6 8 9	111214

[Contd.]

	0	1	2	3	4	5	6	7	8	9	1	2	3	4	5	6	7	8	9
29	4624	4639	4654	4669	4683	4698	4713	4728	4742	4757	1	3	4	6	7	9	10	12	13
30	4771	4786	4800	4814	4829	4843	4857	4871	4886	4900	1	3	4	6	7	9	10	11	13
31	4914	4928	4942	4955	4969	4983	4997	5011	5024	5038	1	3	4	6	7	8	10	11	12
32	5052	5065	5079	5092	5105	5119	5132	5145	5159	5172	1	3	4	5	7	8	9	11	12
33	5185	5198	5211	5224	5237	5250	5263	5276	5289	5302	1	3	4	5	6	8	9	10	12
34	5315	5328	5340	5353	5366	5378	5391	5403	5416	5428	1	3	4	5	6	8	9	10	11
35	5441	5453	5465	5478	5490	5502	5515	5527	5539	5551	1	2	4	5	6	7	9	10	11
36	5563	5575	5587	5599	5611	5623	5635	5647	5658	5670	1	2	4	5	6	7	8	10	11
37	5682	5694	5705	5717	5729	5740	5752	5763	5775	5786	1	2	3	5	6	7	8	9	10
38	5798	5809	5821	5832	5843	5855	5866	5877	5888	5899	1	2	3	5	6	7	8	9	10
39	5911	5922	5933	5944	5955	5966	5977	5988	5999	6010	1	2	3	4	5	7	8	9	10
40	6021	6031	6042	6053	6064	6075	6085	6096	6107	6117	1	2	3	4	5	6	8	9	10
41	6128	6138	6149	6160	6170	6180	6191	6201	6212	6222	1	2	3	4	5	6	7	8	9
42	6232	6243	6253	6263	6274	6284	6294	6304	6314	6325	1	2	3	4	5	6	7	8	9
43	6335	6345	6355	6365	6375	6385	6395	6405	6415	6425	1	2	3	4	5	6	7	8	9
44	6435	6444	6454	6464	6474	6484	6493	6503	6513	6522	1	2	3	4	5	6	7	8	9
45	6532	6542	6551	6561	6571	6580	6590	6599	6609	6618	1	2	3	4	5	6	7	8	9
46	6628	6637	6646	6656	6665	6675	6684	6693	6702	6712	1	2	3	4	5	6	7	7	8
47	6721	6730	6739	6749	6758	6767	6776	6785	6794	6803	1	2	3	4	5	5	6	7	8
48	6812	6821	6830	6839	6848	6857	6866	6875	6884	6893	1	2	3	4	4	5	6	7	8
49	6902	6911	6920	6928	6937	6946	6955	6964	6972	6981	1	2	3	4	4	5	6	7	8

ANTI-LOGARITHMS

(लघुगुणक)

	0	1	2	3	4	5	6	7	8	9	Mean Difference								
											1	2	3	4	5	6	7	8	9
50	6990	6998	7007	7016	7024	7033	7042	7050	7059	7067	1	2	3	3	4	5	6	7	8
51	7076	7084	7093	7101	7110	7118	7126	7135	7143	7152	1	2	3	3	4	5	6	7	8
52	7160	7168	7177	7185	7193	7202	7210	7218	7226	7235	1	2	2	3	4	5	6	7	7
53	7243	7251	7259	7267	7275	7284	7292	7300	7308	7316	1	2	2	3	4	5	6	6	7
54	7324	7332	7340	7348	7356	7364	7372	7380	7388	7396	1	2	2	3	4	5	6	6	7
55	7404	7412	7419	7427	7435	7443	7451	7459	7466	7474	1	2	2	3	4	5	5	6	7
56	7482	7490	7497	7505	7513	7520	7528	7536	7543	7551	1	2	2	3	4	5	5	6	7
57	7559	7566	7574	7582	7589	7597	7604	7612	7619	7627	1	2	2	3	4	5	5	6	7
58	7634	7642	7649	7657	7664	7672	7679	7686	7694	7701	1	1	2	3	4	5	5	6	7
59	7709	7716	7723	7731	7738	7745	7752	7760	7767	7774	1	1	2	3	4	5	5	6	7

[*Contd.*]

60	7782	7789	7796	7803	7810	7818	7825	7832	7839	7846	1	1	2	3	4	4	5	6	6
61	7853	7860	7868	7875	7882	7889	7896	7903	7910	7917	1	1	2	3	4	4	5	6	6
62	7924	7931	7938	7945	7952	7959	7966	7973	7980	7987	1	1	2	3	3	4	5	6	6
63	7993	8000	8007	8014	8021	8028	8035	8041	8048	8055	1	1	2	3	3	4	5	5	6
64	8062	8069	8075	8082	8089	8096	8102	8109	8116	8122	1	1	2	3	3	4	5	5	6
65	8129	8136	8142	8149	8156	8162	8169	8176	8182	8189	1	1	2	3	3	4	5	5	6
66	8195	8202	8209	8215	8222	8228	8235	8241	8248	8254	1	1	2	3	3	4	5	5	6
67	8261	8267	8274	8280	8287	8293	8299	8306	8312	8319	1	1	2	3	3	4	5	5	6
68	8325	8331	8338	8344	8351	8357	8363	8370	8376	8382	1	1	2	3	3	4	4	5	6
69	8388	8395	8401	8407	8414	8420	8426	8432	8439	8445	1	1	2	2	3	4	4	5	6
70	8451	8457	8463	8470	8476	8482	8488	8494	8500	8506	1	1	2	2	3	4	4	5	6
71	8513	8519	8525	8531	8537	8543	8549	8555	8561	8567	1	1	2	2	3	4	4	5	5
72	8573	8579	8585	8591	8597	8603	8609	8615	8621	8627	1	1	2	2	3	4	4	5	5
73	8633	8639	8645	8651	8657	8663	8669	8675	8681	8686	1	1	2	2	3	4	4	5	5
74	8692	8698	8704	8710	8716	8722	8727	8733	8739	8745	1	1	2	2	3	4	4	5	5
75	8751	8756	8762	8768	8774	8779	8785	8791	8797	8802	1	1	2	2	3	3	4	5	5
76	8808	8814	8820	8825	8831	8837	8842	8848	8854	8859	1	1	2	2	3	3	4	5	5
77	8865	8871	8876	8882	8887	8893	8889	8904	8910	8915	1	1	2	2	3	3	4	4	5
78	8921	8927	8932	8938	8943	8949	8954	8960	8965	8971	1	1	2	2	3	3	4	4	5
79	8976	8982	8987	8993	8998	9004	9009	9015	9020	9025	1	1	2	2	3	3	4	4	5
80	9031	9036	9042	9047	9053	9058	9063	9069	9074	9079	1	1	2	2	3	3	4	4	5
81	9085	9090	9096	9101	9106	9112	9117	9122	9128	9133	1	1	2	2	3	3	4	4	5
82	9138	9143	9149	9154	9159	9165	9170	9175	9180	9186	1	1	2	2	3	3	4	4	5
83	9191	9196	9201	9206	9212	9217	9222	9227	9232	9238	1	1	2	2	3	3	4	4	5
84	9243	9248	9253	9258	9263	9269	9274	9279	9284	9289	1	1	2	2	3	3	4	4	5
85	9294	9299	9304	9309	9315	9320	9325	9330	9335	9340	1	1	2	2	3	3	4	4	5
86	9345	9350	9355	9360	9365	9370	9375	9380	9385	9390	1	1	2	2	3	3	4	4	5
87	9395	9400	9405	9410	9415	9420	9425	9430	9435	9440	0	1	1	2	2	3	3	4	4
88	9445	9450	9455	9460	9465	9469	9474	9479	9484	9489	0	1	1	2	2	3	3	4	4
89	9494	9499	9504	9509	9513	9518	9523	9528	9533	9538	0	1	1	2	2	3	3	4	4
90	9542	9547	9552	9557	9562	9566	9571	9576	9581	9586	0	1	1	2	2	3	3	4	4
91	9590	9595	9600	9605	9609	9614	9619	9624	9628	9633	0	1	1	2	2	3	3	4	4
92	9638	9643	9647	9652	9657	9661	9666	9671	9675	9680	0	1	1	2	2	3	3	4	4
93	9685	9689	9694	9699	9703	9708	9713	9717	9722	9727	0	1	1	2	2	3	3	4	4
94	9731	9736	9741	9745	9750	9754	9759	9763	9768	9773	0	1	1	2	2	3	3	4	4

[Contd.]

	0	1	2	3	4	5	6	7	8	9	1	2	3	4	5	6	7	8	9
95	9777	9782	9786	9791	9795	9800	9805	9809	9814	9818	0	1	1	2	2	3	3	4	4
96	9823	9827	9832	9836	9841	9845	9850	9854	9859	9863	0	1	1	2	2	3	3	4	4
97	9868	9872	9877	9881	9886	9890	9894	9899	9903	9908	0	1	1	2	2	3	3	4	4
98	9912	9917	9921	9926	9930	9934	9939	9943	9948	9952	0	1	1	2	2	3	3	4	4
99	9956	9961	9965	9969	9974	9978	9983	9987	9991	9996	0	1	1	2	2	3	3	3	4

LOGARITHMS
(प्रतिलघुगुणक)

	0	1	2	3	4	5	6	7	8	9	Mean Difference								
											1	2	3	4	5	6	7	8	9
.50	3162	3170	3177	3184	3192	3199	3206	3214	3221	3228	1	1	2	3	4	4	5	6	7
.51	3236	3245	3251	3258	3266	3273	3281	3289	3296	3304	1	2	2	3	4	5	5	6	7
.52	3311	3319	3327	3334	3342	3350	3357	3365	3373	3381	1	2	2	3	4	5	5	6	7
.53	3388	3396	3404	3412	3420	3428	3436	3445	3451	3459	1	2	2	3	4	5	6	6	7
.54	3467	3475	3483	3491	3499	3508	3516	3524	3532	3540	1	2	2	3	4	5	6	6	7
.55	3548	3556	3565	3573	3581	3589	3597	3606	3614	3622	1	2	2	3	4	5	6	7	7
.56	3631	3639	3648	3656	3664	3673	3681	3690	3698	3707	1	2	3	3	4	5	6	7	8
.57	3715	3724	3733	3741	3750	3758	3767	3776	3784	3793	1	2	3	3	4	5	6	7	8
.58	3802	3811	3819	3828	3837	3846	3855	3864	3873	3882	1	2	3	4	4	5	6	7	8
.59	3890	3899	3908	3917	3926	3936	3945	3954	3963	3972	1	2	3	4	5	5	6	7	8
.60	3981	3990	3999	4009	4018	4027	4036	4046	4055	4064	1	2	3	4	5	6	6	7	8
.61	4074	4083	4093	4102	4111	4121	4130	4140	4150	4159	1	2	3	4	5	6	7	8	9
.62	4169	4178	4188	4198	4207	4217	4227	4236	4246	4256	1	2	3	4	5	6	7	8	9
.63	4266	4276	4285	4295	4305	4315	4325	4335	4345	4355	1	2	3	4	5	6	7	8	9
.64	4365	4375	4385	4395	4406	4416	4426	4436	4446	4457	1	2	3	4	5	6	7	8	9
.65	4467	4477	4487	4498	4508	4519	4529	4539	4550	4560	1	2	3	4	5	6	7	8	9
.66	4571	4581	4592	4603	4613	4624	4634	4645	4656	4667	1	2	3	4	5	6	7	9	10
.67	4677	4688	4699	4710	4721	4732	4742	4753	4764	4775	1	2	3	4	5	7	8	9	10
.68	4786	4797	4808	4819	4831	4842	4853	4864	4875	4887	1	2	3	4	6	7	8	9	10
.69	4898	4909	4920	4932	4943	4955	4966	4977	4989	5000	1	2	3	5	6	7	8	9	10
.70	5012	5023	5035	5047	5058	5070	5082	5093	5105	5117	1	2	4	5	6	7	8	9	11
.71	5129	5140	5152	5164	5176	5188	5200	5212	5224	5236	1	2	4	5	6	7	8	10	11
.72	5248	5260	5272	5284	5297	5309	5321	5333	5346	5358	1	2	4	5	6	7	9	10	11
.73	5370	5383	5395	5408	5420	5433	5445	5458	5470	5483	1	3	4	5	6	8	9	10	11
.74	5495	5508	5521	5534	5546	5559	5572	5585	5598	5610	1	3	4	5	6	8	9	10	12
.75	5623	5636	5649	5662	5675	5689	5702	5715	5728	5741	1	3	4	5	7	8	9	10	12
.76	5754	5768	5781	5794	5808	5821	5834	5848	5861	5875	1	3	4	5	7	8	9	11	12

[Contd.]

.77	5888	5902	5916	5929	5943	5957	5970	5984	5998	6012	1	3	4	5	7	8	10	11	12
.78	6026	6039	6053	6067	6081	6095	6109	6124	6138	6152	1	3	4	6	7	8	10	11	13
.79	6166	6180	6194	6209	6223	6237	6252	6266	6281	6295	1	3	4	6	7	9	10	11	13
.80	6310	6324	6339	6353	6368	6383	6397	6412	6427	6442	1	3	4	6	7	9	10	12	13
.81	6457	6471	6486	6501	6516	6531	6546	6561	6577	6592	2	3	5	6	8	9	11	12	14
.82	6607	6622	6637	6653	6668	6683	6699	6714	6730	6745	2	3	5	6	8	9	11	12	14
.83	6761	6776	6792	6808	6823	6839	6855	6871	6887	6902	2	3	5	6	8	9	11	13	14
.84	6918	6934	6950	6966	6982	6998	7015	7031	7047	7063	2	3	5	6	8	10	11	13	15
.85	7079	7096	7112	7129	7145	7161	7178	7194	7211	7228	2	3	5	7	8	10	12	13	15
.86	7244	7261	7278	7295	7311	7328	7345	7362	7379	7396	2	3	5	7	8	10	12	13	15
.87	7413	7430	7447	7464	7482	7499	7516	7534	7551	7568	2	3	5	7	9	10	12	14	16
.88	7586	7603	7621	7638	7656	7674	7691	7709	7727	7745	2	4	5	7	9	11	12	14	16
.89	7762	7780	7798	7816	7834	7852	7870	7889	7907	7925	2	4	5	7	9	11	13	14	16
.90	7943	7962	7980	7998	8017	8035	8054	8072	8091	8110	2	4	6	7	9	11	13	15	17
.91	8128	8147	8166	8185	8204	8222	8241	8260	8279	8299	2	4	6	8	9	11	13	15	17
.92	8318	8337	8356	8375	8395	8414	8433	8453	8472	8492	2	4	6	8	10	12	14	15	17
.93	8511	8531	8551	8570	8590	8610	8630	8650	8670	8690	2	4	6	8	10	12	14	16	18
.94	8710	8730	8750	8770	8790	8810	8831	8851	8872	8892	2	4	6	8	10	12	14	16	18
.95	8913	8933	8954	8974	8995	9016	9036	9057	9078	9099	2	4	6	8	10	12	15	17	19
.96	9120	9141	9162	9183	9204	9226	9247	9268	9290	9311	2	4	6	8	11	13	15	17	19
.97	9333	9354	9376	9397	9419	9441	9462	9484	9506	9528	2	4	7	9	11	13	15	17	20
.98	9550	9572	9594	9616	9638	9661	9683	9705	9727	9750	2	4	7	9	11	13	16	18	20
.99	9772	9795	9817	9840	9863	9886	9908	9931	9954	9977	2	5	7	9	11	14	16	18	20